paperweight

paperweight

MEG HASTON

An Imprint of HarperCollinsPublishers

HarperTeen is an imprint of HarperCollins Publishers.

Paperweight
Copyright © 2014 by Meg Haston and Alloy Entertainment

Produced by Alloy Entertainment
1700 Broadway
New York, NY 10019
www.alloyentertainment.com

Library of Congress Control Number: 2015932006

ISBN 978-0-06-233574-6

Typography by Natalie Sousa

15 16 17 18 19   CG/RRDH   10 9 8 7 6 5 4 3 2 1

❖

First Edition

For all the Stevies—
and all the Shrinks who walk beside them.

The art of losing's not too hard to master
though it may look like (Write it!) like disaster.

—ELIZABETH BISHOP, "ONE ART"

day one

TWENTY-SEVEN days to freedom, and I am caged. Suspended in a boxy aluminum prison with gray cloth seats and the synthetic stench of piña colada swinging from the rearview.

Josh—sorry! Josh*ua*—would say I'm being a drama queen. I imagine him saying things like that sometimes. It's not like I can actually hear his words out loud, or he comes to me in my dreams, or some bullshit like that. But if I'm really still, I can almost hear him. The closer I get to the Anniversary, the more I'm trying. I pretend that he's next to me on our rotted wood balcony before dawn, when my shallow breath rattle is the only sound. I conjure him up in the middle of the night, and he's sitting next to the bed when I'm dizzy and sick with Eden and booze. I imagine him rubbing my back in easy circles, whispering these sweet French

1

lullabies our mother used to sing. I can almost feel the warmth of his hand.

I wish he were here now to calm me. I am a hostage in the passenger seat of a white minivan, trapped next to a strange woman with cotton candy hair the color of ginger ale. She is telling me about her granddaughter's masterful performance in the role of Velma Kelly in her middle school production of *Chicago*. As if we were old friends, as if I didn't see her activate the child lock the second we pulled out of the airport parking lot.

In old movies, men in white coats cart the crazies away. I get a woman in a white minivan.

"—just such a *vivid* performance." Cotton Candy's pearly pink acrylics tap the steering wheel at exactly the ten and two positions. "She really trans*formed* herself into the part. Bill— that's my husband—got the whole thing on the camcorder."

I glare out the window at the infinite stretch of two-lane highway. The flat New Mexico desert looks like a kid's drawing: swirls of waxy blue sky over jagged red dirt, leaning cacti like somebody just plunked them down without bothering to make sure they were screwed in right. I even see wavy heat lines like when Josh and our dad used to barbecue behind the house on Broad. But then I blink and they're gone.

"She's the only one in the family with any creativity." Cotton Candy laughs and shakes her head. Her hair doesn't move.

The van veers onto a long, skinny dirt road. To the right is a pasture, the only green I've seen in hours. Beyond the green is a dusty riding ring with several horses tethered to a fence. There are a few square stucco structures with flat roofs scattered across the grounds. They are old and unevenly spaced, like dice slung across a sandy floor and forgotten.

"We'll get you situated at the villa and then I'll take your bags to your cottage," Cotton Candy says.

Villa? Cottage? She makes this place sound like an all-inclusive resort. I almost order a complimentary cocktail. Last night's buzz is starting to wear off.

The bruise above my left eyebrow throbs, and I scrutinize my reflection in the window. The knot has morphed into a purplish welt that looks like Italy, only horizontal. I'd cover it with my hair if I had any. But I got sick of it last week, the way it was wavy in some places and flat in others, like it had no idea what to be. So I got Eden to crop it close to my head. Now uneven, razored layers fall lifelessly around my skull. I can't remember the last time I showered.

The road dead-ends into a circular drive in front of a large stucco building. It's similar to the others but imposing, with a slanted red tile roof.

"There are nineteen other girls with us right now, four girls to a cottage. You'll be in Cottage Three. Great girls in Cottage Three. Just *great* girls," Cotton Candy chirps. "They'll be *thrilled* to show you the ropes as you're getting settled."

God, I hope there's a secret handshake.

"So this is the villa." She parks the van and turns to face me. She's an ex-smoker, redeemed—I can tell from her fake blue-white teeth and the hairline cracks snaking from her pursed lips like barren riverbeds.

"I'm so happy you've chosen to take this step, Stephanie." For a second it seems like she's going to grasp my hands in hers, maybe try to pray with me. But then I think she sees the look on my face and decides against it. "We all are."

"It's Stevie. I go by Stevie." My voice sounds hoarse. Weak, even though I'm suddenly furious. Why didn't Dad tell them when he called? Stevie. Never Stephanie. I am not her.

"Stevie." She sounds uncertain, probably because she's just noticed the outline of my mother on my left forearm. "Stevie," she tries again. "Welcome to the first day of your recovery."

I hear a click and try the handle. The passenger door opens.

I lower my gray flip-flops into red dust and squint into the light. There are two sets of cement steps that lead to a wooden front door with a twisted wrought-iron handle. Between the sets of stairs is a tiered stone fountain that's choking on weak spurts of moldy water.

It reminds me of something I saw on that sucky home renovation show Josh used to half watch while reading for one of his psych classes. That's how smart he was: classes at the university at seventeen, and still he could watch TV and read at the same time.

"Seriously, Josh," I said, lowering myself to the dingy mustard-colored carpet in the living room. It smelled like cat pee and cigarettes. After our mother left, we moved to this run-down apartment on the west side of town. It was nothing like the airy Victorian house the four of us had shared on Broad. Josh and I christened the new place *Le Crâpeau*, which we decided was Franglais for "the Crap Castle." "Can't we watch something else?" On the coffee table was an unopened bag of salt and vinegar chips. Our mother would never have allowed them.

4

"Shouldn't you be writing?" Josh said from the couch, an eighteenth-century French love seat. Like the rest of the furniture, it used to be hers. It didn't exactly fit with the slatted plastic blinds and ugly fluorescent lighting. "Or at least locking yourself in your room with writer's block?"

"Ben says there's no such thing as writer's block. Only writer's 'I really, really, really don't want to do this.'" Bennett Ashe was a novelist friend of our dad's. They'd met when Dad started a men's writing group and advertised it in the local paper, where he worked as an arts and leisure editor. Since then, the group had been predictable: Tuesday nights in our kitchen, bourbon, and too many *In my next novels* to count. Ben was the only real novelist among the group, if you didn't count the three manuscripts stashed at the bottom of Dad's desk drawer like dirty magazines.

"How's, uh . . . the class?" It's not what he wants to ask. Or who he wants to ask about. But there is an unspoken rule between us, and he obeys it.

"Good, I guess." Ben taught a narrative prose seminar to community college kids over the summer and had agreed to let me audit the course. Dad swore that it had everything to do with my talent. Nothing to do with the fact that Ben was basically family—and pitied me for being motherless. Right.

"I could take a look at some of your stuff, if you want."

"It's not ready," I said quickly. "Later, maybe."

I stretched out my legs, pressing my palms into the carpet and feeling the scratchy fiber fingers struggling beneath me. I took a slow, deep breath and tensed the muscles in my legs with intention. The leg lifts had to be exact or they wouldn't count. *One, pause, hold, and down. Two, pause, hold, and down.*

Josh ignored me, staring at the Spanish-style mansion on the screen. It was in Miami, surrounded by palm trees. There was even an infinity pool in the backyard. The owner's shirt was unbuttoned so far you could see his chest hair.

"Look at that fountain in the front there. Nice, huh?" Josh reached for the bag of chips and tore it open. It belched salt and acrid vinegar. My stomach twisted with guilt. *Too much salt*, she would have said. *Too much fat.* Josh didn't care. He acted like it didn't matter, like she was never coming back. "Come on. You love these." He tilted the bag toward me.

"I don't," I spat. "Besides, I already ate." I switched legs. Faster now, double time. I was efficient. A machine. I made sure to breathe through my mouth, so not even the smell of the grease could penetrate me. I was a fortress. "This show is for bored housewives, Josh. Seriously."

"Shut up." He tossed the remote at me, hard, and it whacked me in the shoulder. I grabbed it and switched to A&E. "And it's *Joshua*." Changing to his full name was the first order of business after he'd gotten his acceptance letter from the university. He probably thought it would make the real college kids forget he was seventeen and a virgin.

"Sorry," I snorted. "This show is for bored housewives . . . Josh*uuuuaahhhh*."

Now Cotton Candy opens the front door and ushers me inside. "After you."

A blast of air-conditioning slips under my clothes, leaving a million tiny goose bumps in its wake. It's colder in here than it was on the plane. I can feel my body kicking into overdrive.

Good.

"You can think of the villa as your home base. You'll eat your meals here and spend time between group and other activities. The cottages are for sleeping only. Staff locks them during the day," she explains in a hushed voice as she leads me down a long Spanish-tiled hallway.

We come to a giant room divided by a nurses' station. One side is a dining room with five round tables in light-colored wood. The other side looks like the rec room at Summer Camp for the Criminally Insane and Hopelessly Screwed: mismatched couches facing a television, tables scattered with crayons and construction paper.

Along the back wall, glass-paned double doors look over a patio and a small yard. Beyond that are the riding ring and the pasture, then the emptiness of the desert. I've reached the very end of the earth.

"The other girls are in group right now. You'll meet them at afternoon snack." Her voice echoes a little and the hall starts to sway. I screw my eyes shut and brace for the fall.

"Careful, dear," she says, steadying me. She's got surprisingly quick reflexes.

"I'm fine," I say hastily, jerking away. When I open my eyes, the hall is straight again. "I'm fine."

She presses her lips together until they vanish. "The nurses will get your vitals, take some blood, and do an EKG before your evening meal. But Anna wanted to meet you first, say hello."

"Anna?" *Do I know an Anna?*

"Anna. Your therapist." Slowly, she leads me to an office door on the left side of the hall. "You're lucky. Anna's one of the best we've got here."

Lucky? She's twisted, I'll give her that.

We're standing in front of the door now, and my chaperone raps on the wood three times, fast. *AnnaAnnaAnna*.

"Come in."

Cotton Candy nods at me, then at the doorknob. "Go on in."

I reach for the knob with a shaky hand. Only it isn't really me. I'm detached, a spectator in a cold, dark theater watching an unsuspecting victim approach her end.

Don't do it! I want to yell. *It's a trap!* But the girl on the screen doesn't hear me. Just twists the knob and steps over the threshold. They always do.

day one

"IT'S Stevie," I say, after Cotton Candy has made her exit but before the shrink can get it wrong. I stay pressed against the door for support—and the promise of a quick escape.

"Stevie. I'm Anna. I'll be your individual therapist during your stay here." Shrink smiles warmly but stays put in her red armchair. She is folding a glossy yellow paper square with rapid, sure movements until it starts to take shape. She doesn't try to shake my hand or—maybe there *is* a higher power—hug me. "Officially, we won't start until tomorrow, but I heard you were getting in and wanted to say hi." She places the half-folded paper sculpture on the side table next to her.

I nod. Her reward for Not Touching.

"Why don't you take a seat?" She gestures toward the turquoise

9

love seat facing her chair. On it are two round saffron pillows stitched with tiny brown beads.

I consider not moving. It wouldn't be fair to dangle obedience, then yank it away. But I'm so unbearably tired, so heavy, that I shrug and collapse on the soft cushions. At the moment of impact, I imagine I'm just like any other girl, crashing on the couch after school. I even let my fantasy self have a snack. Ice cream. No. Sugary cereal, the kind my mother always said would give me cancer.

"The first week can feel a bit overwhelming as you become oriented to treatment and the schedule here," Shrink says. She wears loose, ripped blue jeans and a white tank top. A moss-colored cardigan obscures an enviably carved collarbone, but her thighs and ass are soft. Her feet are bare save for a turquoise toe ring. Strawberry waves are piled in a chaotic bun on top of her head. There is a peace sign tattooed on the inside of her right wrist, so we all know she does hot yoga and donates to Planned Parenthood. "Every morning with breakfast, you'll receive a printed schedule that tells you where to be, when. We build some time to relax and reflect into each day. Free time, essentially, though you'll need to stay in the villa or on the lawn."

"So, not free, then." I regret opening my mouth. I can't let her get to me.

"During the first week, you'll meet with everyone on your treatment team: me, your physician, your psychiatrist, and your dietician," she continues unfazed, tucking her feet beneath her. "There will be a lot of paperwork, and some computer testing, as well as some medical tests. This is all to give us a better understanding of your needs while you're here."

Not that I'll be here long. The Anniversary is twenty-seven days from now, exactly. If I make it that long. With any luck, I'll be gone by then. Disappeared, just like my mother before me.

"Once all that is taken care of," Shrink continues, "we'll get you into a more regular routine. You and I will have sessions three times a week, and you'll have group therapy twice each week."

It seems like it is time for me to shrug again.

"It's a lot to take in, I know." When she smiles, I notice that her two front teeth overlap slightly at the bottom. "You can always ask if you have questions. Any questions right now?"

I shake my head.

"Okay." She tilts her head slightly and nods. "So, you must be exhausted."

No way she's a PhD with a line like that. I scan the wall to my right for any sign of a diploma, but there isn't any, probably to make me feel like she's just this girl I know and we're hanging out in her room, flipping through magazines and chatting, like, *"Would bangs look good on me? Be honest."*

And then, *"So . . . sometimes I lock myself in my bathroom and stick my toothbrush down my throat. Is that totally weird? Be honest."*

I slide my right hand across my stomach and count the ribs on the left side. Once, twice, three times. They're not as sharp as yesterday. I have to get out of here. This was such a mistake. I told Dad this was a mistake.

The shrink lifts a folder from the table next to her and scans its contents. "From your intake paperwork, it looks like you didn't have much time to prepare for . . . this. You had about a day to get ready?" The table is painted like a chessboard. On it is one of those Zen fountains. It's loud and kind of erratic, like an elephant with prostate problems trying to pee.

"Wrong." Now the right side. Once, twice, three times. I can hardly feel them beneath the softness. "Eight hours."

"Wow." She leans toward me. "And can you tell me a little bit about how that went? What got you here?"

"My dad got worried, I guess. So he called. I can't—I don't know." It's not a lie. I really don't know how I got here. I run my middle finger down the center of my right thigh. I can feel the scar through the fabric of my jeans, withered and hard.

"Take me through what you can remember. From your point of view, not Dad's." *Dad's*, she says. Like he's our dad, both of ours. Like our histories are the same.

"I never said I couldn't remember." But she fixes me with a look and I know she's not giving up until I give her something. "I got home last night . . . this morning . . . and he was waiting on the couch. This love seat. Watching TV."

"And what time was this?"

"I don't know. Three, four. Whatever time they play reruns of *Dick Van Dyke*."

"You'd been out?"

"With Eden. My . . . this girl Eden. She drove me home." I dig my fingernails into one of the yellow pillows. Speaking Eden's name fills my mouth with liquid rage. But she's all I have left, so I gulp it down.

When I'd gotten home, Dad was smoking in his undershirt and jeans. His mouth was open, but no sound escaped. Maybe it was the booze, but suddenly Josh was in the room with us.

"He's scared," Josh translated. "He didn't know where you were. He never knows where you are anymore."

"Can he tell I'm drunk?" I giggled. "Drunkity-drunk-drunk?"

"He's not a moron, Stevie." I could feel Josh's exhaustion. "You never give him enough credit. You never give anybody enough credit."

"*Ohhh, Rooobbbb!*" Mary Tyler Moore whined on the screen.

"Listen," I said. "Maybe you can hold the pep talk for another day? I've got a lot on my plate. There's an anniversary coming up, you know."

"No shit."

"I'm preparing the sacrifice," I explained solemnly. Then, suddenly racked with laughter, I took a step toward Dad and a wailing Mary Tyler Moore. And everything went dark.

When I don't say any more, Shrink reaches for a plastic Dasani bottle at her feet. "Dad mentioned you'd passed out soon after you got home. Hit your forehead on the edge of the coffee table." She unscrews the cap and takes a sip.

I point to the purple Italy above my eye. *Exhibit A, signorina.*

"Losing consciousness . . . Was that due to your anorexia? Being malnourished? Or had you been drinking as well?"

"Both." I bite the inside of my cheek, but I don't think it hides the smile. The urge to bolt has passed, and now I just want to close my eyes and slide into the word, soak in it until my skin's all pruney. *Anorexia.* Yes. Yes. It's like she's seeing me for the very first time.

"And does that happen a lot?"

"What?" I ask, wanting her to say it again. *Call me by my name.*

"The drinking, or the passing out?"

"Both. Either." Her outline is getting blurry around the edges, dipping from side to side.

"Sometimes."

"And so . . . you get home, you pass out, and when you come to, what do you remember?"

"Um . . ." I close my eyes. "Pretzels or peanuts?" This part I remember: a woman with spidery lashes and orange foundation leaning over my seat with a porcelain smile and a Southern drawl. *Prayt-sels or peenuts, huun?*

"The next thing you remember is being on the plane from Atlanta."

"I didn't have any," I say quickly.

"Any . . ."

"Pretzels or peanuts. I didn't have any." The very thought makes my insides squirm. Again I count the ribs. This time, they are nearly indistinguishable.

"I see." Shrink leans forward a little. "Mind if I ask what you're thinking right now?"

My eyes snap open, and suddenly I see the world with stunning clarity.

"I'm thinking I don't need to be here." Deprivation has made me sharp, like a hawk. I know what needs to happen. I'll call Eden tonight, get her to send me a plane ticket. She'll be pissed after the text I sent before my plane took off this morning, but I'll tell her I was still drunk. Didn't mean it. Just one call, and she'll save me. Cell phones aren't allowed here, but I ducked into the bathroom when I got off the plane and stuffed my phone in my bra, along with a few twenties I swiped from Dad's wallet.

"You don't believe you're sick enough to be here," she says.

"So if you had to put a number, one to ten, on your motivation to seek treatment, what do you think that number would be? Ten being fully motivated."

Oh, I'm motivated. I'm motivated to do everything I need to do before the Anniversary. If she thinks she's going to stop me with hugs and head nods, she's the crazy one.

"So who would I talk to about signing myself out of this place? Like, tonight?"

Her lips part like she's going to say something. Then she closes her mouth for a second. The peeing elephant in the room is getting hard to ignore.

"I can certainly understand that finding yourself in a treatment center across the country would be overwhelming. Especially since you haven't had time to prepare."

"I'm not overwhelmed," I say tightly. My patience is thinning. Ha! Thinning. "I just don't belong here."

She nods. "I know you feel that way. But, Stevie—" She locks her gaze with mine. I hadn't noticed the color of her eyes before. They're a kind of turquoise, almost identical to the couch.

"Stevie," she says again. "Let me assure you that you do, in fact, need to be here. You are incredibly malnourished. If you don't get intensive treatment right now, you are going to die. My guess is that you may even want to die."

Finally, we understand each other.

"So for now, I'll want you to live enough for the both of us. Maybe you could want that too, eventually."

What I *want* is to get back on schedule. Ticktock.

"So . . . signing myself out?"

She clasps her hands together in her lap. "Since you're

15

seventeen, you won't be able to check yourself out. Dad would have to do that. And he's made it clear that he wants you to be here for the full sixty days. Longer, if necessary."

My body caves like she's just knocked the wind out of me.

She's saying something else now, something about "recovery with a capital R." She's probably telling me that this could be the first day of the rest of my life. That's what Dad told me on the way to the airport.

Sixty days. Her schedule is . . . inconvenient. Doesn't she know that the Anniversary is only twenty-seven days away? I've planned this day with exquisite attention to detail. Choreographed my every move—with more than a few missteps, I know—for nearly a year.

I will find a way out of here, I tell myself. I'll call Eden, get her to buy me a ticket. Hitch a ride to the airport. Whatever I have to do to make it home in time to die. I will not betray Josh again. I will not take a single breath on the one-year anniversary of the night I killed my brother.

day one

Friday, July 4, 8:56 P.M.

THE first hours are marked by snacks and meals I refuse, the untouched calories etched in my consciousness like complex equations. I've done the math and know approximately how much weight I'll have to lose before my heart flutters to its silent stop. Death is not an exact science, which is irritating for those of us who appreciate precision.

During dinner and again at evening snack, I am seated at a table in the villa with the other girls from Cottage Three. There are three of them, their names spoken earlier over plates of food and sweaty pitchers of iced tea. Names I will never learn. Why should I? I won't be here long. Eden will figure something out.

One of the girls is a wispy-haired brunette who eats too quickly and who has too much flesh to be an anorectic. The other is more of a threat: a hunched blonde with a clear feeding tube that snakes from her right nostril and hooks over her ear. Her shoulder blades jut out; her bones sharp like exquisite carved marble. The third is the least worthy: a chunky girl with flushed cheeks and a mass of unrestrained white-blond curls. Not strong enough to obey the demands of hunger, she seems desperate to follow the rules here.

There are so many rules, I couldn't remember them all if I wanted to. Slow down, don't eat too fast, hurry up, don't eat too slow. No wearing sweatshirts with pockets at the table, sleeves must be pulled up to the elbows during mealtime. No food talk, no faces or noises at the food. One salt per meal, no more. Two peppers per meal, no more. No cutting food into tiny pieces. Three meals per day, three snacks per day. If meals are refused, supplement is offered. If supplement is refused, it's charted in the maroon binders on the shelves at the nurses' station.

Evening snack is ending. Frothy, anxious chatter swirls around me as the others squeeze empty yogurt containers and shred cellophane wrappers, waiting to be released. The villa's doors and the door to the one restroom won't be unlocked until the staff is sure the patients have digested every calorie.

I steal a loving glance at the red plastic hospital bracelet hanging from my wrist. Stroke it.

DESLISLE, STEPHANIE (STEVIE)

DOA: 7/4

COTTAGE THREE

I have learned that red is the color of power. Red is for the girls who aren't progressing in the program, the girls who haven't gained weight. Yellow is for the girls who are losing ground. They've gained some of the weight their treatment team has recommended.

And green . . . green is for the defeated. The girls who tattoo the recovery symbol on one another's palms in glittery ink, the girls who swear up and down that they won't allow their issues to weigh them down. I pity the Green Girls.

"It's Stevie, right?" a voice says. Reluctantly, I look up.

The other girls have cleared their snack trays, leaving me alone with the thick blond girl. She swipes the clean inner lip of her individual peanut butter container with a wide index finger. Everything about her screams *bulimic*.

"Stevie. Yeah." I eye the girl's wrist. Her plastic is yellow. It catches the light with her every move.

"How are you so far? The first couple days can be rough, I know."

I blink, wondering what she wants from me.

She presses on. "I'm super excited to have a roomie. Seriously, I've been by myself since this girl Jill left, and I'm, like, dying. Teagan and Cate"—she whips her head around and lowers her voice—"they're in the other room in Cottage Three. They're super cool and everything, but they're kind of young and they seem like they have their own thing going, you know?"

I almost laugh. *Roomie*. Like it's summer camp. I focus on the cool plastic of my cell phone, pressed reassuringly against my chest. When they weighed me and hooked me up to the EKG machine like a lab rat, I tucked the phone in the soft folds of my jeans, beneath the pile of my clothes on the floor.

19

"Look—" I stop just short of using her name, even though there are so many to choose from. *Bulimic. Worthless. Waste.*

"Ashlee."

Perfect. She looks like the kind who spells her name with a double *e* at the end. The kind who just barely made it onto the cheerleading squad at school, on unspoken probation for the dimples in her thighs. Ash! Lee!

Before I can tell her that she's wasting her time, a male nurse claps his hands together. "Okay, girls. Nine o'clock. The cottages should be unlocked now. Have a good night."

"Finally." Curly Blonde shoves back her chair and ditches her trash. I follow her outside and into the yard. The icy-cold desert air surprises me. "It was getting claustrophobic in there."

She leads me around the side of the villa and nudges me up a steep, gravelly hill. "Come on. This way."

I hear the rhythmic heave of her step beside me, blending with the thump of my heart as we ascend the hill. Cottage Three sits at the peak. There's a small porch in the back with two rocking chairs.

"So where are you from?" she asks.

"Outside Atlanta."

"Cool. I'm from Dallas." She sucks in greedily, already out of breath. "What do your parents do?"

Parents. Plural.

The gravel under my flip-flops crunches beneath my weight, an echo of a familiar sound—the crinkling of the foil-wrapped truffles my mother used to keep in an etched glass dish on her desk at work. Even as a little girl, I knew better than to take the candy from that dish. There were six truffles there, always six.

Chocolate was for clients only, against the rules for little girls like me. So much was against the rules.

I was almost never allowed to go to work with my mother. A law firm was no place for a child, she told me. I begged every summer. The office was cool and polished and still—everything she was, and everything I wanted to be. On my eighth birthday, she gave in. I packed a tote bag and followed her to a high-rise in downtown Atlanta, all steel and glass perfection. I passed the hours pretending that the glossy mahogany conference table was a ship or a cabin, making forts of dusty books from the used bookstore a few blocks from our house. Anna Karenina and Holden Caulfield and Jo March formed walls of protection around me, and I crouched behind them, breathing in their musty smell while my mother sat behind a desk, bathed in the white light of her computer screen. She wore a crisp collared shirt. She had a long, thin dancer's body and cherry lips that never faded.

She was the only female partner in her firm. Around her, people who mattered whispered words like *Washington* and *judgeship*. She had Promise. I asked her once if it made her proud, the way people talked. Promise was like a precious stone, she told me: hypnotizing, but after a while the weight of it could sink you.

"Mom?" I frowned at the open book in my lap. Flaubert. In her life before law, my mother had majored in French lit. She had promised me that one day we would travel to France, just the two of us. She would show me everything: where she attended classes at Université Paris-Sorbonne, the apartment she rented in the Latin Quarter, the café where she finished editing her thesis.

"Mmm?" Her voice sounded from the other side of the fort.

"Does Madame Bovary love Berthe?"

"Berthe is her daughter, my love. All mothers love their little girls."

"But it doesn't seem like she loves her."

"Well, she's not a happy woman, Madame Bovary."

"But can't Berthe make her happy, Mom?" I felt a tightening in my throat.

"No, sweetness. Children can't make their parents happy. It's not their job."

There was so much I wanted to ask, but we were interrupted. She had a partners' meeting. I stayed alone in my fort as long as I could. But I was weak, even then. I snuck into her desk drawer and reached for the bag of chocolates hidden at the back. The bag was nearly full; she'd never count the truffles in the bag, right? I unwrapped the crinkled foil and crammed the soft milk chocolate spheres in my mouth. With my knees drawn to my chest and my head bowed slightly, I fit beneath her desk. There, folded into myself, a word came to me: *comfort.*

We reach the villa and Curly Blonde thrusts her hip against the door. "Door sticks sometimes, so you have to mess with it a little."

The cottage is tiny, lined with painted cement block walls and a thin, grayish-blue carpet stretched over cement floors. There is a room on each side of the hallway; another door at the end of the hall must lead to the bathroom.

"We're in here." CB bounds into the room on the right and flips a light switch.

The room is sparse, with two beds covered in faded navy quilts. A long, shallow closet borders one side of the room. A sliding glass door looks over the darkness.

Her bed is on the other side of the room, and her space looks like what I always imagined a girls' college dorm room to look like: black-and-white pictures of friends and colorful construction paper cards with *Ashley* (*Oh*, I think, *that spelling doesn't seem right*) written in obese bubble letters plastered to the blue sticky board over her bed. A few self-help books are stacked next to the digital alarm clock on the built-in shelf. A small stuffed dog, blue bear, and one-eared rabbit sit dutifully on the other side of the clock.

On my side, a black suitcase sits at attention at the foot of the bed.

"They unpacked for you." CB kicks off her dirty, Sharpie-decorated Keds. "They have to do a luggage check." She heaves her body onto the bed.

"Are you serious? What for?" My breath is shallow. *Stop.* I will not allow myself to be more than mildly irritated. All of this—the girl, the threadbare carpet, the cement walls—is temporary. I just have to wait until Eden gets me out of here.

"You know, the usual. Razors. Laxatives. Food."

I cross the room and throw open the closet door. A few articles of clothing hang limply from the wooden rod.

"Where the hell are my clothes?" I paw through two pairs of jeans, the oversized sweatshirt that still smells like Josh if I close my eyes, three long-sleeved henleys, and my Braves T-shirt. My running shoes are strewn at an angle on the floor, and I right them carefully, suddenly enraged.

"They probably took some of your stuff. You can't have anything that's too tight or short. Nothing with spaghetti straps, either."

"This is bullshit." I jerk Josh's sweatshirt from a bent wire hanger and pull it over my head.

"I know it sucks, but it's not a bad idea. It would be super triggering for me to see all these skinny girls in tiny little tops and stuff. Wouldn't it suck for you?"

My body goes hot. Of *course* it wouldn't be like that for me. I *am* one of the skinny girls! Has she not noticed? Does she not see me?

"I want my stuff back." This is Dad's fault. My skin feels hot, then cold again, and the room goes fuzzy. My fingertips find my chest, to count the bones. I feel the cell phone in my bra.

"Trust me, it really sucks at first, but—"

"I'm going out."

She's saying something about bed checks, but I slam the door against her words. I don't take another breath until I'm safely outside. The cold air stings my lungs. I can hear voices in the dark, girls giggling outside the villa, but no one is close enough to see. I unearth the phone and power it on.

Eden answers at the last second. In the background is the obnoxious foamy swell of frat-boy alkies and clinking glasses. I know exactly where she is.

"Heyyyy, girl! Craptown USA misses you! What's going on?" she screeches. If she's mad at me, she's too drunk to remember.

I play along, because she's drunk. And playing along when she's drunk is my specialty.

"The food sucks." Not that I would know. I press my back against the exterior of the cottage and let my weight drag me down. "Listen. I can't talk long. I just—do you think maybe you could go over to my house and talk to my dad? He won't listen to me, but maybe if somebody else tells him this isn't a good—"

"Jaaaaaason!" Her drunken laughter makes a buzzing sound in my ear.

"It's Jaden, baby. Jaden." A deep, gravelly voice. He breathes into the phone. "Hello? Who's this?"

"Excellent news," I inform Jaden. "She's a horny drunk."

I hang up. Only two bars left on the tiny battery icon in the top left corner, and I forgot to stash the charger.

day two

"DO you remember your first time?" Shrink asks.

Just like that. We're crossing the lawn behind the villa while she looks for the perfect setting for a therapy session. She carries a limp yellow picnic blanket under one arm. I hold the plastic cup of supplement I refuse to drink. Some of the other patients are sprawled out on the grass on their stomachs, writing in their journals. Everything about me is taut: my breath, my shoulders, my gut. I am bound tight with hate—for this place, for Eden, for my father.

Shrink stops at the edge of the lawn, beneath the stiff yellow talons of a palm tree. Then she spreads the picnic blanket carefully over the grass and settles down.

"My first time." I repeat her words. I place the cup of calories in the grass and draw my knees to my chest.

"My guess is, you never forget the first time you use a behavior."

"You always remember."

"You mean . . . *you* always remember."

"That's what I said." Just as well that she doesn't get it. This way she won't be able to talk about how she's been there, and trust her, recovery has *so* much more to offer.

"No . . ." She scrunches up her nose and glances up at a palm tree. She looks young. "I mean, *you* always remember. As in, you, Stevie, think about the first time a lot. Can't turn it off."

My eyelids drop, and, unbidden, the memory of the first time comes back in smoky shards. The first image is always the same. Me, slumped in the driver's seat of Dad's old Buick. Engine idling, headlights off. The stench of sticky sweet gone rancid. My boozy breath, the supplies, the shame.

"Stevie?" There it is. Shrink's soft, dangerous knock. "Can you describe what's going on for you right now?"

I will never let her near the actual memory. The weight of it is mine alone to bear. I keep my eyes closed, but I shift the scene.

"Show me what you're seeing, Stevie."

"I'm . . . in my bedroom." The lie sounds so realistic, I'm almost proud. "In the apartment."

"Your bedroom. Are you alone, or is someone there with you?"

I know what she's asking before she knows it. She wants to know if someone, maybe a "Very Bad Man," touched me. That's the only possible explanation. Something unspeakable must have happened for me to turn out this way.

"He's there," I say, because nothing else comes. No one ever touched me. No man, anyway. But maybe she's right; maybe I do need a reason. Some glittering thing I can unveil for the crowd—

see, look!—so they can make sense of this insanity. *Ahhh*, they will say, *now we understand.*

"He . . ." Shrink is whispering, afraid she'll scare the revelation away if a single branch snaps beneath her cautious step.

"Joshua."

It's out before I can pull it back in. My eyes snap open. The sun beats down on the back of my neck, and the thin cotton of my henley seals itself to my slick skin.

Fuck. Fuckfuckfuckfuckfuck. My fingers curl into claws, gathering clumps of rough, dry grass. Why did I say that? It's not enough that I killed him? Now I have to lie about him, too? Fuck.

"Your brother. The one who . . . passed away?" She's probably too afraid to say *the one you killed.*

"Josh is my dead brother, yeah." *I'm sorry*, I tell him silently. *I'm so sorry. I don't know why I did that. But she can't tell anybody; it's against the law or something. God, I'm such a worthless little shit. Nobody would believe me anyway. Everybody knows I'm a liar, Josh. Everybody.*

"Okay. And the two of you are in your room." Her voice has this way of lilting at the end of her sentences, like she's asking a question even when she's not.

"Yeah. In my room." Why can't I stop? Why can't I tell her the truth, that yes, fine, Josh was in my room thousands of times for thousands of reasons, but never in the way she's thinking?

"I don't want to talk about it anymore," I tell Shrink.

"Okay. So let's talk about what you want to talk about."

I blink. "I don't want to talk about anything."

"It seems like maybe there's something on your mind."

"Nope."

I place my palm on the picnic blanket. Dad used to have one like it, an old quilt his grandma made before he was born. I remember one August morning when Mom was out of town, Dad took us to the lake for a picnic. Josh sat on the blanket, bent over some paperback, while I made angels in the sand of the bank.

Shrink goes silent, but I can feel her watching me. So intently that for a second I wonder if she's slipped inside me and can hear the crunch of grass under my little-kid bare feet and see the faded yellow pages of that stupid paperback.

"Stevie, flashbacks are nothing more than memories. They can't hurt you. Josh can't hurt you. Not anymore."

I want to pinch myself until I bleed. Josh never hurt me. He was the only one who never hurt me! And here I am, letting her talk about him like he was some sort of monster. My insides seize, and the sun beats down, and I can almost see the cover, but it's just outside the reach of memory.

"Have you ever spoken about what Josh—"

Enough. "He never—I wasn't thinking about that." My voice is sharp. "I was thinking about this paperback book he was reading and I can't remember which one, so don't ask." My chest rises and falls in jagged rhythm. I press my fingers into the scar on my thigh. Rub it desperately, like a child clutching a blanket after a nightmare.

She is silent for a while. Finally she asks, "When was this?"

"At this picnic. Dad used to take Josh and me on picnics at the lake when our mom was out of town for a case or something."

"That sounds like fun."

I wiggle out of my flip-flops. The grass is rough, nothing like it

29

was that day. "Dad said if we couldn't go where Mom was going, we'd bring the country to us. He said we could be just as fancy as she was. The first time we did it, she was in Rome."

"So you made Italian food?"

"Yeah. I was eight and Josh was nine. And Dad took us to this lake just outside of town and we had spaghetti. And those little plastic champagne flutes with grape juice for wine. You know those plastic champagne flutes you screw together?"

"Yup. Those are fun. Festive."

I close my eyes and let the heat from the sun knead my skin. "It's just that I can't remember what book he was reading that day."

"And that detail feels particularly important?"

"Yeah. It's like, if I can't remember all the details, then . . . I don't know." I realize that my arms and legs are moving slightly, like I'm making another sand angel. I freeze.

"Then what? He's slipping away?"

"Are we done yet?"

"We have a few minutes left. Up to you how you want to use them."

I sit up, turn away from Shrink, and survey the lawn. Curly Blonde is sitting at a wrought-iron table outside the patio doors, talking with an old Indian man in a white coat. The psychiatrist, I think.

"I need a new roommate," I say.

"You're not happy with your roommate." One thing I've learned so far: Shrinks do a lot of repeating. Buying a parrot would be cheaper. "Can you tell me what's bothering you, specifically?"

"Nope," I murmur, still watching. CB is gesturing at the psychiatrist with humiliating enthusiasm.

"Stevie, if you don't tell me what the issue is, it's going to be difficult for me to help you resolve it." I can hear the strain tugging at Shrink's voice. "I am a therapist, but for better or worse, I'm not a mind reader."

CB catches sight of me out of the corner of her eye, and breaks away from her conversation to wave excitedly.

"Fine," I sigh, turning back to Shrink. "It's her . . . attitude."

"It'sherattitude! It'sherattitude!" squawks Parrot Shrink. "What is it about her attitude that's frustrating to you?"

I stare at her, willing her to understand. How can I be expected to make progress with a Yellow Girl sleeping in my room? How can I live with a bulimic for a roommate? Everything about her is too much: the bubbly personality, the wild appetite for human contact. And the flesh—all the excess flesh. She is nothing like me. I am contained, self-sustaining. I don't need contact; don't need food. I do not need.

"It's just that she's not going to be helpful to me," I tell her. "To what I'm . . . trying to accomplish in my time here." Already I'm learning recovery-speak; it will be helpful in getting my way. When in Rome.

Her toes curl. "And what are you trying to accomplish in your time here?"

I stare, wondering if I heard correctly. The one and only time I wish she'd repeat herself, and she just stares back.

What am I trying to accomplish? Can't she read my intentions in my jutted angles, see the end goal in my glassy, dead eyes? Doesn't she get it every time I refuse meals and supplement? Or am I not trying hard enough, not achieving enough to make her see my choice, the one I've sworn to with skin and bone?

I choose power. I choose death.

"Stevie? Your goals for treatment?"

I have just one. I've known the truth since last night; it coalesced as I stared through the dark, listening to CB's even snores. I understand now: Eden isn't coming. Dad isn't coming.

The reality of it threatens to rush in, and I try my hardest to block out all the thoughts that come: *I won't get to say good-bye to Dad in person, or tell Eden I blame her for everything, that I've always blamed her.* I try to focus on the only thing that matters.

Josh. I extinguish any spark of regret with the syllable of his name. My plan will be harder to execute here, but I'll do it. I'll do it for him.

I imagine myself dead. Cold. Perfect and unbreathing with a still, stone heart. The weight of my useless body rotting in the ground. My soul lighter than paper and drifting far from its fleshy prison.

I allow myself a small smile. Death won't desert me. It's waiting for me, beckoning. And I'm ready, taking sure steps toward my final act. An intricately choreographed scene that will amaze. I will face the audience: my mother. Eden. My father. Shrink. And with a glimmering cloud of smoke—poof!

I will disappear.

day four

Monday, July 7, 12:10 P.M.

IT'S been only three days and already the nurses purse their thick sausage lips when they see they've been assigned to my table. More paperwork. There's a binder for each girl: the thicker the binder, the stronger the girl. I've been charted eight times already—one entry for each meal since I arrived.

Today at lunch, I am painstakingly careful in my selections: a symmetrical sliver of lettuce, a perfectly dissected bit of carrot. I hold their watery weight on my tongue. At the end of the meal, the Yellow and Green Girls clear their plates and claim their mug of weak coffee as a reward (two creamers! no more!). I'm cold, and coffee, black, would warm my insides. But the nurse on meal duty sits to my right, watching me.

I breathe through my mouth and try not to look down. I know

what's waiting if I slip: thick tomato soup like clotted blood. Rotting vegetables beaded with milky oil. Pale yellow applesauce in a congealed, sugary mass. If I look at it, smell it—or, god forbid, touch it—it will find its way inside me.

Across the table, CB tries to catch my eye. "I know it's hard at first," she sympathizes over her coffee mug. "All you have to do is tryyyy. Just do the best you can. That's good enooough."

The other two girls from Cottage Three, Teagan and Cate or Cate and Teagan, murmur their agreement. The one with the feeding tube whispers something with a vaguely encouraging intonation. I expect something more from a girl like her.

"Are you done, Stephanie?" asks the nurse. There are several nurses, five or six, but this one I remember because her name sounds thick, like flesh: *Hannah*. I've heard some of the other girls whisper *Hammah* behind her back.

"Yeah," I say.

Hammah's narrow eyes dart over my plate, which is nearly untouched.

"How about trying some supplement?" Her voice knows the answer, so I don't respond.

"Just a little? So I can tell them you're trying?"

"No." I already ate the salad. Josh always told me to eat my vegetables. It's the very least I can do, but it threw off my calculations for the day. Pathetic. I stare at the wall behind her for so long that my eyes drift out of focus. I let them. It's nice to see the world that way sometimes, blurred around the edges like I've sunk to the bottom of the ocean and am staring up at the sun.

* * *

After lunch, I head to the lawn. My schedule for the day allows for three thirty-minute sessions of solo *reflection time* before my next session, where I'm supposed to *reflect* with Shrink watching me. Bullshit, all of it. I'm *reflecting* all the time, anyway. About Mom. About Eden. About Josh. I am *reflecting* so much that I can hardly breathe.

Instead of reflecting, I do my exercises to atone for the salad. Teagan or Cate braids Curly Blonde's hair on the other side of the lawn. A carrot-headed girl with thick, pale ankles talks too loudly about how her Spanish teacher *for sure* has a crush on her, which is *kind of creepy but actually? He's kind of hot.* Other girls I haven't bothered to meet gossip or journal or write letters home.

"Hey, Stevie." Shrink is wearing a long, mint-green T-shirt dress and brown sandals. A beaded bracelet sags around her left ankle.

I'll have to be more careful now that she's here. If staff catch you exercising, they chart it and keep you inside for the rest of the day. But the committed among the committed always find a way. I am clenching and releasing every muscle in my body, from my shoulders to my calves. Secret penance.

Stomach: clench, release. Ass: clench, release. I shield my eyes and look up at her.

"Sorry I'm a little late," she says. "Then again, you don't really have any place else to be, am I right?"

I snort. "Cute." *Calves: clench, release.*

She crosses her ankles and drops next to me.

I wait for her to yell at me for refusing so many meals.

35

For growing a thick binder after only a few days here. I wait for her to tell me that I'm not trying hard enough, that I'm failing.

"We could have the session right here, if you'd like."

"Fine."

She stays silent. My insides start to itch. The quiet gets louder and louder, until it's screaming at a fever pitch.

"Josh never raped me," I say.

Her eyebrows lift slightly. Not an arch, like *What the hell, freak?* Just a lift, like *Oh*.

"Or molested me or touched me or anything like that," I say.

"Okay. Maybe when you're ready, you'll tell me about him."

I stiffen. My words have given her the wrong idea. This isn't me starting to open up. "I just wanted you to know. I don't know why I lied."

"I wonder . . ." she speaks slowly, the words crystallizing on her tongue, "if you felt pressure from me. To share something you weren't ready to share. Maybe it felt safer to make something up?"

"I . . ." My breath catches in my throat. "What?"

"Well, I've been thinking about our last session." She kicks off her sandals. "You obviously weren't ready to talk about the first time you used a behavior, and I was pushing you to let me in. Pushing too hard, I think."

I can hear my heart's slow chug in my ears. My chest is throbbing.

"I'll let you in on a little secret about us therapists," she says. "We're just so . . . human. And we make mistakes sometimes—*I* make mistakes sometimes. And the other day, I made the mistake of asking you to tell me too much, too soon. We don't know each other. Why would you share parts of your life with me that you probably haven't shared with anyone?"

I can feel her gaze on my forearm, steady like the sun. I trace the flat purple-black border of my mother from the inside of my pale veined wrist to my elbow. The image calms me and enrages me at the same time.

"You want to know about the tattoo?" I ask.

"Do you want to tell me about it?"

"Not particularly."

"Okay." After a few seconds, Shrink stands up and curtsies.

"What was that?"

She flops back onto the blanket. "You didn't notice?" She pouts like a little kid.

"Notice what?"

"What a good job I was doing not pushing for information. That was almost ten seconds."

"Are you being serious? What, do you want a cookie or something?"

She grins. "I'd rather you have a cookie."

I can't help it—I laugh. The sound is like stale dust rising from the depths. "Good luck."

She doesn't answer, just scrunches her lips together. But not in a disapproving way. More like she's thinking.

"Last session you were trying to remember what book Josh was reading during that picnic. I asked if maybe it felt like forgetting meant he was slipping away." She tucks a lock of reddish hair behind one ear.

"And I said I didn't know."

"I wonder if that's the reason for the tattoo."

I roll my eyes and sit up. "So much for not prying."

"I just think it's beautiful, is all. Hard to take my eyes off her."

Again, I trace the lines from my wrist to my elbow. I could do it blindfolded: my mother's wide eyes, strong Roman nose, and full, red lips. The strand of pearls around her neck. She is exquisite. Permanent.

"I wonder if the tattoo is so you won't forget the details," Shrink suggests.

"I wonder if you read too much into everything."

"Maybe." She flexes her toes. Her calves are white in the sun. It's strange how she doesn't cover them when she sees me looking. How she allows her dress to trace the curves of her ass, to betray the softness of her stomach. "I do think most things have meaning."

I look away. "Doesn't matter, anyway. She's gone."

"How long?" she asks softly.

I point to the two dates below her image: one for birth, and one for the day she left. "A year in May. I was sixteen and Josh was seventeen. I was eating dinner on the back porch," I say.

"When—"

"When my dad told me she was gone."

"And what did he say?" Shrink's face is different from the faces I used to get around the time Josh died. Faces that were twisted in disbelief and even curious fascination. They wanted to know how it happened, exactly how it happened, don't leave anything out. Like his death was the climax of a tragic film, and they'd snuck outside for a smoke and missed the best part.

But Shrink's face is relaxed, blank except for the eyes, which are the color of grass today. They are wide, almost sad.

"I don't know," I say sharply. I don't want to relive this, not with her here. "I don't remember what he said."

"What do you remember?"

"Fried chicken." The words are unexpected, like hot oil on my tongue. "And sweet tea."

Josh was still in class, but I was on the porch swing in the back, at the house on Broad, when I heard Dad's Buick pull into the garage. I was eating fried chicken from the Chicken Shack, a comfort-food place run by a black family from Macon. Little girls with plastic barrettes at the ends of their braids brought the food outside in white paper bags.

The night was humid, the kind of heat that made it feel like you were drowning. Next to me on the swing, Dad smelled like sweat.

"She did the best she could, Stevie," he said. "And for whatever reason, she just . . . needed to go. But you should know that none of this is your fault."

He read that in a book, I thought.

"And it doesn't mean she doesn't love you, little girl. She just . . . doesn't know how."

I sat there, silent with my arms crossed over my chest, until he finally gave up. "Well, I'll give you some time alone," Dad said.

So will she.

He stood up, and the porch swing suddenly felt too light. He went inside.

Hours later, Josh found me leaning over the porch railing, sick with the loss of her, the putrid smell of my own vomit mixed with jasmine from the trellis.

"Get cleaned up, Sass," Josh said quietly. "Go take a shower."

I didn't answer. In the yard, lightning bugs flickered yellow-green around the azaleas. My only thought was: *All this pretty is a goddamn lie.*

"It'll make you feel better."

The lump in my throat tasted like fried flesh. I shook my head.

Josh pulled me in close like a rag doll. His heart was steady.

"Stop." I tried to pull away.

"Nope," he said into my ear, and squeezed even tighter. "Love you. And so does she." I felt his tears hot on my cheek and I pretended they were mine. "Now go on." His voice cracked a little. "And come find me when you get out. I have something for you."

Upstairs in the shower, I convinced myself that maybe when I stepped into the hallway she'd be back. Maybe if I washed my hair just right or made my legs the kind of smooth you see in magazines. Maybe if I could mold myself into the perfect girl, the kind of girl who didn't sneak chocolates or beg for sugary cereal. Maybe then.

I stayed in the shower for over an hour, huddled under the spray long after it turned cold. When I got out and stepped into the hall, the silence was unspeakably loud. The kind of silence that seeps into your bones and tells you that you are alone. My body knew before I did: She was still gone.

On the way to my room I left shiny footprints on the floor planks. Inside, I let the threadbare towel drop to the floor and faced myself in the full-length mirror.

Look at yourself.

The girl in the mirror was too much and not enough. Her lines were soft, curved as though they had buckled under the pressure of being. Weak, her flesh.

It was my fault her absence hurt the way it did. My body was powerless to stop the pain. I turned and slapped my ass, staring in horror at the undulating excess. Punched my stomach, kneaded the flesh there. Too much, all of it. No wonder my mother chose to leave. I took up so much space; she couldn't breathe! I crushed my beautiful mama with the weight of my very existence.

I locked eyes with the girl in the glass.

"No more," I said out loud.

Shrink's voice draws me back. "So food is linked to the memory of your mother leaving."

"You asked what I remembered."

"I did."

"So that's it."

Shrink stays quiet for too long.

"What?" I say, suddenly irritated. Last night after Curly Blonde went to sleep, I figured out that every hour here costs twenty-eight bucks. For that kind of money, Shrink should be speed talking and fanning me with palm fronds.

"I was just thinking about . . . how difficult it must be to lose a parent like that, and then lose a brother. I can't imagine what that must be like for you."

No. She can't. "Do you have brothers or sisters?"

"I have a sister. An identical twin, actually."

It's freaky to think that there's a carbon copy of Shrink out there, sitting in the grass in a T-shirt dress and bobbing her head.

"Josh and I were Irish twins," I say. "Or that's what my dad called us. Have you heard of those?"

"Born in the same year, right?"

"Yeah."

"And he passed away . . ."

That's not what this was. Wrinkled men who breathe last breaths on the cheeks of their sleeping wives *pass away*. "July thirty-first. Last year. Just a couple months after my mom left." Desert dust makes my eyes sting. I blink and stare directly at Shrink. I want her to know I'm not crying.

Ask me, I dare her. *Ask me about how I killed my brother and haven't shed a tear about it since.*

Instead she says, "I imagine you might have felt very alone. Abandoned, even."

I say nothing because there is nothing to be said.

After a minute passes, she tries again.

"What did he say?"

"Huh?"

"The night you found out your mother was gone. What did Josh say?"

"Oh. Nothing. He gave me a journal." I wave her away. "I used it in this writing class I took."

"And do you still use it?"

"Why would I? He's dead." I press the soles of my feet together, hard. Every fiber of every muscle in my thighs is working silently.

"Okay." She sits up straight. "So what would it mean, if you chose to write even though he's not with us anymore?" She eyes my legs.

"He was never with *us*." I roll the hems of my jeans up, then down. Up, then down. Up, then down.

"Even though he's gone, I mean."

Jesus, she's exhausting.

"Okay, I'll cut to the chase," she says. "I'd like it if you'd start journaling again. Would you consider it?"

I cock my head. "Depends on what you want me to write."

"I want you to write about what those days were like for you, after your mother left. About the things that stood out for you. Whatever you—"

"I'll think about it," I cut in.

"Good enough for me." She smiles. Her eyes flicker to the thin gold watch on her wrist. "We're out of time. But we'll meet again day after tomorrow?"

"I'll check my schedule."

She laughs as she fishes for her sandals in the grass. "Our next session will be a little different. We'll meet with your treatment team: the psychiatrist, dietician, and physician. Now that you've had a little time to settle in, we'll spend the hour talking about the best course of treatment and how to move forward during your time here. Sound good?"

"No." I stand up. We are almost the same height.

"Noted. See you then."

As I head for the villa I realize I never finished my exercises. I assign myself triple the reps. I'll have to do them in bed tonight, after CB is asleep.

Just as I reach the double doors of the villa, Shrink's voice floats to me across the lawn.

"Don't forget to journal," she calls.

I yank open the door and let it slam shut behind me. She thinks writing can save me. She never considers that it was writing that got me here in the first place, destroying me from the inside out.

day six

Wednesday, July 9, 6:01 A.M.

TIME is more of a concept here than anything else. It's unreal: blocked out in perfect bold rectangles on the schedules we get every morning. Outside the sun creeps up, glowy over the lawn, then sinks like a sagging balloon losing air fast. I know that time is passing. But there are none of the usual indicators: the erratic beep of the coffee maker in the house on Broad (*Broke & Decker, that's what they should call it,* Dad said), the hollow thunk of a basketball against a backboard in the parking lot at *Le Crâpeau* before the sun slid down. The brittle chorus of crickets at night.

Here, every day feels the same. Each morning at six, we're required to report to the villa for weight and vitals. I leave Cottage Three early, to avoid the golf-cart mafia that lurch across the grounds searching for the disobedient: girls who speed walk, girls who run, girls who make the trip between the cottages and the villa more times than necessary.

Being first to report means I can walk a little fast. Weigh in and have my blood pressure taken before the others arrive. Change from my hospital gown into my clothes without the intrusion of judging eyes.

But this morning, I'm running late. I spent too much time in bed, checking and rechecking the angles of my body beneath the sheets to confirm what I already know: I am becoming soft. It's as if the very act of being here is melting me.

After weight and vitals, I hurry to the small, dimly lit changing room adjacent to the villa's dining room. It's empty. A worn armchair in the corner and a few old desks and side tables are shoved against the dingy walls. Girls have stashed their makeup bags, hair dryers, and flatirons on various surfaces. A ritualistic girl frenzy stirs here every morning before breakfast: the buzz of electric razors (real razors are contraband), the sizzle of flatirons as girls make their hair as slight as their frames.

My fingertips are clumsy as I fumble with the thick cotton ties on my hospital gown. I slip into my jeans and Braves T-shirt just as CB, Teagan, and Cate (I have finally figured out who is who) burst into the room, huddled together and cackling like a trio of escaped mental patients.

"I'm not even kidding. I swear." Cate, the anorectic with the feeding tube, whips her blond hair into a ponytail and gives me a nod. "So that new dude nurse gave me the stuff for constipation—that—what do you call it?"

"I know what you're talking about." Curly Blonde shuffles over the threshold in her filthy inked Keds.

"The stuff that tastes like orange chalk." Cate finds her way to a paisley quilted bag on the desk below the only mirror in the room. It's useless—hung high enough so you can see only your face—but she stations herself in front of it and peers at her reflection, tracing her tube with the tip of her finger. "Anyway, he makes me drink the whole thing in front of him, and when I'm finished, he takes this giant step back. Like shit's about to explode out of me any second."

"Ewwww! Cate!" Teagan rolls her eyes. I inch toward the doorway. The actual door, if there ever was one, has been removed.

"What? It *didn't*! I'm just saying—he acted like I was a freaking time bomb or something!" Cate's smile stretches her lips so tight they turn white.

This is small talk in this bizarre little universe: Girls prattle endlessly about how their hair is falling out, their skin is dry, they can't take a shit. They complain, but deep down, they wear these things like badges of honor.

"Have they made you take that stuff yet, Stevie?" Cate says to the mirror. "The chalky orange stuff?"

I shake my head. "They can't make me take anything."

"She hasn't met with her treatment team yet," CB explains.

"Ohhh," Cate and Teagan murmur in unison. In perfect sync, they reach for their clothes, scurry to separate corners, strip, and re-dress with furtive movements. I steal a glance at the curve of Cate's spine, at her perfect, spindly knees, and the lines of her rib cage that rise up triumphantly from under her skin. I pinch the fat around my midsection until tears come.

"Hey." CB's sudden enthusiasm startles me. "Before breakfast, we're gonna go down to the ring and see the horses. The nurses are too busy with vitals to care, anyway."

"I used to ride," Cate says. The hollows of her cheeks cast a grayish shadow over the rest of her face. She flicks the red plastic bracelet around her wrist. "When you get on yellow, they'll let you ride the horses here. I already picked out my horse. Ernie." She turns on her curling iron. Then she lets her hair down and winds a chunk of it around the barrel.

"You'll get there," Teagan says almost forcefully. She pulls her green bracelet tight, until the puffy flesh around her wrist goes white.

"Morning, girls." The thick-ankled redhead from the lawn stalks past me, twirling the cotton tie on her gown.

"Hey, Jenna. Have you met Stevie? She's in with us now," Cate says.

No, I'm not.

"Cool." Jenna gives me a nod and hunches over her makeup bag. "Anyone need anything?"

"Ooh! Me." Cate finishes curling her hair, flips her head over, and gives it a shake.

"Fine, but make sure they're all hidden, okay?" Jenna clutches something in her grip. I want to know what it is and I don't, all at once. "And if you get busted—"

"I won't tell! Come *on*, Jenna."

Jenna eyes me. "Is she cool?"

"Jesus Christ. I don't *care*," I say.

"Fine. Here." She releases the forbidden item into Cate's outstretched palm, then groans as she tugs on a pair of jeans beneath her gown.

"Ashley? Can you do a topknot?" Cate asks. She hands over the contraband, and I get a glimpse. Bobby pins.

Teagan's watching me. "It's because if you take the little plastic caps off the ends, you could use them to self-harm."

Like I asked. Besides, using hair accessories to self-harm is just . . . uninspired. I don't need tools. My body is both weapon and wound, predator and prey. I will self-destruct without any help.

"So? Wanna come? To see the horses, I mean?" CB bites down on a bobby pin and twists Cate's hair into a feeble knot.

I shake my head. "Nah. No."

"C'mon. I know the first week's been hard for you, but—"

"It's not."

"Huh?" Curly Blonde's brows arch.

"It's not hard." Slowly, I let my eyes trace every indulgent inch of her body. "Not if you have the slightest bit of willpower."

Once I'm outside on the patio, I can breathe again. I hold a notebook in my lap, an empty black-and-white composition book Shrink left on my pillow along with a thin black marker and a pink metallic paper crane. Complimentary chocolates must be out of the question.

The marker is heavy in my hand. It's the first time I've written anything since seminar. I'm not journaling for Shrink. I'm not. I'm writing because I can't stand to be inside the villa with the girls and the noise and glittery clouds of hair spray.

I turn to the first page. Shrink's handwriting is unrestrained.

Write about what changed for you. How you experienced life after the loss of your mother.

* * *

The memory of the first few hours and days after she disappeared is hazy, smeared like pencil marks that have been partially erased. I remember the sounds, mostly: the laughter downstairs as Dad hosted his Tuesday night writing group. The creak of Josh's footsteps outside my door as he debated whether to come in.

On the sixth day he finally did. "Get up, Sass. You have class."

I'd begged him not to make me go. I wasn't ready.

"I'm grieving," I told him from beneath the sheets. "Fuck off."

But he'd said I had to, said Dad needed me to be okay and normal and other things I wasn't. Pushed me until I was dressed and out the door, walking to the Stacks, a bar/coffeehouse in a Victorian-style house just a few blocks from our place. The first floor was a nameless used-book shop where Dad went to read old Hemingway and avoid deadlines. Where my mother bought teetering stacks of classics (*no Hemingway*, she'd told me when I begged. *Hemingway was a misogynist! A drunk!*) to keep me occupied as a child. But the second floor was a bar where Ben taught seminar on Wednesday afternoons in summer.

The bar was dark, with mahogany-paneled walls and dim Tiffany lamps. I stood at the top of the staircase blinking like a moron, waiting for my pupils to adjust. I'd never been in a bar before. Never had a drink. I blamed Josh: Everybody else in my grade already had a fake ID and spent Saturday nights parked behind the soccer field with their friends, chugging a fifth of nobody-cared-what. Not that I had any friends to underage drink with. But still, Josh didn't understand. He was one of those rare breeds who could stay completely straight and everybody loved him anyway. He didn't understand that most of the world wasn't like him—most of us needed a little something extra to be okay.

At the back of the bar, a few community college students were drinking coffee at a long, farmhouse-style table. Students were easy to spot. The rips in their jeans were intentional. They didn't wear the same kind of tired the townies did. My stomach seized. I didn't belong here.

With my every step toward the table came a new awareness: the goose bumps puckering my skin, the way my thighs slapped together as I walked. The girth of my hips, my protruding stomach and back fat spilling over my cutoffs. All of me stitched together and straining at the seams.

There were mostly guys at the table, with only one girl close to my age and a woman with a ropy, gray French braid and a tiny diamond nose stud. The woman smiled at me. I took the chair across from her. I watched the girl out of the corner of my eye. She was thinner than me. Her thick, straight hair was so black it was almost iridescent blue. She had large green eyes winged with creamy layers of chartreuse and electric aqua that came to a point at her temples. A silver shooting star tattoo arced over her right cheekbone. The air around her smelled too sweet.

"You guys read Ashe's latest book?" The popped collar two seats down cut his eyes in my direction. His sunglasses rested on the back of his neck. He wasn't the typical two-year student. Too entitled. A local, probably, with money and a DUI from prom night that had inconveniently sidetracked his Ivy plan.

"I thought he played it a little safe, honestly," the older woman spoke up.

"What do you mean?" I blurted. "I liked it." My dad had spent our final family vacation editing the book.

"I like his early work better," the woman said. "He was hungrier then."

The boy ignored her. "What's your name?" he asked me, balancing his chair on its back legs.

"Stevie." My whisper was dusty. I searched the bar for Ben's familiar outline. He was nowhere.

"Stevie. Nice." The boy reached for his coffee mug and took a too-long sip. Licked the milky foam from his upper lip, slow. "Haven't seen you in any of my classes so far."

"Back it down, Drew." The girl's voice was low and thick. She rolled her eyes at me. "Hey. Eden."

"Stevie," I said again. My cheeks, my whole body, were burning. I reached into my backpack and found the journal Josh had bought me. I scratched at the shadowy sweat stains on the grass cloth cover.

"Just being friendly," Drew murmured. "Buy you a drink, Stevie?"

"Now?" Electricity shot through me.

"Not now. Not on my watch." Ben deposited a stack of composition books at the head of the table. He was about ten years younger than Dad, and Josh's height but thicker, with a shaved head and diamonds in his ears. The sleeves on his white dress shirt were rolled up, almost glowing against the blackness of his skin. He smiled at me, all pity around the eyes and mouth, and my fists curled in my lap. A lump formed in my throat as I nodded back.

"Let's get started." Ben took a folded slip of paper from his shirt pocket and started taking roll. When he got to my name, he called it just like any other, and I relaxed a little.

"God, he's delicious," Eden said under her breath. She straightened up a little and tossed her hair back, and everyone looked except Ben.

I squirmed in my seat and pretended not to hear.

I spent the next three hours not hearing Ben, either, penning four different letters to my mother while the others freewrote on a childhood memory. I wondered if Ben was going to shake his head at my father over a beer.

"I don't feel like going back to my apartment. My roommate's kind of a slut," Eden said after seminar was over and the rest of the class had dispersed. "Want to stick around?"

"Who, me?" I slammed the cover of my journal shut.

"Yeah, you." Eden laughed a little. "Grab that table. I'll be back."

"Okay." I didn't feel like staying, but I didn't feel like going home, either. I tucked myself in the corner booth. A few minutes later, she slid across from me and deposited two short glasses on the table.

"Oh. I don't actually—" I touched the glass with awkward, virgin fingers. "I mean, thanks."

It burned. That's how people always describe the first drink, isn't it? *It burned going down.* But that was exactly it: fire fingers reaching down my throat into my empty gut. I'd been fasting for six days and it felt like some huge transformation was happening inside me.

"Damn, girl." Eden leaned back, impressed as I sputtered. "Take it slow!"

I expected the second sip to go down easier. It didn't. "When did you get that tattoo?" I choked, pointing at the shooting star.

"Couple years ago. Ever thought about getting one?" Her lips curved upward.

"There's nothing to get. Nothing I want on my body forever like that."

"It's just art. Overthink it and you ruin it."

We stayed there in the back corner for hours. I shredded the napkins in front of me, leaving a snowy paper pyramid. She opened my journal without asking and scribbled her cell number on the inside cover in teal ink. *Don't look at what I wrote*, I pleaded silently. She closed the journal and I took a breath.

"I just feel like Ashe is gonna be a really important part of my education," Eden said earnestly. "Like he's really gonna push me past my comfort zone, you know, as a writer." She leaned in. The more she spoke, the closer her lips came to mine.

"And not just because he's black or whatever," she assured me. "It's just, he's so . . . *different*." She pulled back, and her eyes focused in sudden, weird sobriety. "I can't think of anything worse than being ordinary, can you?"

But I wasn't ordinary. Already, I had started to change. My insides a little emptier, my cheeks a little more hollow.

"This is the terrible thing girls like us have in common," she explained. "Parents, upbringings, lifestyles, that are painfully normal. Middle class." It was almost amoral, being raised this way, she told me fiercely. We'd never really understand pain. And wasn't that the human condition? By shielding us from the real world, pressing their palms over our eyes during all the bad parts, our parents—*our parents*—were keeping us separate from humanity. We were something else entirely.

"Animals," I said absently, drawing my belly button toward my spine.

She shook her head. "That's what I'm saying. We're not even allowed to really be animals. Not allowed to experience, like, *raw* things. Because we were raised on fucking Fisher-Price and Splenda and Disney, you know?"

She looked like she might cry, so I said, "I know."

"Haven't you ever wanted to do something . . . This is gonna sound stupid. Don't laugh."

"I won't."

"Something . . . extraordinary? Something that sets you apart just to prove you're, like, different?"

I tensed. Why couldn't she see that something extraordinary had already begun? That once my metamorphosis was complete I would emerge as someone other than me? It wasn't enough, clearly. I had to do more than fast. I would start to run tomorrow. Tonight maybe. Tonight.

"Seriously, though." She lifted her glass to her lips and threw her head back even though the glass was empty. "We should do something. Something real." Her eyes were shining, the wet metallic green of insect wings in summer.

Sitting there in the bar, I realized that I had no idea how many calories were in a glass of scotch. Or even two or three. By then, I was too drunk to panic.

"Like what?"

"Come on." She grabbed my wrist and pulled me out of the booth to the door.

* * *

I put the pen down and tip my face toward the hot New Mexico sun, unable to write the rest. The sounds of that night running together like water. There was the slap of our feet on the pavement and the buzz of the neon sign in the window. Eden's giggles as she passed me her ID before we went inside (*Shh*, Eden said, *shh*). There was the sound of my voice, my words as I described her. There was the hum of the needle.

I'd felt so proud when we'd left. Felt like it was symbolic, the way there was a bandage wrapped around the image of my mother. She was the wound. It was fucking poetry. And then something changed. Eden left to go back to her apartment and I sat alone in my car and I was empty. I was hungry—my god, I hadn't eaten in six days, what did I expect? Somehow, I was lonely for this girl I didn't know, this girl who cared enough to ask me not to laugh, this girl whose black-hole pupils lined up with mine when she spoke. And I ached to be full of something, anything at all. *Hurry, hurry, hurry, fill it up.*

The rest is a blur. It has to be. The drunken ride to the grocery store, wandering the aisles with my throbbing arm, the laughing at nothing and the passing cars. Sitting in Dad's old Buick, parked in the abandoned lot a few blocks from the house. The sound of static radio making my insides quiver. And I knew, in a place deeper than seeing or feeling, that this was a beginning. I was about to do something that could not be undone. Something dangerous. Something toxic.

Something extraordinary.

day six

AFTER breakfast, I'm supposed to meet Shrink on the lawn for a session. But when I shove past Hannah and through the double doors, Shrink's not outside. I survey the grounds for a place to purge. I could care less if anyone catches me. Even though I ate only half of my individual carton of yogurt—I like the way the sweet white yogurt feels cool on the back of my throat—I can still feel it consuming me. At the edge of the lawn, there's a cluster of low shrubs. Perfect.

"Hi, Stevie."

I turn. Shrink is standing directly in front of the sun, so all I can see is the blackness of her outline. She looks like a stained-glass Jesus, standing over me with the sunlight behind her. My Savior, in a white sundress and the usual flat brown sandals.

"You ready for the treatment team meeting?" Shrink is holding my file in one hand. Her creamy cheeks are dusted with peach.

"Oh, right." I slide my fingers through my short, limp hair. My skull is irregular, with divots and ridges.

We cut through the villa and exit the front door. I take the stairs to the right of the fountain. On the steps, recovery slogans are chalked in neon pink and yellow. You Are a Soul with a Body, Not a Body with a Soul! Bite Me, Ed! It's bizarre how they turn the words *eating disorder* into a man's name: Ed. Poor bastard.

"Each of the members of your treatment team will talk for a bit about their assessment of your needs," she says.

"But they don't know me." Not that Shrink does, either. I follow a few feet behind, kicking blood-colored dirt over her tracks. Already the heat is ruthless; the sun feels just inches away. I am slightly dizzy again, which is comforting. My body is obeying the command. I wonder what she'll do if I stop and puke right here.

"True. They don't know you yet." She stops and turns, waiting for me to catch up. "But after taking a look at your testing and blood work, they do know what you need in order to live."

We walk up a small hill toward yet another stucco building with a flat roof. There are a few low shrubs planted in gravel around the perimeter. This is one thing I can appreciate about the desert: It is without pretense. There are few perfumed flowers, or lush green leaves, or other signs of life or beauty. The environment is harsh; the life that has survived is stripped of excess.

"Did you get around to journaling?" Shrink yanks open a small wooden door. I follow her inside.

"Yeah."

"Awesome. That's great." She closes the door behind us and the foyer is plunged into near darkness. It takes my pupils a few seconds to adjust.

"It's not any good, though."

"It's your thoughts and feelings. We don't put a label on those. They are what they are." She flips a switch near the door, and a dim yellow light buzzes overhead.

"Did they teach you that in shrink school?"

She laughs. "As a matter of fact, they did. Still true, though."

The building is composed of only a few carpeted rooms, plus an eat-in kitchen and small bathroom. It could have been someone's home once. In the back room, plastic blinds shield a sliding glass door. They remind me of the blinds we had at *Le Crâpeau*. The room is empty except for a circle of brown metal folding chairs in the center.

"Hi, my name is Stevie, and I'll be dead in twenty-two days."

"Hiii, Stevie."

"Have a seat wherever you'd like." Shrink drops her bag in one of the chairs and kicks off her shoes. It's like her need to be barefoot is biological. She meanders over to the blinds and twists the hanging plastic rod, flooding the room with light. "We'll just hang out and wait for the rest of the team."

I take the seat to the left of her bag and stare at the gashes of outside world between the blinds. In the foyer, the door creaks. Seconds later, two men and a woman enter. The men are wearing white coats. One of the men is the Indian psychiatrist I saw with CB the other day. He has a goatee, wire-rimmed glasses, and bushy eyebrows. He greets me with a deep nod that is almost a bow.

"Miss Deslisle. A pleasure." His accent is thick. "I am Dr. Singh." He takes a seat in one of the chairs in the circle. Shrink and the other two strangers sit, too. We are so close our knees almost touch.

"I'm Dr. Wilkes," says the other man. He is young with slick dark hair and a chin dimple. "I'll be your physician."

"And I'll be your dietician," the woman says. Her long white waves are parted down the center and her smile reveals a gap between her two front teeth. A pair of lime-green reading glasses crowns her nose. "I'm Ms. Dalton."

"Hey." My voice sounds raspy. I clear my throat and cross my arms over my chest. Suddenly, I want to shove my chair back, away from the circle. We are too close, these strangers and me, and I am taking up too much space.

"Okay," Shrink says brightly. "So, Stevie, the four of us make up your treatment team. We are all available to you while you're here—to answer questions, talk, vent, whatever. Okay?"

The dietician chimes in. "This is *your* treatment, Stevie. We want you to be an active participant in your own healing."

My treatment. She is telling me that if this doesn't stick, it will be my fault and mine alone. "You know I'm being forced to stay here, right?"

Dr. Wilkes coughs.

"Just being honest," I say blithely. "You know, about my thoughts and feelings."

Shrink jumps in. "And we want you to be. The hope is that once you've gone through the refeeding process, and as we make progress in therapy, you'll be more motivated to seek recovery."

Refeeding? Even the word sounds inhumane.

"Who wants to start? Sherri?" Shrink nods at Ms. Dalton, who sits to my left.

"Sure." Ms. Dalton reaches into her bag and pulls out a slim black binder. She smells sweet, like the jasmine behind my old house. "From what I can tell on your chart, it's been difficult for you to complete meals or accept supplement since you got here"—she consults her bible—"five days ago."

"This is the sixth day."

"Six days ago. Would you say that's an accurate assessment?"

"No. Not difficult. I *choose* not to eat."

"Okay." She consults the binder in silence for a while. "It looks like you're restricting all food with the exception of yogurt and lettuce?"

Thank you. "Yes."

"So one of my goals for you, obviously, is to get you to the point where you can complete the majority of your meals. The refeeding process—"

"Refeeding means starting you on foods that are easier on your system, to get your body used to food again." I hate that Shrink has read my mind. "It's why we've started you on soup, crackers, applesauce, those sorts of things."

I close my eyes. Soup means a shiny coating of oil over chunks of meat drowned in yellowed noodles. I will not.

Ms. Dalton starts up again. "Given your weight upon your arrival—"

My eyes snap open, and my heart thrums like hummingbird wings. "Tell me."

Her lips wither. "Tell you your weight?"

I nod. That binder holds everything I need. The numbers.

"What would that do for you, Stevie?" Shrink crosses her legs and leans toward me. "To know your weight?"

Everything. I slip my hand around my wrist and squeeze.

"Stevie—" Ms. Dalton falters. "My assessment is that knowing your weight could be more harmful than helpful."

"So you're not going to tell me." She thinks I am fragile. She thinks I will shatter.

"For now, let's focus on getting you through refeeding. After that, it's my recommendation that we put you on a weight-gain meal plan, instead of maintenance."

Good. Maintenance is for the bulimics and the girls who have made half-assed attempts at anorexia. I won't actually gain the weight, of course. But I can appreciate the recognition.

Dr. Singh makes a note on the legal pad in his lap.

"How much?" I ask her. I am cool. Unaffected. "How many pounds?"

I can feel her eyes on me. "We're recommending that you gain somewhere around twenty-five pounds," she says.

The number burns like ice in my veins. It's wrong. The number should be higher. Twenty-five? My god, I'm such a failure.

"Stevie?" Shrink's voice is somewhere at the back of my brain.

Twenty-five. I press my fingertips to my collarbone, frantic. It isn't there, it isn't there. I feel only flesh. Twenty-five. I am spinning.

"Stevie." I feel Shrink's hand pressing down on my right shoulder. "What's happening for you right now? Can you verbalize your thoughts?"

"I'm fine. Keep going." I don't understand. I should be more accomplished by now. But even as I fight it, the truth forces its way to the surface. *Too many binges over the past year.* I thought I had time. I thought I could fix those countless moments of weakness.

"Stevie." Shrink is trying to catch my eye. "Help me understand what's happening."

Ms. Dalton angles her chair so that I am trapped on both sides. "Stevie, I know that the thought of gaining that much weight must feel daunting—"

Wrong. She's so wrong. I am so, so wrong. I should be closer to Josh by now. I've miscalculated. My math—the calculations I've made so painstakingly for the past 343 days—have been all wrong. *If Girl A departs sanity around the time her mother abandons her, assuming she is traveling at full speed toward self-destruction, how long will it take her to reach her dead brother?*

"—but we'll be here to walk with you in this," Ms. Dalton finishes.

Wrong again. I walk alone.

"Keep. Going." I pull my knees to my chest and wrap my arms around them. The metal groans under my thickness. The scar on my thigh pulses, a steady reminder of what I've done.

"I need you to keep your feet on the floor, please," Shrink says. "It will help you to stay grounded."

"Jesus Christ." I slam the soles of my feet on the carpet.

The room goes silent.

"So, what? Are we finished? Can I get out of here?" The light through the window is searing, a serrated blade pressed against my jugular. It takes every bit of strength just to breathe. *In, out. In, out.*

"We're not finished." Ms. Dalton's voice is level. "Can you stick with me just a little bit longer?"

I bite the inside of my cheek until I taste rust. "Fine."

"With the weight you'll need to gain, I'm not recommending use of a feeding tube. I'm confident that you can do this without one. But if you lose any more weight, I'll have to reconsider."

I think Ms. Dalton wants me to nod, so I do. It is the right thing. Across the circle, Dr. Wilkes is starting to talk now, but his words wash over me, unheard.

I'm stuck. I can't afford to have a feeding tube if I'm going to reach Josh by the Anniversary. But if I keep losing weight, they will force me. Strap me down like the mental patient I am.

Dr. Wilkes is saying phrases like *abnormalities in your EKG* and *significant deterioration of the tooth enamel*.

I think of solutions. Water loading is my only real option; there are no pockets in the gowns and the nurse pats me down before weighing to ensure that I am completely naked underneath. But I cannot possibly consume enough water before weighing to fool them. I have to think outside the box, indulge my creative side. Razor blades, maybe, or pills on the day of the Anniversary if absolutely necessary. I could get some; all I'd have to do is tell the doctor I can't sleep. Feel too high, too low, too much, not enough. Hear voices. Bad thoughts.

Next to Dr. Wilkes, Dr. Singh begins to speak. When I hear the word *diagnosis*, the room sharpens. I watch his thin, purple-tinged lips form the words I expect to hear: *post-traumatic stress disorder, dysthymia*. He does not say what I need him to say.

Call me by my name.

He crosses his legs and nudges his glasses down the bridge of his nose, reviewing the chart in his lap.

Say it.

When he looks up, his expression is neutral. "I am, however, changing your Axis One diagnosis in part. It seems that *bulimia nervosa* would be a better diagnostic fit, given that you are not currently below eighty-five percent of your ideal body weight."

Bulimia.

Absurdity. Instantly, the laughter rises up in me and begins to consume. It runs its tongue down my spine, grazes my neck. Scrapes the flesh from my ribs and suddenly, my sides ache.

Dr. Singh has stopped speaking. The room is silent except for my shrill laughter. *Bulimia!* I stand up.

"Stevie." Shrink rises alongside me and reaches for my wrist.

I jerk away. The back of my hand makes a sick slapping sound as it meets her cheek. She stumbles back. Now the rest of them are springing forward. I turn and break through the circle, stumbling toward the door.

Bulimia! A slur, when I've worked so hard to become what I am.

day six

Wednesday, July 9, 11:11 A.M.

IN the hours since Dr. Singh stripped me of my name, I've lain curled up on the gold corduroy couch in the villa, unsealing my lips only for water and the newly prescribed antidepressant that I have stashed under my tongue. They think they fool me by adding Gatorade to the water, but I taste the salty sweetness in the back of my throat.

I lie on my side and stare at my warped reflection on the television screen. The girl on the screen is impotent. She has no control; she has allowed impulse and hunger to rule her. She deserves the label of *bulimia*. I stare into her dead eyes. Maybe if she'd been stronger that night. Maybe if she hadn't been drunk.

She disgusts me. I close my eyes, but she follows me into the depths of memory. *No*, I plead. *Please*. But she drags me back, kicking and screaming, to the very first time. And I am living it again.

Eden was gone, and I was drunk. My arm was throbbing. I was slumped in the driver's seat of Dad's old Buick. Engine idling, headlights off. No one could witness what I was about to do.

The radio was on, but the dial was stuck between stations. The soundtrack was static, peppered with the occasional syllable from Garrison Keillor on NPR. I turned up the volume. Then the static was so loud, I could feel the vibrations at my core. They reminded me that I was alive.

My heart was beating so fast I thought my chest might explode. Beneath the white cotton bandage, my arm throbbed in rhythm with my heart. But my hands were steady and strong.

I reached for the first bag—clawed at it, really—and tore into the package. I found individually wrapped chocolate snack cakes with fluffy white filling. The icing on my fingertips felt taboo, like sugary sex. My mother never let me have these. I crammed the cakes into my mouth, one after the other after the other, until I was breathing them in, positive that without them I would suffocate. I barely took the time to chew, so deep was the need for this oxygen. Too soon, my hands grasped nothing.

Next the bag of round chocolate truffles, each encased in their familiar yellow-gold foil. I pressed the soft globes between my tongue and the ridged roof of my mouth. Their surrender was instant.

Soon fear churned in my gut. It mingled with the processed sugar and booze. I forgot to drink something; this would never

67

work unless I drank something. Rookie mistake. There was a gallon of tea somewhere, I know, somewhere.

Sweet tea. My fingers found the plastic handle. I gulped it down with the kind of urgency only the dying could understand. It spilled down my front, slipped its sticky fingers along my throat and between my breasts. The plastic container buckled, no match for my rabid sucking.

I kept going that way, stuffing myself with all of it—the cheese puffs like bony electric orange fingers, the packets of powdered hot chocolate I tore open with my fangs. It was not human what I was becoming.

The end came only when everything was empty and at last—*at last*—I was full. I turned off the car and stumbled outside. Fell to my knees in the dirt like the feral animal I was.

It was harder than I thought it would be. My thick tongue kept obstructing my index finger. My body prayed, *Please, girl, please. Don't.*

But it didn't take long for my body to submit to my will. With deft fingers, I pulled the strings, commanding my body to empty.

It was almost satisfying, seeing it there on the grassy altar: the swirls of neon orange and frosted bits of cake floating in sugary sweet tea. I crawled a few feet away, twigs and tiny pebbles imprinting my skin with chaotic designs. I flipped onto my back, spent in a moment of peace. It felt almost holy, my body pressed against the earth that way, rising and falling to the irregular chant of my heart. I made an angel in the grass.

Stars came out. At last, my mind was still. So quiet I could hear the crickets in the grass, proclaiming Georgia summer.

* * *

"Stevie?" A woman's voice bubbles to the surface, ripping through me.

I open my eyes, every fiber of my body aching. I look around and realize that Shrink and I are alone in the villa. The other girls are outside on the lawn.

"Stevie."

"What?" My lips and tongue are like rubber.

"I think it's important that we talk." Shrink perches on the edge of the sofa. "Do you want to meet in here? In my office?"

"No session. I don't feel well."

"I'm sorry to bother you. Were you sleeping? Dreaming?"

I shake my head from side to side without opening my eyes. "Remembering."

"Remembering . . . what, exactly?" I can feel her weight on the couch next to me. I pull my knees to my chest.

"'Memory believes before knowing remembers,'" I say, because these are the words that come to mind and I'm not about to talk to her about the first time. Not now, not ever.

"Sorry?"

"Nothing." Just *Faulkner*.

"Outside or in?" she asks quietly.

"I told you, I don't feel well." My voice is louder than I expected. Sweat collects behind my knees, in the ashy cradle of my elbow. I feel sick, shaky, like it's early morning and I'm trying to sleep off a night of drinking with Eden.

"You're angry."

"Because you're not listening to me." I sit up, scramble away to the other end of the couch. With my back pressed against the bony sofa arm, I occupy only one cushion, although technically—

technically—I occupy only half. Less if I pull my knees tight to my chest and scrunch my toes.

"Okay, so you're frustrated with me for pushing. And angry about the treatment team meeting."

"Whatever. I don't care."

"No? Because if I were you, I'd be pissed. I'd be really, really pissed if I finally found an identity that seemed to fit, and then my treatment team took it away."

"Shut up." I spit the words at her.

"Tell me about your reaction," she says in a voice so soft it makes my body spark like a frayed live wire.

"Jesus, it's not a reaction! I'm done talking, okay? That's all."

"Stevie, it's okay to be angry."

I slap one of the throw pillows so hard my hand stings. "Oh. Is it? Is it okay? *Thank you* for your permission to be pissed at your fucking diagnosis."

She doesn't flinch. "*Your* fucking diagnosis."

"It's not mine. It's wrong." I can't bear to look at her.

"You wanted an anorexia diagnosis."

I would puke, if there was anything left inside me. Why is she doing this to me?

"Tell me what it means, Stevie. What does it mean about you, the bulimia diagnosis?"

The words come instantly, rushing past one another on my tongue. "That I'm fat. That I'm lazy. No self-control. Disgusting. Weak. The lowest of the low." For a second, the feeling rushes back into my body. Salty and cold, taking me under like a crashing wave.

"Those are really terrible things to think about yourself."

"They're true."

"I know you believe they are. But I absolutely don't believe those things."

She can believe what she wants. But there is only one absolute truth.

"What did the diagnosis of anorexia mean for you?"

Anorexia. The word sounds intimate and sad. As if we knew each other, once, but are strangers now.

"Stevie? What did it mean?"

"It meant . . . strength. Power. It meant I was better . . . than."

"Mmm. Better than who?"

"Everyone. Myself. Who I used to be." She won't understand. And I don't know how to describe the transformation. It's as if all your life, you've been hiding in a self that wasn't yours. Buried beneath the surface was someone more potent. Someone special. And then one day, it happens. Maybe you're sitting alone in your room, doing your exercises. Maybe you're taking the long way to school, or dissecting the grilled chicken flesh on your plate with a blade. And you hear the word. Your calling.

Anorexic.

And it fits. You have shed the scaly flesh of the imposter. Emerged raw, fresh, and new. You have come into your real self. For the first time, you are alive.

Shrink puts her hand on mine. "You are not your illness," she says. Which proves what I already know: She has no clue.

I tug the ugly afghan from the back of the sofa and cocoon myself in it. Then I look at her. A reddish welt rises just above her right cheekbone. *Did I . . .* Of course I did. I hurt everyone I touch.

71

She catches me looking at her. I think she will make a joke, maybe something about how since my career as a hunger artist isn't exactly taking off, I could always look into professional boxing. But she says, "It's okay, Stevie."

I open my mouth to say something—*whatever, this is bullshit, leave me alone*—and then close it again. The space behind my eyes stings. I clutch my forearms and squeeze until the pain passes.

"It will be time for lunch soon. If you can make a little more effort over the next few days, I can ask Ms. Dalton to let you pick your own meals, and—" She stops. "Stevie? Stevie. Stop." There is urgency in her voice. She reaches beneath the afghan and lifts my forearm.

"What're you—" I look down.

Without realizing it, I have dug my thumbnail into my forearm so forcefully that my mother's lifeless cherry smile balloons with a single drop of blood.

day six

Wednesday, July 9, 9:06 P.M.

BACK in Cottage Three, I reach for the pullout drawer built into the platform bed frame. There are two pills, a white and a yellow, stashed in the left cup of my bra. One is the antidepressant I saved this morning, and the other is the pill they gave me after dinner when I told the nurse I was feeling "very anxious."

"Oh, hey."

I try to slam the drawer shut, but it jams with only an inch to go. CB is standing in the doorway to our room.

"Hey." I nod, eyeing the way her sunburned ankles stick out over her Keds. I reach down and wrap my fingers around my own ankles. Coarse hair has sprouted in prickly tufts from my ankles to my thighs. My armpits, too. I don't have an electric razor and I won't ask any of the girls to borrow theirs.

"I looked for you at the villa so we could walk back together."

"Why?" After the way I talked to her this morning in the changing room, she shouldn't want anything to do with me.

But it's like she's completely forgotten. "I just wanted to see if you were okay. I know you had your treatment team meeting today." She kicks off her Keds and nudges them into her side of the closet. It is stuffed with knit dresses, frilly skirts, and scoop-neck tees.

"Oh."

"Those meetings suck, don't they?" She sighs and heaves her body onto the bed, making the wooden frame shudder. "Must have been rough." She settles onto her stomach, with her head at the end of the foot of the bed so we're only a few feet apart.

I shrug. Next, she'll want to braid each other's hair.

"Yeah." She nods and rests her chin in her hands. It's an irritating habit of hers, this answering as though we're having an actual conversation.

I close my eyes, hoping she'll take the hint and turn off the light.

"I'm glad Anna was there for you, though."

"Anna?"

"Your . . . therapist?"

Right. Shrink. I give up and turn onto my side, facing her. I realize, as I take her in, I've never really seen her before. She is a pudgy child: round, pink cheeks with freckles like tiny grains of sand across the bridge of her small, perfect nose. Her eyes are a liquid, hopeful brown. There is a spark there, flickering but present. Rage suddenly washes over me. It's unthinkable that we should have the same diagnosis. We are not alike.

"She seems so great, Anna. I wish she was my therapist."

"Were."

"Huh?" The skin above her sunburned nose ripples in confusion. *Worthless cow.*

"I wish she *were* my therapist. *Were.*" I say it *slow-ly.* To ensure that she *under-staaaaands.* "It's subjunctive."

"Okay." She blinks. I have hurt her, that much I can see. A fresh wave of anger ignites. I hate her, I hate her, this girl who is still able to feel. "Anyway, she seems really good." She sits up and starts to pick at the pink glitter nail polish on her short stubby toes. "So, when you're quiet for a long time, are you, like, having flashbacks or something?"

"I don't have flashbacks." My voice is thin. "I'm just . . . remembering things."

"That happens to me sometimes, too." The rest of the words rush out of her mouth all at once, like she is unable to restrain herself. "Like, I remember things, things I don't want to remember, actually? Over and over. Sometimes I can't sleep because of it, or can't concentrate or whatever. It's like I can't shut it off, you know? It's like the one thing I want to do, but I can't."

I swallow, keeping my eyes on the polish chips she's now violently flicking from her toes.

"Do you ever feel like that?"

I allow my head to dip in a nod. I do. I hate that I do. I hate that we do.

"Sometimes I wish I could just go to sleep, like, forever, and not dream."

I sit up and face her. "I, uh, have some meds—a pill if you're upset or—if you can't . . . if you need something."

"Really?" She smiles, looking suddenly shy. "Thanks. I mean . . . I'm okay for now. But thanks."

"It's not a big deal." Nearly all of me has no idea why I offered, especially when she could tell on me and get my stash confiscated. But a minuscule part of me knows what it's like to be suspended, half-conscious, in a memory you can't escape. Always remembering. Nobody deserves that. Nobody but me, anyway. "Just don't say anything."

"I won't. Swear."

"Good."

"So, um . . ." CB sits up. Her stomach ripples under her dress, making her look like a girl Buddha statue. *Curly Blonde Buddha.* I almost laugh. "What are yours about?"

"My what?"

"Your flashba—memories."

"You're not serious." I would never tell her about the memory of the first time, or about Josh or Eden or seminar or my mother.

"You don't have to talk about it if you don't want to. It's just that sometimes it helps me to say things out loud. And you haven't really said much since you got here."

I lie down again and close my eyes against the buzzing fluorescent light and her voice.

On the other side of the room, the bed creaks. "You're lucky. It's like nothing gets to you. I have all this stuff trapped inside, and some days I think if I don't get it out as fast I can . . ." She heaves a sigh. "It's like a parasite or something. I don't know."

I do. And I feel the same way. Like my own memories could devour me.

"And the thing is, since my family looks so perfect from the outside, people just assume . . ." Her voice wavers.

I yawn and crack my neck. I need to focus on a new plan, a way to lose weight without alarming Shrink or the rest of my team. No distractions.

"Sorry. Never mind. You're trying to get to sleep." The bed creaks again, and I hear her pad across the carpet. With the click of the light switch, the room plunges into twilight. I keep on the small clip lamp attached to the built-in shelves. Here the dark is too dark. I flip onto my side and face the painted cinder block wall.

"Oh," she whispers. "Before you go to sleep, do you think you could get my zipper? This one always gets stuck."

I roll my eyes at the ceiling. "Fine."

She perches on the edge of my bed, back to me. I cringe at the fleshy curves beneath the thin cotton.

"Here." She scoops the mass of thick blond curls off her back and whips them into a twist so I can reach the zipper. I pinch the cold metal between my fingers and drag it down. The gasp escapes my throat before I can stop it.

Trailing from her hairline to the space between her shoulder blades is a shower of small, perfectly circular scars. Some are purple, some red, and some raised, thick, and white. It looks like someone has taken a hole punch to her, like she's nothing more than a cheap paper doll. Horrified, I reach out to touch one. It's callous beneath my finger.

"Oh. God." She jerks away, reaching for the zipper as she escapes to her side of the room. "Sorry. I didn't think—"

77

"No! It's okay! I . . . what happened to you?" I dig my nails into the mattress, suddenly feeling like I might puke. What am I supposed to do? Go over there? Leave her alone? Call somebody? Shrink, maybe. There's a phone in the hall, I remember.

"Nothing," she says quickly. Her eyes are wide with concern, like she's more worried about me than the meteor shower of scar tissue tumbling down her spine. "Nothing new, anyway. I've had these." And then, as if she's read my mind, "Staff knows already. Don't worry about it."

"Don't *worry* about it?" I rub my face with my hands. My entire body is tensed. "But—"

"Seriously, Stevie." She lets out a hard-edged laugh. "Would you just lie down? You're freaking me out."

I force a laugh, too, but it feels wrong, like I'm the one who put those scars there. Even though I didn't. And she didn't, either. There's no way she could have reached those places on her body.

"Turn the light out? I can't sleep with that thing on." She climbs into bed, still clothed, and buries herself beneath the covers.

I have the sudden urge to climb in with her, to stroke her hair the way Josh used to do for me when I had a nightmare. But that would be weird. So I reach up and turn off the lamp, even though my mind is reeling with questions, and there's this scream churning inside of me like wind, gathering speed.

"It's not, you know," I say into the dark, "normal." I don't say it to make her feel bad. I just say it so she knows it's not okay.

"Yeah." Her voice is a whimper, but she seems to understand. "I know."

"You can tell me if you want," I say to the ceiling, after several minutes have passed. My own marred flesh is aching, and I knead the scar with my fingertips. It does nothing to ease the throbbing.

Across the room, she says nothing. There is only the easy, rhythmic breathing of her sleep. In and out, in and out, like cool water lapping against a rocky shore.

day seven

I lie motionless on top of the covers for hours, my mind filled up to the very edges, spilling over with the knowing of something I'm desperate to unknow. I sync my breathing with Ashley's. *In, out. In, out. In, out.* A small and pointless act of solidarity. Every hour, a faceless nurse dips into the room for bed checks. She reduces us to numbers. *One, two.*

My eyes are tethered to the ceiling, wide and unblinking. I wonder what kind of animal could be capable of that kind of hurt. Her father, maybe. A stock image of a well-dressed asshole flashes through my mind. He sits in a mahogany-paneled office, sipping antique scotch meant for a special occasion that he knows will never come. At the end of his cigarette, a burning pinpoint of fire.

In, out.

Or maybe it was the mother. A woman who looks like Ashley but older, with slightly crepe skin and a thickness around her middle, where she has harbored years of resentment. She stands in the doorway while Ashley sleeps, stalking her prey, exhaling silvery breaths. Waiting for the right time.

In, out.

After the sixth bed check, I can't stand it anymore. I jump out of bed and stretch out on the floor. The cement is cold beneath a paper-thin layer of dusty carpet. I take a measured breath and press my hips into the floor. Lift my right leg slowly, then lower it to the ground. The tightness in my chest dissolves like foam. Next, the left leg. With each exhale, my nearly empty stomach collapses against my backbone. *Nearly empty.* There was the half carton of yogurt this morning and the Gatorade water. Tomorrow will be better.

My thighs are starting to burn, the beginning sparks of an absolving fire. *Forgive me, brother, for I have sinned.* But the exercises don't work the way they should. Soon, the thoughts start to creep in again. *Tomorrow can't be better. They'll tube feed you before they let you get any closer to Josh.* I pick up speed, doubling the reps on each side. *If they skewer you with a tube, pump calories into your gut, you'll lose everything. And if you start to gain on your own, it's over. There is no way out. You are trapped. A caged animal.*

A soft knock brushes against the door, and I jerk upright.

"Who's there?" I gasp into the dark. My skin is clammy. I think I might puke. The thought soothes me.

"It's just me." The door opens a crack and Cate is standing

in the narrow sliver of light. A perfect cartoon stick figure, all spindly lines and protruding joints. Faded pink pajama pants hang from two perfectly jutting hipbones.

"What—are you exercising?" Cate whispers the last word like she is speaking some dirty, delicious sin she can almost remember.

"I can't sleep." I jerk my head toward Ashley, but she doesn't move. *In, out.*

"Oh." Cate's outline bobs and sways. She is dying to lie down next me, to give in just this once. "You have a call. On the hall phone."

My throat goes dry, but I don't move. "I didn't hear it ring."

"It's from Paris." Her voice shudders with childlike excitement. "Who do you know in Paris?"

"Nobody," I say quickly. My heart is hammering in my chest. I hate my body for reacting at all, for betraying me this way. Abs tensed, I lower myself to the floor in degrees and resume my exercises. Let her watch. She's too jealous, too weak to tell on me.

She licks her flaky lips. "But . . . what do you want me to tell—"

"Whatever. Hang up. I don't care." As I deepen the leg lifts, I hear her moving down the hall, then a muffled apology before she appears in the doorway again.

"They said they'd call back later." Her plastic tube glints in the hall light, a phantom limb.

"How does that thing work?" Seamlessly, I shift to abs.

"What thing?"

"The tube. Did you get it as soon as you got here?"

"Right after my treatment team meeting, yeah." She fiddles

with the tie on her pajama pants. "I passed out on the plane on the way here, so I guess they were worried."

I won't reward that kind of arrogance with a response.

"Anyway, at night they hook it up to this machine next to my bed. When they turn it on, this brown liquid stuff goes through the tube and into my stomach. I unhook it in the morning."

"Gross."

"I try not to think about it."

On my last set of crunches, I lift myself to a seated position and hug my knees. "Did it hurt when they put it in?"

"Yeah. You have to lie down on a table while the nurses hold you down and stick it in. They try to get it over with as fast as they can, but sometimes they mess up and have to start over." Her eyes flicker across the room and settle on Curly Blonde's shape beneath the covers. "How can she sleep like that? I wake up every five minutes in this place."

I shrug and squeeze my knees tighter. It's weird, but all of a sudden I want to tell her about Ashley's scars. To describe them in detail—how they looked like snaps on a flesh straitjacket— and not because I want to *process it* or I want Cate to *normalize what I'm feeling* (recovery-speak at its finest! I'm learning!) but because it isn't fair. I have enough inside me: Josh and Eden and the Anniversary and my own vanishing act. I shouldn't have to hold this, too.

Ashley slurs in her sleep.

"It's so funny how she brought all those stuffed animals from home," Cate murmurs.

"So? Maybe they make her feel better," I snap. "Maybe they help her sleep."

Cate's eyes widen. "I didn't mean—I have stuffed animals at home, too. And a blanket I've had since I was five. Binky? Stupid, I know."

I watch Ashley's body rise and fall.

"And they gave me a rubber duck to hold when they were putting the tube in."

I go back to my exercises until Cate mumbles something about weight and vitals, then shuffles down the hallway. Then I get up and wander to Ashley's side of the room. She's got the stuffed dog and the blue bear in a headlock. The one-eared rabbit is sprawled at an unnatural angle in a nest of blond curls, like it got sick and tired of feeling sick and tired and decided to end it all with a spectacular swan dive. I reach for it. The animal has lost most of its stuffing, but it's warm and soft and smells like lavender detergent.

Ashley's mouth is open, her breath like white noise. I stand there for a while, holding the rabbit by its nubby broken neck. Outside, colorless light is starting to rise over the dust. I sink next to the bed and brush her curls from her hot cheek. I stay next to her, watching the tiny sleep twitches of her cheeks and mouth. I let her rest, because it's the most I can do for her. For girls like us, escape from consciousness is our only reprieve.

day seven

AFTER lunch the next day, the air in the villa feels tight, like late afternoon at home before a summer storm splits the sky. I watch Teagan stand sideways in front of the double doors, glaring at her thick rectangle reflection. At one of the round tables, Ashley snaps through the pages of a generic princess coloring book like she's pissed at their happily ever after. I curl into a ball on the couch, trying to blink away the memory of Ashley's scars. All of the girls are waiting. Some pretend not to be.

"Ooh! He's coming!" Cate squeals from the hall, and a girl herd rushes the nurses' station. The mail guy barely has the space to dump his battered plastic bin of letters before the girls start clawing. It's a feeding frenzy: countless jaws unhinged, starved for love and words. It reminds me of this special on killer whales I watched with Josh two nights before I killed him. When an intelligent animal is held in captivity for too long, terrible things can happen. It can get depressed, or even violent. When an animal's world shrinks, the smallest nothings become the biggest somethings. It lives sicker and dies sooner. It gives up before its time.

"Stevie? Mail!" The male nurse is probably supposed to make me come to him, but he's one of the nicer ones. So he holds the red envelope like a Frisbee and when I nod from my spot on the couch, he arcs it over the heads between us. I catch it and toss it on the coffee table without looking. I have five more just like it in my underwear drawer. All unopened. "Oh. And one more today." He sends a second envelope sailing.

"Huh?" I lift my hand just in time to grab it. The envelope is thick and gold. I know this paper. The realization blows through my body like hot desert wind: *Eden*. Without thinking, I lift the envelope to my nose and breathe her in. The sweet smell sends shudders through me. I feel sick and relieved.

"Ashley." The nurse holds up enough postcards to start a collection.

A slow day for Ashley is three postcards, each one glossy with too-blue water and pink cake-frosting script: *Saint-Tropez! Majorca!* She never looks at her mail, either.

"Thanks, Jeff. I'll get them later." Ashley looks up from her princess. The hair is an angry wax red. I wonder if I should say something about last night. But rather than say the wrong thing, I say nothing.

"You're lucky to have a dad who writes you." Teagan slumps

on the couch next to me, nodding morosely at the red envelope on the table. "Don't you want to read it?"

"Not really." Eden's letter is heavy in my hand. I wish everyone else would disappear. Leave me to read her in peace.

"Okay, ladies!" Shrink announces from the nurses' station. "If you have group on your schedule, meet me at the house! Otherwise, you'll be with Kyle in the villa."

I pull my folded schedule from the back pocket of my jeans. *Group.* Maybe I'll have time to sneak a sentence or two, while one of the other girls unravels some knotted childhood revelation. Or maybe I should wait to burrow beneath the light of the clip lamp in Cottage Three tonight. Gather up the covers and her words and arrange them just so in soft tufts around me before I sleep. Deep in my gut is the same tugging I feel just before a binge. I want her words to fill me up and I'm scared that they won't be enough when I'm done.

A group of girls follows Shrink down the hall. Ashley trails behind, alone. Ashley never walks alone.

"Hey." I jump up at the last second, a half step behind her. "Did you, uh, sleep okay?" I slip the letters into my back pocket as we hop down the stairs, two at a time.

"Oh. Hey." She fixes her gaze in front of her, on Teagan's blistered heels. "I'm—if last night was weird for you—sorry. I just forget that those scars are even there sometimes."

"No. I get it." There were plenty of mornings after my mother left when I would wake up and my first thoughts would be totally normal, like, *It feels like Friday* or *Quixotic. I should have played the word quixotic*, and then I would roll onto my side and think, *Oh. I don't have a mother.* It's the one good thing my brain has ever done for me: kept little secrets to give me a second to breathe.

"Do you want to, like, talk about it?" I hold my breath.

"Nah. It's okay. Thanks, though."

We walk in silence the rest of the way, stepping in the shadowy prints of the girls before us. They lead through the front door. Once I cross into the foyer, I know: Group is a trap.

There are too many smells at once. Melted butter, slick dark chocolate, and powdered sugar. Thick, wet grease. Salt and the nuttiness of toasting bread. The scents try to overtake me, to drag me back to *Le Crâpeau*'s kitchen or the front seat of Dad's Buick or Eden's bathroom. I can't go back there. I open my eyes wide, force myself to take in the details.

The kitchen here is somehow bright and dingy at the same time. Fluorescent bulbs fling light over a room of "not quite" colors: ugly light wood cabinets that aren't brown or cream. Laminate countertops that aren't white or yellow. Linoleum floor squares that might have started out eggshell but now have a faint muddy tinge. On the other side of the counter, there's a long, oval-shaped table.

Ms. Dalton, the white-haired dietician from my treatment team meeting, stands behind the counter. Behind the jar of peanut butter and the sagging tube of cookie dough. Behind the boxes of sugary cereal and graham crackers and bloated cheese puffs. Behind the brown bag seeping with grease, like creeping night shadows on a bedroom wall.

What the hell? "Is this a fucking joke?" I ask.

"Stevie. Please be mindful of your language." Shrink stands next to the dietician. "Come on in, girls. Welcome to group."

The rest take their places on the other side of the counter: Teagan, Jenna the bobby pin dealer, and countless faceless others. They look like dumb, glaze-eyed animals that don't realize they are heading for slaughter.

"Seriously," I hiss in Ashley's ear. "What. *Is* this?"

"BG," she whispers back. "Bulimia group."

"But I'm not—I think my schedule is wrong," I say loudly. "Wait. Where's Cate?" My eyes snap across the room, frantic. "Shouldn't this be a cottage thing?" *I should be nicer to Cate*, I think. *Since we're more alike than anybody else here.*

"You okay?" Ashley rests her hand on my arm.

On my other side, Teagan says, "It'll be *alright*," or some other lie.

"So as you've probably guessed by now," Shrink says, "today's group will be a binge experiential."

I picture a row of girls bent over toilets, Shrink rubbing each girl's back as she moves down the line, correcting form and holding back hair.

"Some of you have experienced this group before," she continues.

Jenna moos her agreement, flicking the yellow plastic on her wrist.

"And for some of you, this is your first time."

I clear my throat.

"Excuse me? My *schedule* is wrong," I say again, louder this time.

The others are silent.

"I should be in the villa. With Kyle." I stuff my hand in my back pocket and pinch Eden's letter. She'd know just what to say to talk her way out of this. She'd use honeyed words and jokes and she'd slip outside into the sun before anyone knew what had happened.

"You're in the appropriate place, Stevie," Shrink says evenly. "As you all can see, on the counter are several different types of foods that you may have used during a binge. But these foods don't have to be used as binge foods. They can be enjoyed in appropriate amounts, and that's what Ms. Dalton and I want to share with you today."

I cut my eyes from Ashley to Teagan, and back to Ashley again. Their faces are blank and obedient. Their mouths have lolled open, making space. Do they *want* this? An excuse to indulge, permission to cram themselves full, all in the name of health? How can Shrink possibly think that these girls and I belong in the same cage?

In front of me, Jenna murmurs something to a girl who is crying. Teagan plucks a hair from a spot above her ear. For the first time, I notice: She has a bald spot there. A strange vacant spot where hair should be.

"Please take a few moments to make your choices," Ms. Dalton says.

Finally, Jenna steps to the front and takes a paper plate.

"Good, Jenna," says Shrink, in a voice like she knows the girl's secrets. I wonder if Shrink says the same kinds of things to Jenna as she says to me. I wonder who she thinks is better, stronger, worthier.

Ashley falls in line behind Jenna. She lifts a gallon of red fruit punch from the counter and tilts it over a paper cup. The syrupy red flows. I see my mother's lips.

"Stevie?" Shrink finds me, pulls me aside while the Green

Girls graze and the Yellow Girls hover, and then there is me, the Red Girl, and I don't belong. How can no one else see that? "Do you think you could give this a shot?"

My gaze bounces from the stack of paper plates to the heaps of food. The calculations make my brain hurt and I don't think they're right anyway because I can't think straight. Gummy worms with grainy sugar scales. Melting vanilla ice cream in its soft cardboard container. Salt and vinegar chips, the kind Josh loves. *Loved.* I take a gaspy breath.

"Stevie, what's going on for you right now?" Shrink's voice finds its way to me.

I cross my arms over my chest and will myself to think about other things. But the other things that come are nightmarish thoughts in lightning flashes: the call from Paris and Ashley's withered scars and the way Josh's face looked just before he died and the way his blood felt sticky running down my palm. I scrunch my eyes shut, but it doesn't help. He's still there, dying and dying and dying beneath me. I can't take it anymore. I want all these girls to leave me here with the food. *Just one more time.* I'll shove it down just one more time, and for a second I will forget. I'm not a bulimic. Sometimes I just need the thoughts to go away.

"Stevie. Let's take a break, okay?" Shrink's palm nudges me out the door, past the other girls and into the still heat outside. I bend over, palms pressed over my knees. Dry heave at the dust.

"I'm going insane," I breathe. My stomach buckles, and I heave again. I thought it would feel better to say it out loud. It doesn't.

"You're not insane. You're here with me and you're safe.

Here." Shrink sits on a dirty concrete stoop and guides me down next to her. She hands me a paper cup of water and I drink it. My whole body is swooping and untethered. One violent gust and I will come undone.

"You're not crazy," she says again. "I think the smells are triggering for you. Bringing back memories that are tied to food, or particularly traumatic times during your eating disorder. But you're perfectly sane, and you're safe here. Do you hear me?"

"I hear you." Hearing and believing are two different things.

"Would you take a few deep breaths for me?" she asks. "In through the nose and out through the mouth?"

I obey her because I don't know what else to do. My heartbeat slows a little. I still want it all in me: the sugar and the salt and the bread. I need to fill myself up until there is no more room for the past.

"Can you put into words what was happening for you in th—"

"Don't make me go back," I beg. "Please."

She angles her body toward me. I can feel her gaze on my face, almost like she's touching me. "What could happen if you tried this exercise, Stevie? What's the worst thing that could happen?"

"Nothing. I don't know. I just . . . Don't make me go back in there."

Finally, she looks straight ahead. She stretches her legs out in front of her and crosses her ankles. "It can feel really scary, trying to find that middle ground."

I shrug and stare at the dirt.

"It could even feel impossible. For over a year now, you've dealt in extremes, right? Restricting or bingeing and purging. No in-between, no gray."

I shrug again. What she doesn't understand is this: I have no choice. For me, the middle ground doesn't exist. I starve or I stuff myself. I'm blacked-out drunk or pissed-off sober. I worship Josh and I hate myself. I blame Eden and I need her. If I can't live, then I'll die. There is no middle—not for me.

"I think, though, that if you try this exercise, you'll see that you're capable of moderation, Stevie. I really believe that."

"Yeah." There's no point in explaining to someone who is okay.

"Stevie, if this group is too much for you today, we could stay out here and talk."

I shake my head. I don't want to talk to her anymore. I don't want to open my mouth, not for food and not for words.

"So are you willing to give it a shot?" she asks.

My skin starts to hum. *I'll fake it*, I tell myself. *Slip some food under the table*.

"I guess."

"Good. I'm really proud of you for pushing yourself." Shrink stands and offers me a hand. It's small, and colder than I thought it would be.

Inside, I pretend not to notice as the other girls' eyes follow me to the counter. I breathe through my mouth and peel a thin paper plate from the stack. It's silent at the table. Then Jenna speaks.

"It's weird," she says. "The last time I ate this stuff at home was in my room, by myself. I would hide food all around my room and then binge on it at night. And I know my mom found the wrappers and stuff when she was cleaning. But she never said anything." Her voice gets small. "I still can't figure out why she never said anything."

Simple. She doesn't think you're worth saving, I think.

Ashley's voice: "I feel like maybe . . . your mom just couldn't admit to herself what was going on with you. Maybe it was just, like, too hard for her." Her voice is pinched.

I force myself to look at the food again. It's even uglier now than it was before: the ice cream misshapen in the carton, the chip bag concave and shimmering with grease. At the end of the line, an unmarked brown bag. I peer inside. The smell alone is enough to make me sick.

Fried chicken.

Shrink did this on purpose. She wants to keep sending me back to that day on the porch and she doesn't get that it hurts exactly the same every time I remember. I am filled with spitting rage.

"But it's like, she's my *mother*," Jenna says. "Mothers are supposed to take care of their kids, no matter what."

Some other voice at the table snorts. "*Supposed* to."

I sweep a plastic fork from the counter and stab the first piece of chicken in the bag. I fling it on the plate, already feeling the hot grease soaking through and staining my palms. If she wants to hurt me like this, fine. I don't care enough to stop her.

"Good, Stevie," Shrink approves quietly. "You're really challenging yourself."

I turn away from her. There's an empty seat between Jenna and Ashley, and I squeeze between them. I dump my plate on the table and wipe my palms on my jeans, leaving dark swipes on my thighs. The fat burrows between the denim fibers.

"So let's try a second bite." Ms. Dalton circles the table. Slowly, like a shark. "Again, lift a bite from your plate. Notice the smell. Does it smell salty, or sweet? What spices have been used to season the food?"

I drive the fork into the chicken flesh and rip a piece from the bone. I won't breathe it in. If I breathe it in, I'll break down and consume it all.

"Now place the bite on your tongue and hold it there for just a moment," Ms. Dalton instructs. "What tastes arise for you?"

I stare at the speared meat. Purse my lips together to contain the scream.

"Give it a try, Stevie," Shrink prods quietly behind me. "You're doing great." There is a scream inside of me, building. Rattling my insides. I stuff it down with the chicken. When I cram the bite into my mouth, my stomach heaves, and I am back on the porch at the house on Broad. My mother has left me.

That night, it just happened naturally. I was sitting on the porch swing full of chicken and tea, and my belly kept twisting into itself and I couldn't sit still. I made it to the edge of the porch just in time. I folded over the railing and emptied myself into the earth.

Shrink pipes up behind me. "Girls, notice that you can take a bite—that you can experience this food—without overdoing it, and without dissociating; meaning that you can stay fully present in this moment."

The air on the porch was heavy enough to crush me.

"We're so very proud of you guys for trying this," Ms. Dalton adds. "The strength in this room is palpable."

There is still fried animal on my tongue. I swallow it and the scream. The meat lodges in my throat and for a second I think it will stay there. Maybe it will stop my breath. Maybe the food will actually kill me. But my body takes over and swallows again. I can feel the weighty flesh worming its way down to my gut. My stomach coils, desperate to reject it.

I whisper, "Excuse me. I need some air," and I shove back my chair and run outside. Shrink thinks I can do this, but she's wrong. My body won't allow it. I stumble around the side of the house. Next to the stucco wall, I bow my head and my body gives it up; I don't even have to ask. I feel the familiar click, the moment when my body knows everything is going to be okay. When I'm done I kick fiery dirt over pale meat and I think, *It's like riding a bike*. Which is weird because I never learned to ride a bike. Josh crashed his and broke his arm when he was seven and I was six, and that was that.

I come around the corner, rubbing the damp from my eyes and wiping my mouth with the back of my hand. Finally, my insides are quiet.

"Oh." Suddenly Ashley is standing there, wobbly and gray in the too-bright sun. "I . . . um . . . wanted to check on you. I told Anna I'd come so she could stay with the group." Her lower lip twitches.

"Okay."

"Stevie." She whispers it.

I should feel something. A real girl would feel something. Scared she'll rat me out to Shrink, or pissed at her pudgy-lipped disappointment.

"Tell on me if you want." I can't even look at her.

"What?" I can hear her pout getting deeper. "Stevie, what are you—"

"Anna. Tell her if you want. I really don't care."

"Are you being serious right now? I was just—I wanted to see if you were okay. I want to help!"

"I'm okay. Okay?" I snap at my feet. "And I don't need your help."

"Yeah. Okay. 'Cause you're doing such an awesome job on your own." She stomps back into the house, letting the door slam behind her.

day seven

Thursday, July 10, 9:45 p.m.

I avoid Ashley for the rest of the day, but it doesn't matter. I can feel her disappointment clinging to me, a sticky residue that won't come clean, like dirty salt water baked into my skin. It's not that I care what she thinks. It's that she had the balls to act upset— sad, even—that I'd purged. Like she pities me. A Yellow Girl! Pitying me! I should pity her. All afternoon and through dinner and snack, I am a live wire, ready to blaze at the slightest spark. I need a drink. I need to get wasted with Eden, to forget the way only we know how, together.

When the nurses release us to the cottages at the end of the night, I take my time gathering Josh's sweatshirt and my journal and the handout on mindful eating Shrink brought me after group. I slip my meds into the pocket of my jeans and I wait until the villa empties. The building feels strange like this, with no sick girls to give it purpose. The nurses talk and laugh a little louder without the patients here. Their life sounds make my skin squirm.

"Stevie, my friend! Anything I can do to help?" The nice male nurse (Jeff, right? Jeff.) looks up from his chart and smiles. Jeff the Nice Male Nurse is always smiling. "Need to talk to someone? I can call a therapist if you'd like."

"Nah. Thanks, though, Jeff. Night." I clutch my sweatshirt to my chest and get out of there fast, before he can say more nice things.

I stand in the yard until Cottage Three goes dark. Then I make my way up the hill and lean against the cold stucco. Eden's letter feels weighty in my pocket, keeping me grounded. After a few more minutes, I sneak inside. Ashley's almost-snores seep beneath the bedroom door.

I creep to my side of the room, peel off my jeans and leave them in a pile on the floor. I pull Josh's sweatshirt over my head and slide between the sheets, then flick the switch on my clip lamp and run my fingertips over the bumpy pen strokes that make my name. They are warm.

Eden's drawn a crude lightning bolt on the back flap and colored it in with neon green ink. I smile. She would never draw a heart, or scrawl Miss you! like everyone else on the planet.

I peel the flap so slowly. When I was little, my mother had our Christmas gifts wrapped professionally, with fat wired gold ribbon and glittery sprigs of silver holly that left fairy-dust trails in the living room until March. The unwrapping was always the saddest part. The promise of what was inside was always better than the actual gift.

Inside the envelope, the letter is folded around a picture. A real picture, printed with sharp corners and a glossy finish. My stomach gets twisty when I see it: Eden and me, arms slung around each other in her kitchen. Grinning and red-faced, like fucked-up idiots. I have no idea when we took this.

Finally, the letter. Her handwriting is nothing like it should be; it's boxy and small, contained.

Hey, girl.

Got your message the other day. Your cell's going straight to voice mail, so I had to look up the place on my phone. Hope fat camp is everything you dreamed it would be. (Too soon?) This place sucks without you, so you'd better get your ass back here soon. It's totally dead in summer, you know? You know. Mostly I'm just hanging with the boys at night and taking this Intro to Anthro course during the day. It's decent; a gen ed requirement, plus I figured it would help me write characters better, to understand groups of people on a different level. The professor is a total fox, which never hurts. He thinks I don't see him checking me out during his slide shows of tribal women with their tits hanging out. Please.

Listen. About what you texted before you left. I know you didn't mean it. You were pissed off about having to leave and everything. I get it. But the thing is, sometimes I think you're right. I think maybe what happened that night was partly because of me. I mean, we both know I didn't kill him. But still . . . we never really talked about it, you know? Maybe when you get back, we can.

*Either way, I just wanted to say that we're good, even after
everything you said. When you get back I'm taking you out for
a drink. Or six. Whatever you need. Just tell me. I'll take care
of you, like you deserve. You know I will.*

E

*P.S. Write me back, bitch. I know you have nothing better
to do in there.*

I read the letter so many times. She's talking to me like nothing's
changed, like I'm not even in this place. I'm not sure if I love
her for this, or hate her for it. She has a way of doing that to me:
dizzying me until I don't know which way is up. It was always that
way between us, from the first seminar to the night before Dad
sent me here. If only I had gotten my bearings sooner. If only I
had stood firm and told her *no. No. We can't do this.* If I'd had the
power to refuse her, Josh would still be alive.

"I can't stay," I told Eden after our second seminar. We bobbed
in the rocking chairs on the porch of the Stacks while the
other students filtered onto the street and headed to Milo's
or the Royale or the organic co-op down the block. When
Drew banged through the door, his gaze slid sticky between
Eden and me. "My brother would kill me." I didn't want to
bail on Josh, but I hated being home. The house on Broad
was too dark, too quiet. Even with Josh and Dad and me
there, the windows and doors bulged with emptiness, ready
to blow.

"You didn't say anything about a brother last week." Eden slid
a cigarette between her Pepto-pink lips and propped her feet on

the porch railing. She tilted her head toward me and lifted an eyebrow, like, *This okay?* I nodded.

"Josh," I said. "We play Scrabble every Wednesday night. And I already missed last week." I flicked at the grayed edge of the bandage over my mother's face. The ink had ached all week.

"God, that's adorable." She lit the cigarette, looking like a print ad for Cool in her ripped jean cutoffs and low black tank that showed off the pink lace of her bra. Her hair was gathered carelessly on top of her head. "Tell him it's for class. I need your help with this piece I'm working on, anyway."

I closed my eyes. It was a zillion degrees outside, and I was woozy from the heat. Beads of sweat formed at my hairline and under my bra. I straightened up and pressed my knees together. The tops of my thighs smashed together and stuck there. *Stupid bitch loser,* I thought. *If you hadn't binged last week . . .*

In my back pocket, my cell buzzed.

"My brother," I told her, and rocked myself to standing. I had to grip the railing to stay upright. Maybe I'd done something right this week after all.

"I'll be upstairs when you're done," she said, like I'd already given in. She waved me away with a chrome wisp of smoke.

"Hello?" I hurried down the steps to the street. I thought about running the steps while we talked, but he'd hear me. "Hey."

"Hey, Sass. You okay? You sound—"

"Yeah. I'm good. What's up?" I paced.

"I just wanted to see if you wanted to grab dinner before we play," he said. "Milo's, maybe?"

"Oh." I froze. "I . . . Actually? Some of us are staying late to finish up peer edits. So I'm staying at the Stacks. And, uh, we'll get food after." Sweat poured down the greasy slope of my nose, landing salty on my upper lip.

His silence on the other end was heavy. Finally, he said, "Yeah. Okay. Just make sure you eat something, Sass. And if you're not too late, we can still play."

"Yeah. Okay. Later." I held the End button long enough for the screen to go dark.

Upstairs, Eden had already ordered drinks and littered the table with her seminar notebooks. The bar was starting to fill, and I let the clinking beer mugs and townie chatter relax me.

"So I'm writing these song lyrics for my friends, these guys Nic and Reid." She slid a purple pen between her perfect teeth. "They're in a halfway decent band, and they're playing the Pit this weekend."

I sat across from her and rolled my glass against the back of my neck before I took a sip. "Josh and I do the Pit together every year." The Pit was short for PeachPitPalooza, an annual local music festival and our town's only cultural event, if local stoner garage bands counted as culture.

"If you want, you guys can come with me this year. The boys got me tickets to all the good acts."

"Is one of them, like, your boyfriend or something?" I opened my throat and let my drink slide down. It was better that way.

She laughed and waved over a bartender. "Hell no. It's just, I hang out with guys most of the time. Girls can be such bitches."

"Yeah," I said, even though I'd never understood girls and had no room to talk on the subject. As a kid I'd spent most of my lunchtimes and recesses watching girl clusters from afar, from the back table in the cafeteria where I read alone, or the edge of the playground. Other girls seemed to know when to laugh or how to toss their hair so it seemed like an afterthought. But no matter how long I studied them, I never understood. It felt like they were playing a game and no one had bothered to tell me the rules. It wasn't that the other girls had been mean to me, exactly. They just never seemed to know I was there. In high school, nothing had changed.

"Hey, babe," Eden said when the bartender neared our table. He was young, with a beard and a shiny wedding ring that was either cheap or brand-new. I watched Eden's eyes catch on it. "Another round for my girl Stevie here? And I'll want one in a second."

My girl Stevie. I smiled into the bottom of my glass. It felt good to be someone's something.

"You got it, Eden." The guy headed back to the bar without even looking at me. That was the thing I'd noticed about Eden—everybody knew her name, and she knew no one's. She picked her own names for other people: *doll* and *honey* and *babe* and *sugar* and other candied words she used when she couldn't be bothered.

"So I'm stuck on the bridge—total writer's block." She slid down in her seat, and our knees touched. Neither of us moved. Her skin was warm and the perfect kind of slick. "The song's about this girl—from the point of view of a guy—and he's telling her that she doesn't have to be ashamed of her past or her flaws or whatever. That he loves her no matter what."

"Girls blush, sometimes, because they are alive," I blurted.

Her head snapped up. "That's like—"

"It's Elizabeth Barrett Browning," I said quickly. "I didn't make it up or anything. "It's from a poem. I swirled my fingertip over the rim of my glass. "*Girls blush, sometimes, because they are alive. Half wishing they were dead to save the shame. The sudden blush devours them, neck and brow*—" I stared up at the ceiling. "I forget the rest."

"Oh my god, that's incredible," she said. She looked at me as if the words were mine. "Hold on." She slid out of the booth and back in again on my side. "It's hard to hear you over there."

Now it was our thighs and hips fused together, and I squirmed because my legs were goose-bumped and thick, and she must have been able to tell.

The bartender brought new drinks, and I drank mine fast.

"Another?" he asked.

I nodded.

"Got it."

I should have stopped then. I was the perfect kind of drunk: Eden's face was soft and my body felt good and loose and nothing seemed particularly important. But I was greedy and wanted more. So I reached for Eden's drink and took a sip, and she let me.

"I like, relate to that poem," I said. My words were thick. "I feel like that's why my mom left. Because there was something wrong with me or she couldn't stand to be around me or something." I didn't mean to say it. But the booze made things that were true a little easier to say.

"Yeah," she said. "Sometimes I look at my parents and their effing perfect marriage and I think the same thing. Like, I must seem so messed up to them."

The room dipped, and I leaned closer to her.

"But here's the thing." She turned toward me, her eyes blazing, living green. "People like you and me? We're *real*. So, okay, that means flawed or whatever. But wouldn't you rather be real and flawed, then some synthetic perfect girl who never really *lived*?"

I was close enough to breathe her in, to consume her sweet, smoky breath. I wanted to believe her more than anything.

"Yes," I said, to make it true. "Yes."

"That's why I dig you, you know?" she whispered, like we— just the two of us—were a secret the rest of the world could never hear. "You, baby girl, are *real*. I can tell. And if your own mother never saw that?" She ripped the bandage from my arm without taking her gaze from me. It burned. "Then fuck. Her."

I copied the movements of her lips like a child, forming the words on my own. "Fuck her." I wished my mother could see me, drunk and whispering close with this mystery of a girl.

"That's right." She slipped one hand around the back of my neck and leaned even closer. We breathed each other in. I wanted everything about her—wanted to exist exactly as she did, wild and unapologetic, giving the world the finger.

"Here you go. Two more."

I jumped when the bartender set down our drinks with a deliberate thud; my body flooded with shame for all the things I wanted.

Looking back now, I realize just how stupid I was then: I had no idea that I was already losing myself in her. Disappearing into her wide electric eyes and philosophical musings and open mouth. Of course I couldn't see it. She drew me in slowly, and by the time I realized how dangerous she could be, it was too late.

day eight

Friday, July 11, 5:32 a.m.

I'M first to the villa for weight and vitals the next morning. I yank the ties on my hospital gown into unforgiving knots. The fabric sticks to the curve of my belly and the tops of my thighs and my ass. I can even see the outline of my scar. My eyes are dry, my head cotton-stuffed. I lie still like a corpse on one of the couches in the villa while Hannah pumps the bulb on my blood pressure cuff. When I sit up, she slides a stethoscope over my back. She takes notes in a black three-ring binder, the kind I used for school. It's strange, knowing I'll never buy another binder. So I don't think about it.

"You look tired this morning, Stephanie," Hannah says as she leads me into the tiny room with the upright scale. She closes the door behind us, and there is barely enough room for both our bodies. She is too much at this hour—her lips slathered with frosty drugstore magenta, her every breath an effort. Her short orange hair is curled into perfect hard semi-circles.

"Didn't sleep," I mutter at my feet. I hate weight and vitals. So much measuring and recording, the nurses gathering up numbers as if they are desperate to solve some mystery. There is no mystery. I am dying.

"Sorry to hear that," she says too cheerfully.

I stiffen when she slides her palms along my ribcage and over my hips, to be sure I'm not wearing underwear or hiding anything beneath my gown.

"On the scale for me?" she prompts.

The scale rattles beneath my weight as I step onto it, turned away from the numbers. The seconds here are always torture, as she slides the weights on the scale back and forth, back and forth, until they are just right. I hate that she can see the numbers and I can't. It isn't fair. They aren't hers. They're mine.

"Alright! Thank you, Stephanie." As she records my weight, she purses her lips together for a fraction of a second. She recovers quickly, but it's too late. I've read her. And I understand: I've lost weight. The realization shoots through me potent and fast, as good as the first high.

Good girl, I think, stepping off the scale and onto the cold tile floor.

Then, *Oh, shit. I don't want a tube. They'll give me a tube.*

I dress quickly and go outside, lying in the cold spongy grass beyond the patio. I have to think—the important kind of thinking that can only be done in secret. When other people know you're thinking, they start to think for you. And the last thing I need is Shrink's *you can do it*s and *I'm so proud*s because I *am* doing it, my way.

It's dark, still. I blink at the sky. One eye, then the other, so it looks like the stars are jumping. In the riding ring, the horses are restless.

"Doing a little stargazing?" At the sound of Shrink's voice I suck in a cold, hard breath that makes my lungs feel like they're the wrong size.

"Holy shit." I sit up fast.

"I didn't mean to scare you. Mind if I sit?" She settles next to me, in jeans and sneakers and a hoodie that's dark green or navy or black. Her hair is damp and smells like coconut, which I know because she's too close.

"What are you doing here so early? Do you live here or something?" My heartbeat is clumsy, like it's trying to clap a rhythm it can't quite find.

"Feels that way sometimes. But no." She leans back on her palms and looks up at the sky. "I got here early, to see if you had any interest in a trail ride."

"Like, on a horse?"

"Like, on a horse."

"But I'm still on red," I say, all panicked, like, *I am still on red, right?* Right? I check my wrist to make sure. "It's against the rules."

"Promise I won't tell," she says. "I just thought we could do something special."

"Why?" A reward after my behavior in group yesterday seems unlikely. I eye her warily. Is she going to yell at me for purging? Ashley must have told. I'd prefer yelling to this gal pal routine, anyway.

"Because I know the binge experiential yesterday was difficult for you. So I'm asking you to take some time to do something relaxing. Something fun. Treatment is hard work. I know that, Stevie."

I can feel the warm red blood humming just below surface of my skin. If she's going to bust me, I'd rather she just get it over with. "I don't think so."

"Why not?"

"I've never been on a horse." It's almost not a lie. I've only ridden a horse once, when I was seven. At a birthday party for Emily P., who was the most popular girl in my class and who only invited me because her mother was the kind of mother who made homemade valentines for every kid in the grade.

"I'll be right there with you. And it's a chance to get out a little. Come on, it'll be fun." Shrink springs to her feet and extends her hand. "We have to get moving, or you'll miss breakfast."

I get up without touching her.

"That would be tragic," I say.

Shrink takes a horse named Whimsy and I get Ernie, a coffee-two-creams-colored horse whose name sounds familiar, but I can't remember why. I clutch the reins clumsily in one hand and gather a fistful of mane in the other. The hair is coarse and oily.

We do a lap around the ring, my horse following Shrink's, and everything is coiled like a snake: my muscles, my hands, the too-small riding helmet that smells like another girl's sweat. The line of raised flesh on my leg is tight, as if it's ready to burst.

"Doing okay back there?" Shrink calls without turning around.

She leads the way out of the ring and cuts across the pasture, toward the main road.

"Yeah." I can see my breath in the early morning air, which seems out of place in the desert. "I'm fine." I focus on an invisible line on the horizon, where the watery pink meets the just yellow, and go back to thinking. Technically, I should want a feeding tube. Tubes are reserved for the very best girls, the ones who are so close to death that they can reach out and almost stroke it with their skeleton fingers. But I have to prioritize, and what I want more than the honor of being almost dead is to be actually dead.

". . . I know yesterday was difficult," Shrink is saying. She tugs the reins on Whimsy until we're just two girls riding side by side, carefree into the desert sunrise. We're practically a tampon commercial.

"It's fine." *Just say it*. Does she really not know that I purged yesterday? Maybe I should have given Ashley more credit. *Focus, Stevie*. If I don't want a tube, then the only option is to fake getting better until the Anniversary. By then, I can stash enough pills to do the trick. I hate this plan. It means that I'll have to eat at least a little, and after yesterday I'm starting to think that I can't. As in, I have trained my body so well that it will carry on the crusade, with or without me.

Mostly, though, I hate this plan because this ending is wrong.

"What was it like for you, the experiential?" Shrink takes her eyes from the road. Her cheeks are the same pink as the sky; the welt beneath her eye is turning green.

"Sucked." I don't give her any more than that. She doesn't deserve it, after she's taken away my ending. The one I designed was perfect. Poetic. And Shrink stole it. Every person should be able to choose her own particular brand of suffering. It's a fundamental human right. Death. Liberty. The pursuit of unhappiness.

"Stevie, I want you to know that I understand—"

"You don't." I stare straight ahead, but I've lost the invisible line on the horizon. She ruins everything.

"I'm sorry?"

"You don't understand because you're not me, so seriously, just . . ." I don't finish, because I don't think the words are coming out in the right order and she won't get it anyway. I chew the inside of my cheek, trying to slow the erratic flutter of my heart in my chest. It feels untethered, like it's this angry captive bird that's going to find a way to fly out of my body at any second.

"You're right. I'm not you."

"I'm not getting a feeding tube," I inform her. "I decided."

She doesn't answer.

"It's disgusting," I say. "I'm not letting some nurse shove plastic in me." In that moment, I know for sure. Whatever I do, I do on my terms.

"Okay, so you don't want a tube."

"That's what I said." My voice quivers as Ernie, then Whimsy, head up a small hill, kicking pebbles in their wake. I grip the reins so tight my hands start to tingle.

"Good. What do you need to do to make that a reality, then?" She steers Whimsy until we are side by side again. The sun pushes higher.

"Don't ask questions you already know the answer to."

"But I don't know the answer. I don't know your answer, anyway."

"I guess I'll try not to lose more weight. But I'm not gaining."

Shrink's head lists to one side, like her helmet is too heavy. "I am really, really proud of you for making an effort to maintain your weight, Stevie. That's awesome." Her eyes are searching.

"You don't think I can do it." Why am I arguing with her? I don't care what she thinks. I care only about Josh. About finding a way to get to him when everyone here insists on keeping us apart.

"Stevie . . ." She pauses. "I get the impression often that you think I'm not being honest with you. Game playing, maybe. I've gotten that feeling a few times since you started treatment."

"Perceptive."

"Here's the thing, though. I'm not game playing. I will always be honest with you." She pats her horse on the neck, and he tosses his head at her touch. "Do you know what I want for you during your time here?"

"Doesn't matter." I shrug.

"Well, I'll tell you anyway. Here's what I want. I want you to want to get better. I want you to learn how to eat and how to feel—and trust me, both will feel like absolute shit. I want you to get pissed when you need to and to feel sad when you need to. I want you to heal, Stevie. Okay? So there it is. No hidden agendas."

Jesus, she has a talent for making things weird in record time. I wonder if this is what she's like on a date. I picture her in some vegan café, and the guy across from her is like, *Hi, my name is Dylan*, and she's like, *I'm going to be completely transparent with you, Dylan. These tofu nuggets are making me saaaad.*

"Why do you even do this?" I ask, before she gets any more TV-movie moment on me.

"Do what?"

"This. This." I flap one of my hands between us. "Therapy or whatever. To fix people?" My stomach swoops a little and the desert around us suddenly feels faded and out of focus.

"No." She squishes her lips together. "I think . . . I do it because I know that we all carry heavy burdens in life. I'm not naïve enough to think that I could shoulder someone's burden for them. I have my own weight to carry."

"What do you mean?"

"I mean, I've got my own problems, just like everybody."

I don't think shrinks are supposed to say that kind of thing out loud.

"But I do feel honored to walk beside someone as they learn how to carry their own particular burden. Maybe they figure out how to adjust the straps on their pack, or how to lighten their load by unpacking a few things they don't really need anymore."

"So what do people need you for?"

"To share skills or offer suggestions. Or maybe to ask good questions or make observations. And always to offer support. Because we're not meant to walk alone in this life. We're meant to be part of a *we*. Something bigger, something outside of ourselves."

My *we* died with Josh. She doesn't get to step in, the homely girl understudy who slaps on an extra coat of makeup on opening night.

"What's yours?" I ask.

"My what?"

"Your burden." *World hunger*, I expect her to say, or maybe, *My twin sister steals my favorite sweater sometimes. You have no idea how* annoying *that is.*

115

"I'm an alcoholic. Recovering."

"Oh." I'm almost positive shrinks aren't supposed to say *that* kind of thing out loud. What am I supposed to say? Probably something murmury and sympathetic. But what comes out is, "You're fucked up, too."

I'm surprised when she laughs. Her laugh is fat and unapologetic.

"I'm human, Stevie. And I used to have not-so-good ways of coping with life, and now I have better ways and I try really hard to use them. That's it. It's not magic."

I picture Shrink in the Stacks, laughing too loud on wobbly high heels. It makes me want to laugh and cry.

"So, what's it like to know that about me?"

"I don't know. You don't seem like an alcoholic. Eden is one. Or will be, I don't know."

She pulls Whimsy to a stop, and Ernie follows. I shield my eyes and look around. There is nothing here, just a few pathetic scrubby plants beneath us, and the occasional cactus. It's too quiet out here.

"You spent a lot of time with Eden, didn't you? At the bar, after the class you took. What was that like?"

"It was . . ." I know what she's doing, but I give it thought anyway, because she's just shared some deep shit or whatever and it will be awkward if I don't play. "She sent me a letter. Yesterday."

Shrink bobs her head, once.

I shift on my saddle. "And I couldn't really sleep that well last night 'cause I kept thinking about it. She acted like I'm not even here."

"Like you don't exist? Or like you're not in treatment?"

"Like I'm not in treatment. She acted that way when I was home, too. Like I didn't have a problem. She didn't even notice that I was losing a lot of weight. She just would say how good and skinny I looked, and stuff."

"She didn't see that you were really sick." Shrink strokes Whimsy's mane, softly.

"It wasn't her fault. I think she just didn't want me to feel messed up. I needed that."

Shrink is silent. My skin is starting to pinken—a slow, dry burn.

"Plus I hid it well, I think. My dad didn't say much, either. The only person who kept saying stuff about it was—" His name catches in my throat.

"Josh," she says.

"Josh," I say. We fought about it the night I killed him. I close my eyes and his words come rushing back.

You look like shit, by the way. Everybody thinks so and Dad's too scared to say it. This whole food thing—it's selfish and crazy and you look like . . . shit.

My fists curl into balls at my side.

"What do you think about that? That he was the only one who was brave enough to say something?" Shrink asks.

"Like I said, Eden was the only one who accepted all of me." I want to turn back. It's too hot here; I want to bury my face in one of the villa's couches and go to sleep. I want to press Ashley's bunny to my cheek and smell the lavender.

"This is where we see things differently, Stevie. I don't believe your eating disorder is the real you. I think there are some things we shouldn't accept. And living sick is one of those things. It sounds like Josh thought you deserved better. Maybe he wasn't willing to see you live sick."

"Well, he didn't have to," I snap. "I made sure of that, didn't I?"

I've stunned her into silence, I can see that. Maybe now she's starting to understand the *real me*. I have bad blood running through my veins. I'm not a good Green Girl. I'm not sharp like my mother or decent like my father or extraordinary like Josh. My mother knew it, and I know it: I am a monster. And when Josh looked up at me in his last moments, his vision clouded with his own blood and me just staring down at him, I think he finally knew it, too.

day nine

I imagine letters to Eden all day, only I have no idea exactly what I want to say. Shrink screwed with my brain this morning, sliding in her questions and her *maybes* just so, and toppling everything I'd ordered so neatly in my skull. She doesn't get Eden. She doesn't get that I *needed* to feel like fucked up was okay and I wasn't the only one. I needed a break from Dad's avoidance and the way Josh tried to gauge how much weight I'd lost when he hugged me.

In the evening snack line I stand alone. The line jitters, all shuffling feet and flitting hands. Two girls ahead of me, Ashley French braids Cate's limp noodle hair while Teagan watches. I should say something about how Ashley didn't rat me out, but every time I open my mouth, one of the girls bursts out laughing and I feel stupid.

"Stephanie? Stephanie D.?" The woman standing behind the serving window hasn't learned my name yet. To be fair, I've never corrected her. She reminds me a little of the cafeteria lady at my school: crumpled skin and a smile that is crooked and a hairnet draped over her wispy dishwater hair.

I step up to the window, which looks like a dumpy concession stand. Snack foods perch on the ledge: a small bag of pretzels, an apple with an individual container of peanut butter, a baggie of trail mix, chocolate cookies, a tiny bag of jelly beans. They are clustered in groups, index cards assigning each group a point value between one and three.

"How are you, Stephanie?" She slides a tray in my direction.

"Not hungry."

"You can do it." She smiles and consults a clipboard. Nothing is done around here without consultation of a goddamned clipboard. "Ms. Dalton has you down for six points for evening snack."

I scan the choices, searching for an acceptable combination, as if there is one. I reach for the package of jelly beans, then pull away before my fingers graze the cellophane. It reminds me of that game Josh and I used to play when we were kids, where you build a tower with wooden blocks and remove one block at a time until the tower falls. Once you touched a block, you're committed. You can't go back.

"Wait. Can I do the apple? But without the peanut butter." I point but don't touch.

"No, ma'am." She turns around and reappears with an apple, a container of peanut butter, and a plastic knife. "And what else?"

Behind me, the line of girls is shifting, rolling against me in stronger and stronger waves. I want to whirl around, tell them all to take about five giant steps back so I can think. "I can't—I don't know. The trail mix? Wait. No."

"Trail mix it is." She slides a bag across the ledge. "And I'll get your supplement."

"No. No." I shake my head. The apple and peanut butter and trail mix are already too much. "No supplement. Not tonight."

She doesn't argue, just makes a note on the form.

I clutch my tray and move slowly toward the table where Ashley, Cate, and Teagan are examining their selections.

"Uh, hey. Can I—"

"Sit." Ashley kicks out the chair across from her and half smiles, like she's totally forgotten what a bitch I was yesterday. "What'd you get? Ooh. I love that trail mix. Especially the dried cranberries. They're so good."

"Me, too." Cate combs the braid out of her hair. She reaches for the supplement, then nudges it away again. "I got the jelly beans, but I hate the licorice ones. Do you think I'll get charted for that? It's not, like, an ED thing. I just hate licorice." She chews her lower lip.

"I'll trade you licorice for cherry." Teagan's eyes cut across the room, scanning for nurses.

Cate shakes her head. "I should've gotten the apple."

"Want mine?" I interlace my fingers behind my neck and peer at my tray.

She snorts. "Right."

I knead the clear package of trail mix, studying the contents. Someone has tried to sneak chocolate covered peanuts beneath the raisins and almonds, I can tell. I shove it to the side and contemplate the apple. It's medium sized. I lift the plastic knife and saw carefully around the core. Then I slice those chunks in half, then do it again. And again.

"Stephanie." A heavy hand lands on my shoulder. "I need you to stop cutting up your food, please. That's enough."

I turn and shake Hannah's hand away. Cheap turquoise liner borders her eyes and squirms when she glares.

"Fine. Okay." I lift the first apple slice. The inside is pale and grainy. I bite it in half and chew as fast as I can. "*Mmmmmm. Food.*"

She sighs and shuffles away. Teagan catches my eye and grins.

I swallow the mealy mash, then peel back the gold foil on the peanut butter container and sink the knife into the gooey square. When I pull it out again, it stretches like caramel. I try to spread the peanut butter on an apple slice, but most of it sticks to the knife.

"Hey. Ashley. Thanks, um . . . thanks," I say, widening my eyes at Ashley. But Cate is too busy separating out black jelly beans to care. "Or, you know?"

She nods, all serious. "If you ever need help, like, distracting or something, we could do it together."

"You sound like you work here." I contemplate my next bite. It doesn't look right. I try to remember a time before all this when I ate peanut butter and apple together. People do that, right? It seems like a little kid snack. Maybe at school once. I pop the apple-peanut-butter chunk into my mouth and screw my eyes shut because maybe that will make it easier. The fat coats my tongue instantly. I chew frantically. *I'm doing it for Josh. I can't have a tube. I'm doing it for Josh. I can't have a tube.*

"Actually, I think working here would be kind of cool. I wonder what you have to do to get a therapist job." She pops a handful of pretzels—I don't think she even counts first—into her mouth and chews.

"When I get out of here, I'm never coming back." More accurately: *When I get out of here, I'm never going anywhere else.* The thought feels good and warm. I force myself to reach for another slice. The bitter apple skin pricks my throat on the way down.

"I hope I never have to come back, either," Cate says without looking up from her jelly bean piles.

"I don't know." Ashley smashes the empty pretzel bag flat with her palm. "I don't really want to leave. I like it better than being home, actually."

"Yeah," Teagan says to her lap. "The people here are nice."

Ashley nods. "And I like the schedule here or whatever." Her words start to tumble fast. "It's like school: You know exactly where you're supposed to be and what you're supposed to eat, so you can't really screw it up if you just follow the rules."

I don't disagree. We just follow different rules.

"Out there, it's way worse because it's like, there's everything and you can have anything at all, so it's easy to have too much and it's hard to stop and not safe like it is here."

I watch her expression go hard and her pink cheeks deepen. Even Cate has stopped her organizing. Teagan lifts her eyes.

"But I think when I get out I'm gonna buy, like, a bunch of individual peanut butter containers, so I know." She's not really looking at me anymore. "I'll stack them high."

"When are you supposed to go home?" I ask.

"Well, my Ninety-Six is in a couple weeks, but they probably won't come to that." She grimaces.

"Your what?"

Teagan pops a pink jelly bean into her mouth. "Her Ninety-Six. About a week before you're supposed to get out, your parents come out for four days and do, like, family therapy and stuff. Plus you can stay with them at their hotel if you want, and go off grounds during the day."

"Ashley. Maybe you could stay with a relative when you get out," I say carefully.

"Maybe," she mumbles. "Who are you going home to?"

No one. "My dad, I guess." It's what she expects to hear. "I'm serious, though. Do you have someone else you can stay with? Someone who can look out for you?" I cover her hand with mine. It's clammy, and when I touch her, she jumps and sucks in fast. Her eyes go wide. She looks up at me like she's seeing me for the very first time.

"No. No, no, no," she mutters. "I don't have anybody. No one like that." Her face is pleading, desperate. Begging me to help her or save her or some other heroic feat.

"It's okay," I say stupidly. "It's gonna be okay." I pull away, my hand sweaty with her panic, and I just want to get out of there. The villa feels too small for all of these girls and their demons, and it's insane for me to think for a second that I could help this one. We are all a collection of lost causes, stashed here so no one has to see just how wounded we are.

When I finish snack, I take my journal to my corner of the gold couch. Ashley's words play on loop in my broken brain. *Who are you going home to?* Even if I wanted to go home, there's almost no one left. *If.* There are too many *ifs* in my head to think straight: *if Josh were alive. If I'd never taken seminar. If I hadn't introduced Eden and Josh that night. If.*

The night of the Pit, I got ready in a silent house, scurrying back and forth between my mother's bathroom and mine in the dark, ears pricked for the slam of the front door. When it never came, I thought maybe Josh had forgotten about the Pit this year, and part of me was relieved. I liked the idea of slipping in to see all the good shows, just Eden and me. I grabbed my keys and my cell. I thought about leaving a note for Dad, then decided it didn't matter.

I'd barely twisted the key in the front door when I heard Josh pounding up the porch steps.

"Sass. Wait. You leaving for the Pit already?"

"Oh," I said vaguely. "Yeah. I thought you were busy or something."

He stopped and peered at me under the unforgiving porch light.

"What is that, lipstick? Since when do you wear lipstick?" He reached for my arm, but his hand found my shoulder, and his face got tight. His eyes fell on the tattoo. He hadn't said a word since I'd come home with it. Neither had my dad.

"It's not—screw you." I shook him off. The air was wet, already threatening to smear the foundation and blush I'd stolen from our mother's makeup drawer. I'd curled my hair with her curling iron, but I didn't know how because that's something you have to learn, and my hair was already sticking to my neck.

"Sass! I didn't—I'm just not used to your face like that is all. What did Dad say?"

"I don't need his permission."

"Yeah, no, I know," he said quietly.

We stared at each other. He looked like plain old regular Josh, in his T-shirt and jeans and sneakers, and suddenly I felt stupid and embarrassed beneath all the makeup. *Let's just forget it this year,* I wanted to say. *We can watch whatever channel you want and you can pick the snacks, too. And I won't be weird about them. Just for tonight.*

"I'm meeting my friend from seminar at eight," I said instead. "So I have to go. You probably don't have enough time to—"

"No, I'm ready. I'm good."

"You don't have to come if you don't want to." I didn't like the idea of hanging with Eden and Josh at the same time. I didn't know why. Josh would judge, probably. He wouldn't understand her, just like lately he couldn't understand me. She wasn't his type. She was mine.

"Of course I'm coming." He sounded hurt. "We do the Pit together every year."

"Okay, then." I sighed. "Come on." I hurried down the front steps and past the For Rent sign Dad had stabbed in the front yard and never mentioned. I'd heard him on the phone a few times, saying *original hardwood floors* and *wraparound porch* in this fake, bright voice. I tried to walk fast enough to feel a breeze on my face, but the air was too still.

"For real. Your—you look good, with your hair like that." His voice lilted up like a girl's on the word *good.* "Hey, when we get downtown do you want to grab something at Milo's? Did you have dinner yet? I didn't have dinner yet." He tosses the words on the cement in front of us, extra casual. No big deal.

"Nah, I'm not hungry." It was true, and I was proud. My hunger pangs had actually started to fade. I sped up a little, feeling my muscles hum.

"Sass. *Slow down.*"

"I don't want to be late, Josh. Okay?" My face burned. I wished he would just give up. A few blocks away, the music bubbled up: different songs and instruments and good-time noises layered one on top of the other.

"So your friend. Is she just hanging out, or is she playing or singing or something?" Josh huffed.

"She wrote lyrics for this band. During Ben's class."

"Cool. Cool." He reached over and fake patted my back, leaving his hand there long enough to evaluate how much my shoulder blades were jutting. I dropped to one knee, pretending to fuss over a shoelace that wasn't untied.

Downtown looked the way it always did this time of year. Nicer than usual but also kind of pathetic, like an ugly girl wearing sequins to prom. The same tired PeachPitPalooza banner sagged over Broad. Along the sidewalk, white Christmas lights were nestled in the trees like uneven strands of fake pearls. There was a main stage set up at the far edge of downtown, where people settled into rows of metal folding chairs. The shops and bars and restaurants were all open, tables and patrons and pitchers of beer spilling onto the sidewalk.

Every fourth storefront or so was dark, dusty windowed, and deserted. It had been that way for a couple years: Businesses snuck out in the middle of the night and never came back. The streets were clogged with people and they blurred together and I was light-headed, which felt good.

"Stevie!" Eden waved from her seat at a patio table a few bars down. She was siting alone. I waved back, then turned to Josh.

"Don't be weird. She's my friend, okay?"

"What do you mean, *weird?*"

"Just . . . " I raised my palm for emphasis. "Just."

He snorted. "Yeah. Got it."

Eden didn't get up when we reached her table. She shielded her eyes, even though it was dark out and there was already an umbrella over the table.

"Hey." She grinned at Josh. "Is this the brother?"

"Hey. Joshua." Josh lifted his hand in a half wave.

"God," I muttered under my breath.

"Eden."

I sat next to her. Josh took the seat on the other side of the table.

"So, you wrote lyrics for one of the bands? That's really cool." Josh smoothed his gray T-shirt, leaned back in his chair, then hunched forward. Inside the bar, somebody tuned an electric guitar. "Have you written for the festival before? During other years?"

During other years? I shot him a look. He sounded like he'd just asked her about her stock portfolio, or her thoughts on health-care reform.

Eden swirled melting ice in an empty glass and shook her head. "This is my very first time. Can you believe it?" She lifted her glass, shook a cube onto her tongue, and held it glistening between her teeth.

Even in the dark, I could see Josh go red.

"When does the band go on?" I asked too loudly.

"I think around nine." She crushed the ice and swallowed

it. She turned to Josh. "It's my friend Reid and my other friend Nic—they have this cool electric sound. I turned some of my freewriting from seminar into lyrics, and they liked them, so . . ."

"Impressive," Josh said, like he was forty. "So how's the class going?" He flagged down a waiter at the next table. Something our mother would do.

"Really good, I think. Ben's amazing. And it's been cool getting to know your sister." She cut her eyes at me and winked.

"Hey. Hold still." I leaned over and pressed the outer corner of her eye with my thumb. When I pulled away, there was a black glitter smudge on the tip. Fallout from her newest look: a dark, glinting, smoky eye. Along with her star tattoo, it made her eyes look like a supernova. You could get sucked in and disappear.

"Thanks." She searched my face. "You curled your hair and did your makeup."

"Oh," I said. "Yeah."

"Can I get you guys something to drink?" The waiter stood behind Eden.

"I'll have another." She raised her glass in the air like a torch.

"Sweet tea," Josh said, which was humiliating. "And can we get, like, an order of fries or something?"

The silver star over Eden's eye shuddered.

Josh turned his whole body toward me and lowered his voice. "What do you want to eat, Sass? Anything. Dad gave me money."

"I'm not hungry." I glanced at the waiter. "What are your drink specials?"

"You mean, like . . . *drink* drinks?" the waiter asked.

Eden was quiet.

"No," Josh said, his eyes on me. "She doesn't. She'll have tea, too. And the fries. Bring the fries."

"Josh." I hated the way my voice trembled, but I couldn't straighten it out. "I don't want the fucking fries."

"Don't curse, Sass."

"Sooo . . ." The waiter glanced back and forth between us.

"She'll—" Josh's mouth crumpled and his eyes looked like colored glass. "Just bring them. Please," he muttered.

The waiter looked at me.

"Water with lemon," I whispered.

The waiter practically sprinted inside.

I stared into the crowd, too embarrassed to look at Eden and too pissed to look at Josh. When Josh got up to go to the bathroom I felt her hand just above my knee, burning hot through the fabric of my jeans. I stiffened.

"Sorry. He's, like, overprotective sometimes," I said.

"Actually, I think it's sweet." She didn't move her hand, but leaned close enough for me to feel her breath on my ear. "Your brother seems like a really good guy. I'm glad he's looking out for you. Somebody has to."

Back on the couch, I let my pen drop and rub my eyes, trying to erase the memory of that night. I didn't need Josh to look out for me. I didn't need anyone. I was getting stronger every day, more self-reliant. In the end, it was Josh who needed protection. Only neither of us knew he would need protection from me.

day ten

I twist beneath the sheets for hours, desperate for sleep and afraid of it.

I want a pill from my stash. Hell, I want six or ten or however many it will take for me to forget myself and where I am and what—god, if there is one, help me—I've done. I want to forget the way the lines and angles of my body have bowed into curves, how my belly arcs toward the ceiling, a pale, sweaty crescent moon. The precious space between my thighs is crumbling. And I can feel the hard-edged fruit and oil weighing me down. Taking me further from my Josh.

But every time I near sleep, I'm scared shitless. Because the memories are coming faster now, pouring through me, as if I've broken the handle on the faucet. They are coming, no matter how much it hurts. And all I can do is hold my breath and try not to drown.

I'm close to sleep when the overhead light in our bedroom clicks on. Fluorescent light brings tears to my eyes.

"Hey." I press the heels of my hands into my eye sockets until I see stars. "Turn it off, okay?"

"Sorry. Sorry." Her whisper sounds like a yell. The light stays on.

"Seriously. Turn it off. Go in the hall or something if you need a light."

"I would, Stevie. But I just need to finish, okay? Just . . . sorry."

"Ashley." I sit up. It takes a few seconds for my eyes to adjust. She is sitting cross-legged in the center of the room. Around her, a mass explosion. Every single item of clothing both of us owns is strewn across the floor. Her mattress is bare.

"What the hell?" I flatten my back against the wall and bring my knees to my chest. "Ashley, are you . . . Are you okay?"

"Stevie, ohmygod. I'm better than okay. I'm, like, amazing." She's fully dressed, in jeans and a white T-shirt. In full makeup and dripping hair. "I'm just getting some stuff done because our days are so busy, so I'm just straightening up so our room looks nice." Her voice drops to a low whisper. "I tried to be quiet."

I check the clock by my bed. 1:15 A.M. I look away and check it again. Josh taught me that trick, when I was little and had nightmares. If the time on the clock is the same when you look the second time, you're not dreaming.

I'm not dreaming.

"Ashley." I keep my voice even, like she is a frantic child and I am the adult. But I'm not an adult, and she's scaring me. "You need to go to sleep, okay? You need to go to bed." I rack my brain for the right thing. Should I call a nurse? *Hello, my roommate is batshit crazy. Symptoms? Straightening up. But trust me.*

"I'm not tired!" she assures me. "It's like, I haven't had much energy since I got here and now all of a sudden? Listen. Listen. I'm going to arrange our clothes by color, okay? That's how my closet is at home and it makes it so easy to find everything. I'll do yours, too. Okay?" She's talking too fast, the words like dry sand pouring from her mouth.

"Okay," I whisper. I stay pressed against the wall as she folds the clothes. A rainbow starts to form in uneven piles around her. "But tomorrow we should talk to your therapist."

"God. Kyle. Can you believe I got the only man here? I think they want me to feel better about my dad or something. Did you know I have father hunger?" She hiccups a laugh. "You know what I thought of when they told me that? A chocolate dad wrapped in foil, like Easter candy."

"That's funny. We'll talk to Kyle, okay? In the morning." I glance at the door. My skin is slick.

"Ohmygod." She claps her hands together. "I started journaling! Because Anna told you to journal, and so I brought it up to Kyle and he said okay." She jumps up and sweeps everything off of the wall shelf until she gets to a spiral notebook. Then she opens it and flips the pages one after the other after the other, too fast to read. "This is bullshit, though. Seriously." Her face darkens.

"Ashley. I think maybe you need something to help you sleep. I can help you."

"Can't. I have to switch my laundry." She tears the pages from her notebook and they drop to the floor. "But I'll be back." She hurries to my side of the bed and grasps my hands in hers.

"I can't remember the last time I felt this good. I'm getting *better*, Stevie." Her eyes are bright and loose, like fortunes rolling in a Magic 8 Ball.

"That's good, Ashley. That's really good."

When she leaves, I jump out of bed and scoop up the journal pages. There are words everywhere, covering every inch of the page in different directions, pinks and greens and baby blues, fat and schoolgirlish. I can make out the words, but I can't find a sentence. The back of my throat tastes like peanut butter and sick. I can't be here anymore.

In the hall, the dryer door slams. I wind my bedsheet around me and grab my journal. Sneak down the hall to the small porch outside the front door. Screw bed checks. Let them catch me. I flop into one of the rocking chairs and pull my sheet tighter. It does nothing to stop the cold. I angle the other chair perpendicular to mine and prop my feet on the armrest.

In the distance, just above my left big toe, a string of white lights from a nearby city bobs in the dark, like the Christmas lights draped over downtown for the Pit. I count them left to right, right to left. Remember the way Eden's face looked under those lights. She was beautiful, the way two plus two is four. It was simple fact, and I wasn't the only one who knew it.

Eden,

I got your letter. Obviously. Maybe sometime we could talk on the phone or something. I don't really use the phone here, but I could, if I wanted to. After dinner, which is going-out time at home, I guess.

I've been thinking about you. A lot, actually. About what happened to Josh, and why it happened. I think it started that night at the Pit. I keep replaying the night again and again in my head and every time I want to know: Why did you do it? Just for fun? To prove you could?

My fingers are trembling with cold and anger, and I nestle the pen in the center of the journal. I go through the night of the Pit once more, combing through the sandy details to find a shell I hadn't seen before. Maybe if I remember just one more time. Maybe then I'll understand how everything unraveled.

Josh and Eden and I hung around long enough to hear her friends play the patio of a dive bar. Christmas lights sagged overhead. Around us, the hipster set crammed around patio furniture, drinking soapy-smelling beer. I sat between Eden and Josh, ignoring my brother and watching Eden watch the show. She bobbed her head in perfect rhythm, strands of hair around her face pressed against her damp skin. I'd never seen anyone more comfortable existing.

"Sass," Josh hissed, leaning close. "What did I—are you seriously mad at me?"

I shushed him and stared straight ahead. "I'm trying to watch. Could you not ruin this, too?"

"I should be mad at you, you know that? We do the Pit together every year—you and me. As a family," he whispered accusingly.

"Josh, please." I glared at the band. "We haven't been a family since Mom left."

"Bullshit." His voice cracked, which made me feel awful. "Bullshit."

I'm sorry, I should have said. *I didn't mean it*. But instead I gritted my teeth and pretended to listen to the music and pretended not to think about what an asshole I was, or about the way my thighs stuck to the cheap plastic patio furniture. I wanted to be alone with Eden, and buzzed. Josh was screwing everything up.

When everyone around me clapped, I clapped, too. I leaned toward Eden when the music got loud again and muttered, "God, I need a drink, you know?"

"Get one, then," she said, her voice low. Everything was just that simple for her. You want something, you make it yours. "I love these tools, but I couldn't listen to this shit sober. I have no idea how you're doing it."

"My chaperone'll kill me."

"Just say you're going to the bathroom. I'll chat him up. He'll never know."

I hesitated, looked over at Josh. Under the lights his face shone like a freaking altar boy's, serene while my insides churned. I thought about the psychology class I'd taken the year before, when we discussed nature and nurture. Josh and me, we'd both been raised the same way. We'd had the same parents, anyway, though sometimes I thought that didn't mean what it should. My mother had always loved Josh better.

If we'd basically had the same nurture, the only thing that was different was the nature. Who we'd been, from the moment we sucked in our first breath. The thought was actually kind of freeing. I'd never been stupid enough to believe that all people were equal. Some were just plain better than others. And if Josh was born better than me, if good was part of his DNA, that wasn't my fault. I couldn't help it.

"I'm going to the bathroom," I announced in the middle of the next song.

"That's cool." Eden grinned. Josh didn't say anything.

The inside of the bar was dark, and damp with humidity. There was an old video game machine in the corner that spewed alien sounds. A few guys circled a pool table. The bartender didn't bother asking for my ID. I ordered two shots of whisky. Quicker. Fewer calories. I'd run tomorrow, I promised myself. I waited until he turned to watch TV before I took them. Then I ordered one more, and took that, too.

I sagged on the barstool and waited for the warmth to take over. I hated Josh for making me do this in secret. Why couldn't he be like everybody else's older brother, getting me my first fake ID, or at least pretending not to know? I stared at the TV above the bar for a while. The Braves were playing some other team. I watched the ball bounce like a pearl against the green.

When I felt loose enough, I slid off the stool and went back outside. Eden was sitting in my seat, gesturing wildly at Josh. He was laughing like a moron.

"Move, bitch. You stole my seat." I grinned, nudging her foot with mine.

"Stevie," Josh said, like a dad.

"Jesus, Josh. Take a break or something, okay?" I said.

I felt his eyes on me. When Eden didn't move, I sat on the very edge of her seat, my body angled toward them. The lights above us were a little hazier, Eden's outline liquid.

"So I'm having some people over after this." Eden stretched out in my chair. "You guys down?"

"I don't think we can." Josh was still staring at me. "We should get home."

"I'm down, for sure." I stretched out next to her and knocked my sneaker against her sandal. "Sounds fun."

"*Stevie*," Josh said. "I don't think we should. I think you need to get some rest."

I slid down low in Eden's chair and blinked at the glowing jewels above me. "And I think *you* need to chill the fuck out, *Joshua*."

"No need to fight, children," Eden said playfully. "Especially not over my little old party."

"Stevie, seriously." Josh's voice got quiet and pleading. "Let's go home. I think you need to get to bed. I'll walk you back."

My face burned under the lights. "This is bullshit," I snapped. I jumped out of my chair, stumbling over a crack in the patio where green peeked through. "Leave me alone."

"Easy, tiger." Eden reached out and wrapped her hand around my wrist.

"I'm fine. I'm fine. I'm just leaving, okay? I'm sorry about"—I flapped my hand in Josh's direction without looking at him—"this." I whipped my head around, looking for the exit. "I'll call you tomorrow."

"Stevie." Josh reached for me, but I slapped him away.

"Get off, Josh." I could hear my words slurring together, but I didn't care anymore. "I'm going home, and you'd better not follow me."

Head down, I charged into the street, weaving around wasted frat boys on every block. I hated Josh for humiliating me this way. It was my life, didn't he get that? My life, my call. He wasn't my dad. He didn't have a say.

"Stevie!" Josh's voice found its way to me, but I kept walking. The whole way home, I heard him, calling my name again and again. I never turned around.

"Stevie! Stevie." When I open my eyes, Ashley is there. "Ohmygod, when I couldn't find you I got totally freaked out." She leans over me, her wet hair dripping through my sheet and dotting my chilled skin.

"I'm here. It's fine. I just . . . couldn't sleep." I slam my notebook shut.

"Me neither," she chirps. "But the closets look great. Wanna see?"

"Yeah, okay. I'm coming." I follow her inside. "But then I think you need to get some sleep, okay? I think we both need to get some sleep."

I watch her scurry down the hallway, and I wish Josh were here. Wish I could just snap my fingers and bring him back for a second. I'd ask him what to do, and he'd know, because he knew how to take care of people in a way I never did. Or at least he knew how to try.

day ten

AT breakfast I watch Ashley while I prick rubbery scrambled
eggs with my fork. She flounces from the serving window,
bright-eyed in a sundress and cardigan. I'm positive neither one
of us got any sleep. I heard her tossing and turning beneath her
hot, just-dried sheets all night. I must have dozed off for a few
minutes, because when I woke for weight and vitals she was
gone, her bed made so tightly I couldn't have slid between the
sheets if I tried.

"Morning, girls." She lets her tray clatter to the table, next
to me and across from Teagan and Cate. "OJ, pleeease." She
reaches for the plastic pitcher.

"Morning." I saw off a corner of my eggs and force it
down. I don't think about my numbers this morning, or how

140

Hannah actually looked pleased when she jotted them down in her binder. Instead I picture the colored pills pooling at the bottom of my drawer like lethal candy. I take another bite.

"You're in a good mood this morning." Teagan yawns and nudges the last bite on her plate. She wants to eat it, I know. But then she'd be the first one finished.

"I got a lot done yesterday." Ashley pours a too-full glass and leans into me. "Hey. I'm sorry if I freaked you out last night. It's just that I've had a little extra energy lately, which is awesome! Because, like, I totally think treatment is working." She spins the yellow circle around her wrist. "Pretty soon, I'll be on greeeen."

"Okay." I search her for any sign of the wildness I'd seen last night. But her eyes are clear. "But maybe you should still talk to Kyle. You seemed pretty . . . hyper." I select my words carefully.

"Oh, for sure," she agrees. "For sure. We have a session this afternoon."

I glance at Cate and Teagan, just to see. But they're talking coffee creamer combinations and don't notice. But I know what I saw wasn't right.

After breakfast, I get to the lawn before Shrink for our session. I stretch out in the grass and let the sun burn my skin. Clutch my journal to my chest and close my eyes, exhausted.

"Good morning."

I look up. Shrink is Hippie Shrink today, in a chambray shirt and a navy tie-dyed maxi skirt I could have made during craft hour.

"How are you this morning?" she asks, and squats down next to me.

"I'm tired." It's the truth, but not the whole truth. I feel disgusting, the scrambled eggs like cement-filled balloons in my gut. "I could use some coffee." I lick my lips and taste the syrup I couldn't swallow.

"You'll have another shot at lunch." She smiles. "Didn't get much sleep last night?"

I search her face, looking for the twitch of an eyebrow, something that will show me I should tell her about Ashley. Only Ashley didn't rat me out after I purged. And really, this isn't my business. I have my own problems. My own preparations to make. Ashley will only be a distraction.

"I'm having trouble sleeping," I say.

"I'm sorry to hear that. You can always let Dr. Singh know the next time you meet with him."

"I need a higher dose of meds."

"Hm." I can feel her eyes on me. "So how do you want to use your time?"

"I don't know. I'm kind of . . . Could we take a break? Not have a session?"

She tries to sit next to me. "It seems like you're struggling today. But I'm going to encourage you to push through any discomfort you're feeling and—"

"My stomach is the fucking size of a bowling ball, okay?" I sit up, my outburst surprising even me. My hands find my midsection. My gut is round and hard. For the first time, I can't rest my arm across my hips without feeling my stomach underneath. "I feel like shit." I close my eyes again.

142

"I know you do. This is the really hard part, when your body's getting used to food again."

"Is it like sobering up?"

I feel her tighten next to me. "Let's keep the focus on you, Stevie."

"I could journal," I say to the sky. "Or write letters. I was working on a letter to Eden last night. I could finish that." I squint up at her. *Please. I can't talk today. It's just too much.*

She pauses. "Rest, Stevie. We'll meet later this afternoon. I'll be in my office if you decide you want to talk. If nothing else, I'll see you in group tomorrow. We can make up the session later, okay?"

"Yeah. Thanks," I say. I flop onto my stomach and press my cheek into the grass. I can hear the living earth humming beneath me. I make the tiniest grass angel. Then I sit up and go back to the letter.

Here's the really shitty thing about it all, Eden: I was going to apologize to him. Can you believe it? For being a bitch to him that night and storming off. I'd thought about it, thought maybe he was just trying to be a good big brother, and I was going to skip time with you to apologize to him. God, I was so stupid.

Josh and I hardly spoke to each other the week after the Pit, which wasn't hard to accomplish. By Monday morning, Dad had rented our house to some yuppie couple from Atlanta without even asking us. Josh had classes during the day, so I lugged boxes into one of my dad's writing buddy's pickup trucks, then out again. I dropped them in the "front hall" of the new place, if you could call it that. I heard some things shatter, and so did Dad. He didn't say a word, like usual.

By Tuesday morning, I was getting sick of the silence again. I scribbled two words on the back of the electric bill, and pinned it beneath the coffee maker.

Scrabble Wednesday?

The next afternoon before I left for seminar, I checked.

You're on, he'd written.

I left seminar early, made some excuse to Eden and Ben about a doctor's appointment. Practically gunned the Buick all the way home from the Stacks. I was sick of not speaking to Josh. We'd never been this way. It was as if our family had existed in a bubble before. We weren't perfect, but we managed and everything was okay. And then my mother decided to walk out—burst the bubble and send the rest of us skittering and spinning, soapy and confused.

She hadn't called since she left, either. Not once. Sometimes I would dial the number I found in Dad's desk drawer and listen to the unfamiliar beep until I heard her voice. And then I'd hang up, because I had nothing to say unless she was going to come home.

When I unlocked the door to the new place, the *click* was flimsy. Inside, it was hot and dark and smelled powdery, like generic carpet cleaner.

"Hello?" I pawed at the switch by the door, then turned it off when the fluorescent light was too much. In the kitchen, I found a note from my dad, scribbled on a Post-it note. It was as if the only way our family knew how to talk anymore was through sentence fragments penned on the back of scratch paper.

Having a beer with the guys. Dinner in freezer. Love, Dad

I found two frozen dinners, as promised. In the dark, I tore off the cardboard and stabbed the plastic with a fork I found in the sink. I wouldn't eat it, but seeing the food on the table would make Josh happy. And I hadn't been doing much of that lately. While the teal numbers ticked down, I took out the Scrabble board. When the microwave bleated, I took out the trays and spooned the indistinguishable contents onto the first plates I could find: my mother's dinner party china. I poured us both a Diet Coke. In wine glasses, with ice.

I sat at the dining room table and waited, nudging the tiles around the Scrabble board in exotic combinations. I texted him four times. After the third time, he texted that he was running late, which was obvious, because it was past nine. *Could we play the next night instead?* I took both dinners back into the kitchen. Devoured them over the sink, then puked and rinsed it all down the drain. Back in the dining room I sucked on the ice from my empty glass.

It was after ten when I heard the front door slam.

"Sass? You up still?"

I didn't say anything, just sat there in the too-small dining room with my glass of Diet Coke water.

"Hey," he said, breathless even though he was just standing in the doorway. He smelled like something too sweet that I couldn't quite place. "Where's Dad?"

"Out."

"So. Sorry I'm so late. I was out and lost track of time." His eyes fell on the table. "Did you eat? It smells like meat loaf."

"Nah. Not hungry."

"Come on. Don't be mad." He walked over to my side of the table slowly, like he was scared of something. Rested his hand on my back. When I looked up, something glinted on his shoulder. The tiniest smudge of black glitter. And that's when I knew, when it was big and looming, staring me in the face. I wish I could say I knew the second I saw him. Or that I had a feeling, deep down. But I had no idea, which made it so much worse.

"Oh," I said. "So, are you guys fucking, or what? Behind my back?"

He went white, like I'd slapped him. The air in the apartment was so thick, I could hardly breathe. My *brother*. And my—Eden.

"No. Stevie." He swiped at his shoulder, but the stain remained. "No, I swear. I just—I was running late to meet you, and she called, and—"

"She *called*?"

"She asked for my number the other night at the Pit, okay? It was no big deal."

I tried to shove my chair back, which didn't work because of the stupid, cheap, stained carpet in the hellhole we now inhabited. I squeezed out of the space between the chair and table, and couldn't get past him without touching him.

"I was gonna tell you, okay?" He gripped my shoulders. "God, would you please *eat* something? You're like—"

"Yeah. Good. Make this about me." I wrenched out of his grip. If I'd been capable of tears, I would have cried.

"Stevie, stop! I just wanna talk, okay? That's all." He blocked the apartment door.

"Move, Josh. I'm not talking about this now. I'm never talking about this." I shoved him, hard. He stumbled back. "Just . . . leave me the hell alone." I twisted the ugly gold door handle and fell outside, into the hall. I needed space from him the way I needed air. I needed him to be gone. It would just be so much easier.

day eleven

Monday, July 14, 11:57 a.m.

GROUP the next day is held in the kitchen again, which makes me want to bail. But this time, there are no caving cereal boxes, no dripping cylinders of ice cream, no hardened syrup stains on the counter. So I step inside, next to the other girls in Cottage Three.

We wait. Leaning against the counter, Ashley tugs her knit tee over her belly. Teagan plucks a single strand of hair from her head and examines the white-bulbed root. Cate flicks the tube coming out of her nose. We're huddled together like the world's most pathetic peewee football team, silently debating our final play. It won't matter. We'll get our asses kicked.

"Welcome to group, Cottage Three!" Shrink says brightly, joining the huddle.

We all make a noise like *mehhh*.

"Today's group is a meal group," she says. "We'll cook our lunch together and then process as we eat."

"What are we making? Do we get to pick?" I pinch my hospital bracelet between my index finger and thumb. It occurs to me that maintaining my weight this way could make me a Yellow Girl. *But I'm not a Yellow Girl*, I think, suddenly pissed. I look at the only other Red Girl here—Cate—but she's nodding, like *okay, okay*.

Shrink shakes her head. "Here's the menu: spaghetti with salad, and brownies for dessert."

I purse my lips together to contain the burst of laughter that's waiting behind the pink flesh like machine gun fire. Pasta? Salad, with dressing of course, slick, greasy calories that ruin the vegetables. Brownies? I look around to see if anyone else gets the joke. No one's laughing.

"Before we divvy up the jobs, I'd like you all to choose something to drink." Shrink nods at the refrigerator.

Ashley steps up first. The refrigerator makes a slurping sound when she jerks the door open. Standing at attention are rows of shiny aluminum cans—Coke, Sprite, Dr Pepper. I don't even have to summon the numbers. They come instantly. *140calories 39gramsofcarbs39gramsofsugar.Toomuchtoomuchtoomuch.*

"Where's the diet?" I ask.

"There is no diet," Shrink says evenly. "Can we pause for a second? Check in with how everyone's doing?"

"Oh." Ashley is already clutching a fat red can.

"Seriously, though. That stuff is *bad* for you," I say.

Ashley's face crumples like a crushed can.

"I mean, I'm sorry. But like, isn't the goal to get us to be healthy"—*fat!*—"or whatever? Because this isn't. It *isn't*." I hate the way I sound, like a shitty whiny kid, even though I'm the only one here who's thinking clearly.

Ashley closes the refrigerator door. She's still holding the can.

"The goal is to start to take the fear out of food, out of eating." I hate the way Shrink's voice gets all gooey when she's saying the worst things. "The goal is to show you that you can start to take the power away from some of your fear foods."

"Do we have to?" Cate says quietly, pinching her tube. She's staring at the floor.

Thank you.

Shrink shakes her head. "You don't have to. But if you're feeling some anxiety around the idea of taking a soda, then I would encourage you to challenge yourself."

I hate words like *process* and *encourage* and *challenge*.

"Stevie? On a scale of one to ten, where's your anxiety right now?" Shrink says it like the electricity in me is nothing more than a set of lost house keys—*where's your anxiety right now?*—instead of this hot squirmy thing in me that makes me shaky and dizzy and sick. Forcing down a few bites at meals is one thing. But cooking is another.

"I don't know." My head is too jumbled up to answer.

"I'm at like an eight," Cate volunteers. "Soda was one of the first things I cut out when I started to restrict, so . . ."

"So your anxiety is pretty high right now. Would you consider taking a soda?"

Cate bites her bottom lip. "Maybe like a Sprite?"

"Good, Cate. Go ahead."

When the other girls are all clutching their soda cans, Shrink glances at me.

"No." I wince at the metallic *pop* of the cans opening. I'll try the salad, maybe. Some sauce without the noodles. But soda? *Soda?*

"Absolutely your choice, Stevie. So we need to divide up the jobs. I'll make the salad, if a couple of you can take the pasta. And then who wants the brownies?"

"We'll help with the pasta," Cate offers. Teagan threads her thick wrist through Cate's angular elbow.

"And we'll do brownies?" Ashley almost asks. "Right, Stevie?"

"I guess," I mutter at the floor.

"Great. You'll find everything you need in the cabinets." Shrink claps her hands together, breaking our huddle, and the other girls scatter. I don't understand. Not figuratively, but literally. My brain isn't wired right, can't make sense of how the others are pulling ingredients from the refrigerator and boiling pots of water and snapping pasta in half when I can't move. Maintaining my weight is too hard. I need a break. Just for today.

"Okayyyy." Ashley stands on tiptoe and opens the corner cabinet, unearthing a box of brownie mix, a measuring cup, and a plastic bottle of oil. "Can you grab the eggs?"

As she walks by, Shrink squeezes my shoulder. I dip out of her reach and jerk open the fridge door. Standing in the cold white light, I try to focus. Almost impossible, when there are more cans and bottles and cartons and all the numbers zooming around inside my head. Somehow my fingers find the foam carton of eggs, and I retrieve it and hand it to Ashley.

"Thanks." She reaches for a knife and stabs the plastic bag

of brownie mix. Chalky brown dust escapes, and I hold my breath.

After we're all finished with our tasks, we serve our plates and take them to the table. It feels fake sitting around a table in this semi-house with these girls and Shrink at the head of the table, like we're playing a TV family and she's the single mom who's behind on the mortgage but still makes time for family dinner. I'm starting to have second thoughts about this whole compliance thing. Maybe a tube would be the better option. Maybe I could disconnect it at night.

No. The night nurse would notice.

"So, what was that like for you all, making the food?" Shrink's eyes sweep around the table.

"Okay, I guess." Teagan's fingers find their way to her hairline. "It's kind of weird making food *together*."

"Not being alone, you mean?" Shrink twirls pasta around her fork, sending tiny spatters of sauce to her placemat. She doesn't even notice.

"Yeah. Before I got here, I can't remember the last time I ate around people, you know? Like it was just something I did by myself. Bingeing or purging or restricting. Whatever I was doing, I just didn't want anybody to see."

"Same," Ashley blurts over a mouthful of wilted greens. "It's embarrassing, and nobody understands."

My chin drops to my chest in a half nod. After our mother left, I ate almost exclusively in the dark. Or drunk, which is almost the same.

"You felt a lot of shame around eating or preparing food or engaging in behaviors." Shrink nods her understanding. "It's exhausting, isn't it? Carrying that kind of shame?" Her eyes flick to me, like *Stevie?*

"I don't want to talk about it." I look just beyond my plate. The smells are too much and all the food is touching and really, tomorrow is a much better day to stop losing weight. "Is it hot in here? It's hot in here."

Shrink reaches overhead and yanks a beaded brass chain, sending the ceiling fan above us in reluctant circles. "Better?"

I shrug.

The table goes silent, except for the clinking of forks that are not mine.

"You're not the only one, Stevie," Cate says quietly.

Shrink puts her fork down. "What do you mean, Cate?"

"I just mean . . . it's hard for all of us, that's all. Maybe if you talked about it some, it would make it easier. Or you'd see that you weren't the only one feeling . . . whatever."

I stare at my plate. "I'm feeling like . . . this pasta sucks," I say, and the other girls laugh, but the laughter is too shallow to be real.

"Stevie, I notice that you're having trouble with your meal," Shrink says.

I look around, and the other girls are halfway through their pasta.

"I wonder if it would be helpful to you if we played a game to distract while you eat. Could we give that a try?"

I've looked at her before, but now I really *look* at her. I hold her turquoise gaze without looking away, like there is a silky thread strung from my pupils to hers, and I do the unthinkable: I beg. *Please don't make me do this. Not today.* I try to make her understand what I know deep down: *I can't. Get it?*

She gives me an almost imperceptible head nod that proves she doesn't.

"We can play the alphabet game." Ashley reaches over and squeezes my wrist. For a second, my red bracelet disappears. I don't breathe again until she lets go. "Books. You like books, right? I'll go. A: *Alexander and the Terrible, Horrible, No Good, Very Bad Day*. It's a kid's book. I used to read it when—I was a kid."

"I don't want to play," I mumble. Accidentally, my gaze falls on my plate. The pasta writhing beneath chunks of sauce. The salad limp and slick.

"B: *Breaking Dawn*. From Twilight," Cate says before carefully pressing the tines of her fork into a pale, fleshy tomato.

"C: *Charlie and the Chocolate Factory*," Shrink says. "My absolute favorite. Give it a shot, Stevie. I know you can do it."

I lift my fork, all the while thinking *nonononono*, but fuck I have to, there's no other choice. *It'sforJoshit'sforJosh*. And I stab a chunk of carrot with my fork. It feels like lead on my tongue and I chew and swallow fast. The oil from the dressing coats the inside of my mouth, and Shrink smiles.

"Can I do a movie?" Teagan's voice sounds far away. "D: *Dirty Dancing*. My older sister used to watch that movie all the time. The main guy's dead from cancer."

My fingers still frozen around the fork, I try again. Twirl the pasta around the tines while I think about anything other than the whiteness of it, the carbs, the butter. I stab and twirl, then slip the fork past my unwilling lips.

It should feel like something more than this. It should be a monumental moment, but it isn't. One minute I'm taking a bite of pasta, and then next Shrink is saying G: *Great Expectations* and I can feel everything mixing around together in my gut and my stomach surges a few times—false starts.

At the end of the meal, we clear our plates and leave them in the sink.

"Excellent job, girls. I'm proud of all of you," Shrink says. She drains the last of her Coke, which surprises me, because she seems like a coconut water kind of chick. "You can head back to the villa together, if you'd like. I'll finish up here."

Outside, I squint into the heat. I can feel my stomach expanding, my belly fighting against the waistband of my jeans. I hate this, all of it. I hate Shrink and I hate myself and I even hate Josh a little, which I know is unfair, but there it is.

day twelve

Tuesday, July 15, 11:01 AM

BEFORE I sit on Shrink's love seat, I warn her: "I definitely don't want to talk about group yesterday."

"Okay." She looks up from the paper crane she's folding and nods. For the first time, I notice that the desk behind her and the windowsill are littered with her paper cranes, each a different color and pattern. I read a book about them in elementary school. I don't remember the story, exactly. Just that the girl died.

"For what it's worth," she says, "I think the fact that you don't want to talk about group yesterday means that at some point, we should talk about group yesterday—"

"I knew you'd say that." I plop onto the couch and grab one of the pillows, to obscure my expanding belly. My jeans are getting too tight, but I only brought jeans. One of many humiliations.

"Let me finish." She smiles. "Of course, you don't have to talk about anything you don't want to talk about, and I'm glad you're taking charge of your session. So." She rests the unfinished bird on the side table, next to a flickering candle that smells like rain. I think about asking her to teach me to fold paper like that, but then I think there's no point in knowing how to do something for just sixteen days. "What do you want to talk about?"

"Eden," I blurt. It just comes out. "I don't know what to say to Eden." Her name on my tongue makes me a deep kind of tired.

"I was wondering," she says. "It seems like she's come up for you a lot lately. You started a letter to her, right?"

"Yeah. But I haven't finished it."

"What do you think's getting in your way?"

"Confusion." I stretch on out on the love seat with my head propped against one arm and my legs dangling over the other. But that's not comfortable, either, so I sit up again.

"What's your confusion about, you think?"

"Like, about how I feel about her. Or what she was—or is, or whatever—to me. And Josh made things even more confusing, so . . ."

"How's that?" She leans forward in her chair, which is Shrink-speak for *tell me more*.

"He was, like, dating her. Or something. I don't know exactly what was going on between them, but I know it was something."

"How do you know?"

"Because—" I let my head drop back and I stare at the ceiling. "Because he didn't deny it, and neither did she."

"Okay. So they were . . . romantically involved, possibly.

157

What was the nature of your relationship with Eden? You've never really said."

"I don't *know*." I'm sorry I brought it up. How could Shrink possibly understand, when I can't even wrap my head around what we were? "But I was pissed that she was hanging out with Josh."

"How is it that their relationship made you so angry?" What she really wants to know is *why*. But shrinks don't ask *why*, even when they should. It's against their code or something.

"It's just . . ." I close my eyes and am back in *Le Crâpeau*, its walls closing in around me. I remember the glittery glint on Josh's shoulder, and the rage returns, fresh. It's been here all along. "She was *mine*. Just . . . a friend that was just mine. I needed that, you know? I never had it before."

"You felt . . . almost territorial. Did you ever tell Josh or Eden how angry you felt about their relationship?"

"Josh knew I was pissed. He kept seeing her, though. I would find pieces of her on him—like he would smell like her some nights when he came home. But Wednesday nights after seminar were my nights with her."

"Is that what you all decided?" she asks.

"It was just kind of an unspoken rule," I say. "I mean, I didn't even tell her I knew about her and Josh. Until this one Wednesday toward the end of seminar. When she took me to her place."

"So, here it is. Nothing special." Eden had made a half-assed *ta-da* motion with her arms, showcasing the airy converted loft she shared with a girl she despised.

158

"Eden. This is amazing." The place was one big room, with a few tapestries knotted together and hanging from the high beams to separate the space. The cool was in the details: hardwood floors painted light green. Dying potted plants that proved her total disregard for life and tiny colored glass bottles along the windowsill. There was an exposed brick wall, hung with framed squares of metallic gold paper. There were candid pictures of pretty people I didn't know doing interesting things. It looked like life after high school, the way it was on a television.

"I'm thinking of kicking my roommate out." She pushed off her flats and nudged them out of the way. "She keeps stealing my soy milk and lying about it. I'm fine if she wants some, but just ask, you know?"

"Mhmm." There was a bookshelf on the wall near the front door. I ran my fingers over the spines and unearthed *Anna Karenina*. "This used to be one of my favorites." The cover was glossy. The spine was smooth, unlined.

"Me, too. Anna's so tragic."

I flipped through the volume. The pages were creamy and perfect.

"I'll get us a drink. What do you want?"

"Whatever's fine," I murmured. I returned the book to its space and tried another: Camus. *The Stranger.* It was pristine, too. "You take really good care of your books," I said lamely.

She clanged around in the kitchen for a few minutes, and I took a seat at the counter. She nudged a Mason jar toward me. I lifted it to my lips. Vodka with a hint of something sweet. Lime. Tiny fleshy bits clung to the edge of the glass. My cheeks felt hot.

"What are you reading next week?" I asked after the first

159

few sips. Our final seminar was the following week, and it was tradition for Ben's students to do a reading for family and friends.

"I'm trying to decide." She came around to my side and sat on the counter, her feet dangling. My wrist grazed her knee. "I kind of spent most of my time on those lyrics. I'll have to polish something up. Maybe we could get together this week and work on stuff."

"I don't really have anything, either," I admitted. I hadn't been working. I was having trouble focusing, and to be honest, I didn't really care about writing anymore. The really shitty thing about it was that I knew Ben had noticed. And he hadn't said a word.

"I know," she said. "Unless you want to read one of those letters you've been writing to your mom."

I wondered how much she'd read over my shoulder while someone else read aloud and everyone nodded along.

I finished the rest of my drink. Staring into the bottom of the glass made everything blurry. I could feel my stomach fighting my waistband. I sucked in.

"Your mom should've told you to your face that she was leaving. She didn't say anything before she left?"

"Nah. She was too scared or something." My throat was tight. "That's what my dad said, anyway."

"That's bullshit." She refilled my glass.

I told myself to go slow. "Yeah."

"People should just say what they mean, you know? She should have sat you down and just said, *Stevie*—"

"'I want something better.'" My voice was flat.

"She'll never be happy, you know. I can tell she's that kind of person, like, immediately. I don't know if that makes you feel any better."

It didn't, but I nodded anyway.

"People like her . . ." She finished her drink and poured herself a shot. "Women like her want whatever they don't have."

The accusation stung for just a second, until I remembered that I wasn't supposed to care about my mother enough to defend her.

"Yeah." I slid off the stool. "Where's your bathroom?"

"Right around the corner, there."

Behind the closed bathroom door, I surveyed her belongings. Tiny glass bottles and jars lined the sink: perfume samples and face creams and hair masks and other girl potions that were foreign to me. I spritzed my wrists with a scent that smelled like amber. I stared at my reflection in the mirror. My face was too pink; my hair plastered with sweat to the back of my neck. I found a hair tie in her medicine cabinet and pulled my hair into a high knot. Examined the lines of my neck. I could see my pulse in my neck, pumping.

I stared deep into my pupils until they could have been someone else's. *You are not enough for her*, I told myself. *You weren't enough for your mother, and you aren't enough for her.* I wondered if Josh had been here first, if his reflection had existed here.

I flushed the toilet and turned the faucet for a few seconds. I took a slow, deep breath and went back into the kitchen, the words pouring from my mouth before I could chicken out.

"How come you're hanging out with my brother? You could have any guy you want."

Her features twisted into something I couldn't quite recognize. I didn't know if she looked angry or guilty or what. I hoped it wasn't angry. Angry belonged to me.

"He's sweet." Her voice was sharp. Pissed. "What do you care?"

"I don't," I snapped. "It's just that he's my brother, and—"

"Oh my *god*." She jumped down effortlessly. "You're *jealous*."

"What?" My face burned. "You're fucking insane, you know that?" I turned away from her. My brain was sober, humiliated. My body was drunk. I tripped and almost knocked over the lamp next to her couch. "Jesus. I have to get home." I was halfway to the door, trying to figure out where I'd put my purse and my keys, when she laughed.

"Hey. Wait." She dipped toward me, a colorful blur: pink lips and cheeks and a shimmery beige over her eyes and all the black hair that fluttered around her shoulders when she walked. "I'm sorry."

"Whatever. I need my keys."

"Stevie. I didn't mean to laugh, okay? I'm sorry." She gripped my arm and pulled me into her. "Don't leave." She hugged me.

"I'm not—I was just asking." I said it into her collarbone. I reached out my fingertip and traced it, because it was so beautiful. Long and angular.

"I know." She pulled back a little. "I'm sorry, okay? I'm sorry."

And then her mouth was on mine, and my breath caught in my throat. We stayed like that for a long time: her top lip pressed between my top and bottom lip, unmoving. She tasted tart and good. My whole body was knotted into itself. In the corners of my eyes, hot tears gathered and slid down my cheeks.

"Hey. It's okay," she whispered into my mouth before she

kissed me, really kissed me. I could feel the parts of myself that she was touching because she was touching them: My lips burned where her lips were and the back of my neck where her cold, small hand rested. I was there because she was there. She kissed the wet salt from my cheeks. I kissed her back, found her tongue with mine. I rested my hands on her shoulders.

"I'm drunk." I shuddered at the ceiling as she kissed my neck. "I'm really drunk, okay?" I let her press me into the door, felt my body harden against hers. I let her consume me.

"And what was that like for you?" Shrink asks, and I find myself in her office again, my knees drawn to my chest and my ankles crossed over each other.

"That's the wrong question," I say to my lap. "The question is, *What were you thinking while you kissed her?*"

"Okay. So what were you thinking?"

"I was thinking I wanted to kiss her better than Josh kissed her." I can't even look at her as I say it. "And I was thinking, *I can't believe she wants me.*" Me. An amateur, a fumbling idiot with no perfumes or face creams on her bathroom counter. I'd never kissed anyone before. Other girls had their first kisses in middle school, in basements, sucking the punch-stained mouths of the boys they'd grown up with. But nobody had ever wanted me before Eden, and maybe that was part of it.

There's a knock at the door. Shrink jumps, but I'm grateful.

"I'm in session," Shrink calls, irritated. The door opens anyway.

"Anna? I'm sorry. We need you for just a second. Quickly." A nurse's voice. Jeff's, I think.

"I'm sorry, Stevie. I'll be back as soon as I can," Shrink says. "Sit tight for me, okay?"

"Yeah." When the door closes behind them, I stand up and stretch. My body aches from the synthetic, air-conditioned cold. I bend over the candle on her side table and warm my hands. I wander around Shrink's office, running my fingers over book spines and picture frames. On her desk are small flocks of paper cranes. I pick up a shiny green one, tap its angles with my fingertip.

I put it down next to a small notebook. The notebook is open, with a number scribbled in pencil on the first line. I only have to see the first few digits to know what it means. I look away. I look again. It's still there. I am not having a nightmare.

I expect to feel angry, enraged. I expect to feel a fire in me. But instead, there is a void.

"Stevie, I'm sorry about—" Shrink stops when she sees me.

"What are you doing calling Paris?" I ask. Quietly.

She's silent for a while. I wonder if she's thinking about lying.

"She's your mother, Stevie. She has a right to know how your treatment is progressing."

"What did you tell her?" I whisper.

"Stevie, please turn around."

"What did you *tell* her?" I can't turn around. I can't face her.

"Stevie."

"Tell me." The silvery lead marks run together on the page.

"I haven't told her anything yet. We've been playing phone tag. It's difficult with the time difference." Shrink takes a few steps toward me. "Stevie, I think we should talk about how you're feeling about this, okay?"

Finally, I turn. "Do you talk to my dad?"

"I've spoken with him once. I don't divulge specifics. But he cares about you and wants to make sure you're getting what you need while you're here."

"Fine," I say evenly. "Fine. But not her. She hasn't even called once since the funeral, did you know that?" I can tell from her face that she doesn't. "So it's pretty obvious that she *doesn't* care about me, so there's no reason for you to be talking to her."

"Stevie, I understand that she's hurt you—"

"Don't you dare defend her." I'm remarkably calm, considering.

"I won't. I understand that she has wounded you."

"She doesn't have the right!" Is that me yelling? Is that my voice?

"She does. She's your parent and she's assuming the cost of treatment, so—" She stops. Knows she's just said something she can't take back.

Of *course* she's paying. I'm such a moron. Why didn't I realize? Like my father could shell out this kind of cash? No. No. I can't believe how stupid I've been. Of course it was her. I picture her writing a check in her Paris apartment, feeling smug and redeemed. Fuck her. I won't take another cent of her money.

"Stevie. Please. I can see that you're upset, and I want us to talk about this. If you're angry with me, we should talk about it."

"I think I'm done talking," I say. I stare past her, focusing on the flickering candle flame. With the slightest movement, I could tip it as I'm walking toward the door. I could make everything go up in flames.

day twelve

Tuesday, July 15, 6:47 P.M.

ON Christmas and Easter, my mother forced Josh and me to wear fancy clothes made out of heavy, unfamiliar fabrics—velvet and taffeta for me, wool for Josh—and to go to church. My father always stayed home and labored over his latest manuscript. *You go listen to your stories,* he told her, *and I'll stay here and work on mine.* When I was very little, I worried about his soul for saying that.

It was a performance, twice a year, on schedule: clacking down the aisle in too-tight Mary Janes, sitting up straight, bowing my head at the appropriate times, sneaking games of hangman with Josh when our mother wasn't paying attention, which was almost never. We were her puppets, all gangly legs and big bright eyes, bobbing our heads on command.

No more. She can't control me, not even from Paris. I will not spend another night in this place. I'll leave tonight. No one can stop me.

At dinner, I execute a performance of my own. It is truly remarkable. I am calm. Composed. I sit across from the Cottage Three girls and Hannah and I slice my rubbery chicken breast with the artificial grill lines into pieces. I eat just enough. Slowly enough. Fearfully enough.

"You had a session today, right?" Next to me, Ashley pours a second glass of tea. She cuts her chicken breast in quarters and shoves one of the pieces in her mouth. "With Anna?"

Hannah's burgundy-penciled brows arc. "Chew and swallow before you speak, dear."

"Sorry," Ashley says, without chewing or swallowing.

"Yeah." I stab a flat green bean.

"How'd it go?"

I shrug. "Fine."

Ashley gulps her last few chunks of chicken in rapid succession. "I'm finished. May I get coffee, please?"

Hannah frowns at Ashley's plate. "Go ahead."

While the others work their way toward coffee, I debate actually finishing my meal and getting a coffee of my own. It is, after all, the Last Supper. And I could use the caffeine tonight. But there's so much left on my plate and already I feel sick. And there are other things to worry about. I slip my hand into the pocket of my jeans to find the pills I've stashed there. I feel a quick, hot flash of guilt.

Ashley returns with her porcelain mug and individual creamers.

"Hazelnut and vanilla," she announces, and the others murmur their approval. "Tomorrow, though? I'm doing two hazelnuts. Or a hazelnut and a peppermint."

"That's disgusting." Teagan scrunches her nose.

"Whatever. It's good." Ashley empties the creamers into her coffee and wraps her hands around the mug.

"Are you getting coffee, Hannah?" I ask.

"As soon as the rest of you are finished," she says.

"We are." Teagan nods at her plate, then Cate's.

"And I won't be requiring my usual after-dinner cappuccino," I say.

I think Hannah's squinting at me, but it's hard to tell the difference between her disapproving face and her normal face. I smile. With a labored breath, she heaves her whale body out of the chair and goes to stand in the coffee line. Cate and Teagan follow.

"Hey." I widen my eyes at Ashley's mug. "Can I have a sip?"

Ashley trains her gaze on Hannah's back. "I dunno."

"Come on," I plead. "I was like a caffeine addict at home. I never get coffee here. I'm in withdrawal or something."

"You could always finish your dinner," she says pointedly.

"It's . . ." I avert my eyes. She doesn't deserve this, I know. But I can't tell her the truth. ". . . still really *hard* for me, you know?" I make my voice small. "Just a sip. Please."

Ashley slides her mug in my direction. "If I get charted, I'm telling."

"Thanks." It's easier than I thought it would be. In one smooth motion, I pull my hand from my pocket. Lift the mug to my lips and take a small sip. It's shitty coffee, but it really does taste incredible. Before I lower the mug, the pills go in and disappear. Simple. "Thanks," I say again. I swallow the guilt. It had to be done. She's been too frantic at night lately.

"So how're things going with Kyle?" I ask. I'm talking too fast. I can't help it. "Is it weird, having a male shrink?"

"I guess. Anna's better, I think. I tried to put in a request to change therapists."

"What happened?"

"I got it back with a note on it that said *Thank you for using your voice*." She takes a sip. I hold my breath. She takes another sip.

"But nothing happened?" I'm practically sweating.

"Kyle's still my therapist. But at least I used my voice, right?" She laughs, and her whole face opens up. I'm glad, because that's the way I want to leave her.

The pills work quickly. Ashley is yawning during evening snack and can barely keep her eyes open as we trudge up the hill to the cottage. I let her lean on me for support.

Minutes after lights-out, I hear the even, steady sounds that tell me she is asleep. In the dark, I dress in my jeans and Josh's sweatshirt, then gather a few things and pack them in the backpack I brought on the plane. My cell, the money I stole from Dad before I left, my wallet, the journal, a pen, and a change of underwear. I leave the pills in the drawer. I won't need them anymore. I'll be home for the Anniversary. I'll come to my end the way I've always planned. I tug Ashley's bunny from her grip and stuff it in the backpack. Then I go back to my bed. Pull the covers up to my chin and wait.

I count the seconds, and right on schedule the bedroom door opens. I almost feel the heat of the flashlight. *One, two.* Then the door closes. Silently, I peel back the covers, put on my sneakers, and slip into the hall.

I haven't even reached the cottage door when I turn back. I ditch my backpack on the floor and riffle through it. I tear a small piece of paper from the journal and scribble my cell number on the back. Then I take out the bunny. Carefully, I tuck it next to Ashley and pin the scrap of paper beneath the digital clock on her shelf. Then I'm gone.

day twelve

Tuesday, July 15, 11:26 PM

OUTSIDE, I move low and fast. I suck in dry, cold air every few seconds when I realize it's time to breathe again. There are enough nurses crisscrossing the property that I know I'll be lucky to make it to the main road. I shouldn't have eaten tonight. I would be quicker, lighter.

I hurry alongside the fence that borders the pasture and the red dirt road. My path gets darker as I leave the shuddering porch lights of the cottages behind. I curse my mother with every step. She thinks paying for this place will erase her sins. I hope they call her as soon as they realize I'm gone. I hope she feels powerless. I hope she knows: She did this. This is her fault.

The ground turns solid beneath me as the tip of my sneaker meets asphalt. I think I'm supposed to turn left. Isn't that the way I came in, strapped next to Cotton Candy in her shiny white van? But I don't remember exactly. . . . Maybe it's right. No. Left. I'm almost positive. One last look behind me, and then I start to run.

I run as fast as I can toward nothing. It's dark—too dark to see anything but the dingy white of my sneakers as they hit the asphalt. There are no cars, no streetlights. Just a few stars above me, which makes it hard to tell how far I've gone. That's the thing about progress: it's relative.

The desert yawns on either side of me, purplish cactus shadows spearing the sky. My backpack slaps against my spine.

If you do it right, running is supposed to be what Shrink calls a "*healthy coping skill*." As long as you don't freak out and accidentally run twenty-eight miles on the treadmill before you pass out and fall off (*ahem*, Cate), running is supposed to release these feel-good chemicals in your brain. According to Dr. Singh, people like me don't have enough of these chemicals. So hypothetically, if a person wakes up one day wanting to kill herself because she feels bad about her dead sibling, there's an easy solution: Go for a run!

Running is supposed to loosen you up, bring anger to the surface, send it splashing to the pavement like sweat. Tonight the reverse happens. The farther I go, the tighter I get. My lungs are bursting and my legs are throbbing. My body opens up and absorbs all the anger in the universe. Sucks it in like I'm this desperate, empty human sponge. It seeps into my bones, into the deepest part of me. I picture the anger cells, with their oozing irregular edges, multiplying in my body like cancer.

I gasp for breath, but if I stop I may never start again—or I might come to the conclusion that I've lost my mind. I've been teetering on the edge of crazy for a while now, but this! This is new. Heading into the empty desert in the middle of the night with no real plan. It's enough to make me laugh out loud.

Without losing pace, I pull out my cell phone and money, counting the bills. It's not enough to take a cab to the airport. I'll have to hitchhike at least part of the way. Eden. I need to call Eden. I stop for a second, bending over and spitting into the dust. I dig for my cell and power it on. I'll ask her to buy me a ticket. She can do it; I've seen her plunk down her dad's credit card at the end of a marathon booze session. Just a ticket, and I'll pay her back and I won't owe her anything. I can get myself to the airport if she can get me home. I press and hold the two. Imagine Shrink's face when she realizes I'm gone.

Hey, boys and girls, it's Eden. You know what to do.

"Eden," I wheeze into phone. "I really need—I have to—can you call me? Call me back, okay? Call me."

I press the two again. It's late there. Or is it early?

Hey, boys and girls, it's Eden. You know what to do.

Okay. Okay, okay, okay. She'll call back. She'll get the message and she'll call back.

In some deep part of me, though, I know she might not. Not if helping me will ruin her buzz or sidetrack a hookup or inconvenience her in the slightest. Because Eden serves Eden, and no one else.

Why didn't I see it back then? Why didn't Josh see it? If only one of us had understood her, Josh would still be alive. But we didn't, because she was just too intoxicating. She played us both, because it was nothing more than a game to her.

* * *

On the last night of seminar, Eden captivated the crowd. Her voice was dark and syrupy, and the bar was silent. She read something that she thought was deep, something about a relationship with a younger man. I watched her and tried to pretend she wasn't talking about Josh.

"His naïveté was white and temporary, like snow," she murmured into the mic.

God, I thought. *Seriously?* But then she smiled, just for me. I stared at her lips. Tonight they were tangerine and wet. My mouth puckered, like I was sucking something sour.

"She's really good." Josh's hot wintergreen breath on my ear made me jump.

"Yeah," I whispered at my hands. "I guess." I wondered if he was here for me or for her.

"So, this is where you guys had class every week? Cool." He was trying too hard, like he had been for weeks. Things had been weird between us ever since he'd come home late that night. Weirder still since I'd kissed Eden for the first time. And in the week since the kiss in her apartment, there had been more. More hands on each other, sneaking deep into places they never should have gone. I couldn't stop. I didn't know how.

"Yeah," I said. "It was alright." The Stacks looked different tonight: the tables shoved against the far wall, replaced with rows of rickety mismatched chairs facing the podium in front of the bar. The floor was scuffed but clean. There were two leafy plants on either side of the podium. Pinkish punch in a cloudy plastic bowl in the back, with finger sandwiches and limp celery sticks.

"Sass." I heard his little boy voice like when we were kids. "I think I might like her."

I looked at the ceiling. There was a brownish water stain directly above us.

"I know it's weird for you, the idea of us . . . together."

I nodded.

"It's just . . . She's so *pretty*. And nice and funny, you know?"

Pretty. Nice. Funny. For a second—just a second, it didn't last—I was furious. He was my older brother. He was supposed to say disgusting things like *hot piece* and *pussy*. He wasn't supposed to say *pretty* and *nice*. That made it so much worse.

He was looking at me, and I couldn't stand to look back. "I think this could be something real. Something good."

Please. Don't. But I couldn't ask him. He deserved whatever he wanted. I'd known all my life that he was better than me, in a deep-rooted way. He was what our dad would call *good people*. You could slice him down the middle and even the very center of him would be fresh and green and good. My center was rotten.

"I . . . think she likes you, too." I'd tell her tonight. Soon.

"For real?"

I didn't have to answer, because Eden looked up and then everyone behind us was clapping. So I just nodded and clapped, too. Next to me, Josh lifted his thumb and middle finger to his mouth and whistled. I didn't know he could do that. Maybe he'd done it before. Maybe I hadn't been paying attention.

"I'm not supposed to tell you, but Dad's out right now, getting champagne," Josh said as everyone stood up. The bar was crowded. Almost everyone held a mini-plate in one hand and a

175

plastic cup of punch in the other. I reached for a plate and some dead-looking celery.

"Huh?" I heard Eden's throaty laugh bubble up from somewhere in the crowd. It made my body spark in places, and it felt good and it hurt at the same time, like a static shock.

"Real champagne. Pretend to be surprised. You could read us whatever you were supposed to read tonight."

"Yeah. Sure." I'd told my dad not to come. Told him it wouldn't be worth it since I wasn't reading. *There just wasn't enough time for everyone*, I'd lied. "Um, I have to tell Eden something really quick. Unless you and Eden want to go out after?" I pinched my mini-plate. It was a prop and we both knew it. Inside me, something welled up: a scream or a cry. Nothing would have felt better than to release it.

"Nah." He scanned the crowd for her. "Tonight's your big night, Sass. Whatever you want to do, I'm down." He gave me a side squeeze. We didn't really hug anymore. Neither of us could handle it. "Tell her I said congratulations?"

"Got it."

Eden was chatting up a guy in a waiter's uniform at the very end of the bar. Even more than not wanting to share her, I didn't want Josh to be just another guy in her collection. He was too good for that.

She was wearing black jeans and a white V-neck. A black blazer. I could see her every line.

"Hey," I said. "That was really good."

"*Good?*" The corner of one side of her mouth inched up slowly. "You can do better than that. Jake here said my reading was . . ." She pouted, pretending to forget. "Remind me?"

176

"Inspired," Jake repeated on cue.

"Inspiiiired, dahhling."

She's drunk. Already.

"Can I talk to you?" I asked. "Like, alone."

We left Jake and ducked into the hallway that led to the bathrooms. There were no signs on the doors, just two doors: one on the left and one on the right. You had to guess which was which.

"Wecan'tdothisanymore," I said, all one word. It came out easier than I thought it would.

"What? Stevie—" She reached for me. I stepped back, just in time. I just wanted her to accept it, to let me go home. "What are you talking about?"

"This," I whispered. "Whatever we're—it has to stop."

"What are you, religious or something? People are people, Stevie."

I didn't say anything.

"Is this about Jack the waiter?" she teased.

"Jake!"

"I *know*, Stevie. I'm screwing around. Just—what's going on with you?" This time, when she reached for me, I reached back. It was the wrong thing, but it was a reflex, the way when someone says "how are you?" you say "fine," even though you're not. Her skin was hot and soft. My mouth opened a little.

"Josh likes you," I said to the toes of her black boots.

"I like him, too," she said. *Simple.* "But not the way I like you." The boots took two steps forward, and then she put her hand on my throat and it fit perfectly. "And the fact that you're looking out for your brother like this makes me like you even more. Of course, that's not the only thing I like." She dragged her finger up to my chin and bottom lip.

"I'm fucked up," I said.

"Me, too." She took another step, pressing me against the wall. Lowered her mouth to my ear. "I don't think I'd like you as much if you weren't."

My insides crumpled like foil.

"He'd want you to be happy, right?" Her breath was spicy with liquor.

It was selfish, but standing in the hallway with her heart beating against my chest and my heart beating back, I wasn't sorry. Josh had always been better at everything: Rows of plastic gold statues and ribbons and certificates in his room announced his glory. But this time, it was me. I was the best at being broken, and Eden wanted my kind of best.

I nodded. "But I can't." I'd been carrying our lie for seven days now, and already it was too heavy. Eventually, I would drop it. It would shatter. Best to put it down softly now, while I still had control. "He's my brother, Eden." I said it to the soft flesh of her earlobe. "You know? I can't."

She exhaled, like she'd been holding her breath. "Yeah."

"Sorry. I'm sorry." I'd never been a crier, so I thought about everyday things, normal things: the way the sunlight leaked through the slatted blinds at *Le Crâpeau* and made backslashes on the carpet, the paperweight on Dad's desk that held everything in place, the perfect rows of bloody-red lipstick in my mother's makeup drawer. It didn't work; my body felt hot and full, like it could burst at any second.

"Me, too. I'm sorry, too." Eden pressed her hand to my throat and kissed me. Slowly, the way you linger in beautiful places you know you'll never visit again. I mapped her mouth with my tongue, swearing I'd remember every pink detail. I even let myself touch her, the white hollow of her throat, the way her bones made a perfect V above her heart. When she gasped, when her body stiffened, I thought maybe I'd done something right.

"What the hell?" Eden's mouth was open, but the voice leaking from her lips was my brother's. It was disorienting. It took me too long to understand.

It was Josh.

day thirteen

I don't know how long I walk before I see lights. I look up at the sky once, to see the position of the moon. But I can't find it and anyway, I don't know what I'd do if I could. My heels are bleeding—I can feel the sticky warm wet pooling in my sneakers—and I'm dizzy, so when the lights appear I have to blink a few times to make sure. There are a few streetlamps within sight, arranged along the perimeter of a roundabout, the closest thing this area has to a downtown.

I need someplace to think. I need water or a cup of coffee, black. A place to come up with a plan. I hobble the wrong way around the roundabout onto the main street. There are almost no cars in the angled parking spaces, and the storefronts are dark. At the far end of the street, there's a shell of a gas station. The pumps are rusty and still in the ground. The sign out front says simply: Beer.

I relax a little when I see a diner across the street. It's small, but the lights are on and I can see the outline of a man in the third window. There's a counter with stools. There's a woman in an apron behind the counter. I bet there's pie. It seems like there should be pie.

I half expect the waitress to say, *Have a seat wherever you'd like, hon*, because that seems like something that would happen here. But when the bell over the door announces me, she doesn't even turn around. Better that way.

I choose the counter stool closest to the door. I need something to calm me down, but I don't think this place serves booze. "What can I get—" The woman stops when she sees me, then picks up again but slower this time. "For you?"

"Water, please. With lemon." I smooth out my voice, and I think it sounds like a normal person's. I'm out of breath, of course. But that happens to normal people.

"Anything else?"

"Coffee. Black," I say quickly.

She nods and turns around.

While she gets the coffee, I take out my cell phone and count my money again. Eden still hasn't called back. My hands are shaking, and when the waitress deposits a cup and saucer in front of me, she looks at me funny.

"You alright, sweetie?" She's pretty, in a tired way.

"It's cold out there!" I say. I wrap my hands around the mug and take a shuddery breath. What the hell am I supposed to do now?

"Would you like a menu?"

My head bobs before I can stop it. *It's okay, it's okay, because I'll start again tomorrow and I have to come up with a plan right now and so I should eat something, but only something small.* I take the sticky laminated menu and scan the options. It's a nightmare. So many words and I'm too tired to do the math.

"Just . . . a house salad, please. No cheese, no dressing. And where's your restroom?"

She points somewhere.

"Okay. Thanks. I'll be right back." I shovel the money and my cell into my backpack and try to focus on the neon sign in the back corner. My heels sting as I walk.

The restroom is weirdly clean for a place like this. There's a paper towel dispenser, but somebody also hung a mauve-colored hand towel from the rack next to the sink. The edges are embroidered with crooked white lace. There's a lavender candle on the back of the toilet that's almost burned down, and a can of room spray next to it, which is probably a fire hazard.

I bend over the sink and blink into the mirror. No wonder the waitress stared when she saw me. I look like shit. My hair is sweat-soaked and plastered to my pale skull. My eyes too big for my head. My cheeks are puffy. I look like a strung-out runaway in a made-for-TV movie. I tear a few paper towels from the dispenser, wet them, and pump the pearly bubblegum soap. Scrub my face and the back of my neck, and pat the sweat from my hair with a wad of fresh dry towels.

"Your salad's up." There's a knock at the door. "You alright in there?"

"Yeah! Yes. Yeah. Thank you." I stare down at my hands. The knuckles are cracking like it's winter.

At the counter, I push down the panic that keeps welling up in the back of my throat. I need a drink. I need something to calm me down. *IneedIneedIneed*. I know what I need. Fuck it. I consult the menu.

"Can I also get a—*think, Stevie, be smart*—cup of the vegetable soup and the cheeseburger with fries? Medium rare. And then, like, do you have pie or something? Any kind of pie?"

"Peach or cherry?"

"Peach!" I almost squeal. It's like, *symbolism* or something, and I want to tell somebody, but of course she can't know I'm from Georgia! That would ruin everything! "With vanilla ice cream and a Diet Coke, please. Do you have free refills?"

"Sure, honey. Sure."

"Okay, great." I should've sat in one of the booths, but if I move now it will look strange. I check my phone about a million times before the food arrives. Nothing. When she sets the meal in front of me, I have to force myself to go slow. Because she's watching me, I can tell, her gaze lighting on every part of me.

I almost want to look up at her, but instead I stare at my plate. Take a bite of the burger, slow and easy. My hands are shaking. The meat juice runs down my chin and I'm in the backyard of the house behind Broad when we were a family. There is so much hurt snaking through me that I can't stand it. I take another bite, and another, and another. Inhale the Diet Coke. The soup I swallow in three large gulps. The pie is buttery and the filling too hot. It burns as it slides down my throat.

I don't want to do this anymore—I don't have the energy—but it's too late to stop. I wish Josh were here to stop me. To hold me and count my bones and get pissed. I'd curl up against his chest like a baby and listen to his heartbeat.

"Gosh. All that Diet Coke," I say to no one, and slide off the stool. One foot in front of the other in front of the other until I'm back in the bathroom. I turn the lock on the door and lean against it, feeling the familiar desperation welling up. I have to do it, I know I have to do it, but I'm almost too tired to move.

I'm bent over the toilet, breathing in the sharp smell of watered-down bleach, when I hear another knock.

"Just a second!"

"Stevie? Stevie, I need you to open the door for me, please."

Shrink. My gut withers at the sound of her voice.

"Hold on!" I practically scream, lunging for the sink.

"Stevie, if you won't open the door, I'll ask management to unlock it. Please open this door right now."

"Wait!" I turn on the water full blast and fall to my knees in front of the toilet. My body understands me, knows what has to be done. But I don't even get to enjoy the aftercalm. I flush just as the door handle turns and Shrink barges in.

I don't acknowledge her. Just bend over the sink and shovel a handful of metallic water into my sour mouth. Swish and spit. No use trying to hide it. She's too late, anyway.

day thirteen

Wednesday, July 16, 2:27 A.M.

"STEVIE."

When I finally turn around, Shrink looks strange: jeans and a hoodie and no makeup. *Oh. It's late,* I remember.

"I'm not leaving here," I tell her.

"Stevie, look at me, please." She grasps my skull in her hands and peers into my face like it's a crystal ball.

"Quit." I shrug her off. "I'm not drunk or high or whatever you think." I don't think I can stand anymore, so I arc around her and lean against the door. Shrink reaches for me and we sink to the floor.

"How'd you know?" I ask after a while.

"The waitress saw your treatment bracelet."

"Oh." I think I'm supposed to be upset or something. I dig deep for it, but nothing comes. "What time is it?"

"Two thirty."

"Sorry you had to get out of bed." I really am.

She shakes her head. "I wanted to come find you. I am very concerned about you, Stevie." The last part comes out breathy. "But I'm glad you're safe. I'd like to give you a hug. Would that be okay?"

I shrug.

She pulls me into her in an awkward sort of side hug and it's gentle. The kind of single tap that makes the whole pane shatter. There's a weird choking sound—me, I think—and I feel my face get hot and twisty and it feels so tight and awful to be in my skin that I wish I could just stop breathing.

"Okay," she says into my hair, in a way that makes me moan in the ugliest way. "Okay." Her sweatshirt is wet and smells like puke.

My sobs come out in these violent shuddery bursts. It's so stupid, all of it—that I thought I could get away with this, that I'm so weak and useless. That I thought Eden might be able to help me. I pull away, wiping the snot bubbles from my nose with the back of my hand. I stare at my knees.

"I killed my brother," I tell her after a while.

"Tell me," she says.

"He caught me kissing her," I say. "The night he died, he caught me kissing her."

For a moment, he'd just stood there, stricken. Staring at me like I was a stranger.

"Oh my god." Eden said it with an almost smile.

That's when he turned and ran, like I was something to be escaped.

"Josh!" I called, but he was already gone, pushing through the thinning crowd of parents and roommates. "Shit."

I ran after him, through the wake he'd created. I hurried down the steps calling his name, and at the last step, my fingers came close to grazing his T-shirt. Not close enough.

"Josh! Wait. Please."

He threw the door open and stormed outside, into the parking lot. He kicked up gravel as he walked, tiny bullets launching behind him. "Go back upstairs with your goddamned *girlfriend*, Stevie." His voice cracked over my name.

"Josh! She kissed me, okay? I'm sorry!"

He stopped when he got to the Buick, digging through his pockets for his keys. "I told you I liked her. I *just* told you. Don't you care about anybody other than yourself?"

Anger reared up, even though I had no right. "Don't *you*? You *stole* her. She was my friend first, Josh! She was my only friend, and you *knew* that!"

"Your *friend*?" His laugh was accusing. "Okay, Stevie. If that's what you do with your *friends*, it's a good thing you never had any."

"Shut up, Josh. Not everybody's perfect like you, okay? So just . . . quit being so judgmental." I gasped for air, but I couldn't get a real breath. "You're just like Mom."

"Judgmental? Is that what you call telling the truth? Here's the truth, Stevie." He glared at me, hate flashing in his eyes. "You're selfish. You're a selfish bitch and for once in your life,

187

it's time someone told you: You can't always get what you want."

His words were a slap, knocking me back. Josh never cursed—never used those words with me or even around me.

"And you look like shit, by the way. Everybody thinks so and Dad's too scared to say it. This whole food thing—it's selfish and crazy and you look like . . . shit." He spit on the ground next to his shoe and yanked the driver's side door open so hard I thought he might rip it off.

There wasn't time for it, but I thought, *Do people really think I look like shit?* I ran around to the passenger side and jerked my door open before his fingers hit the lock.

"Josh. Wait. Please." *Josh. Wait. Please. Wait. Please. Josh.* I was a baby, reduced to a few simple, meaningless phrases. I dove inside and slammed the door as he forced the key into the ignition and gunned out of the parking lot onto the street. The wheels squealed against the pavement. I jammed the seat belt into the buckle four times before it took.

"I was telling her, Josh. I was telling her and she wouldn't listen. I swear. I was ending it." My words didn't make sense, even to me, and I was desperate to find a way to make him understand that I was not the girl he thought I was. *I'm not I'm not I'm not.*

"*You're* the one who's just like Mom, you know?" He was crying and he didn't care. He leaned over the steering wheel, slammed his fist into the dashboard over and over until I heard a sickening crack.

"What are you *talking* about? Fuck you." My blood thundered through me, searching for a way out.

"Please. Like you don't know." He made a wide right turn, swerving onto a deserted one-way street.

"I don't! Josh, stop! Stop it!"

"You think she just left, moved to Paris for no reason? Are you seriously that naïve?" Another turn, barreling onto the two-lane road that stretched through the dark like a thread, stringing nameless towns together. The Buick's headlights like two white pearls, rolling fast.

"I don't know why she left!" I screamed at the windshield, clawing at the ugly cloth seats like an animal. "Nobody tells me anything!"

"She moved 'cause she was screwing some piece-of-shit partner at the Paris branch! She's a whore who doesn't care about this family." The Buick weaved in a seamless dance with the yellow line. "You're the same, Stevie. You're just like Mom. A heartless slut."

"Shut up!" I screamed. "You shut up!"

I saw the truck first, because I wasn't crying. It was a semi. The headlights were getting too close, too fast.

"Josh!" I lunged over the console and jerked the steering wheel toward me, the truck's blaring horn bleeding past.

Time seemed to stand still, people say. Or *It all happened so fast.* Lies. It took exactly the amount of time it took, and I felt all of it. Every millisecond. The whoosh of the car, airborne, a cheap aluminum toy.

Weird, I thought.

We hit the road three times: roof, wheels, roof. Slammed into a solid, unmoving wall. The impact was instant, aftershocks pulsed through me. There were too many sounds at once:

shattering glass and crumpling tin and a high-pitched noise that was shrill and constant. And then everything stopped— everything but the noise. And I was upside down, still strapped in, and blood rushed to my head. I was dizzy and I thought, *What is that? What the hell is that sound?* and then, *Josh. Where's Josh?* and then, *The noise is me*, and I stopped screaming, at least out loud.

I felt nothing, only the adrenaline drowning my senses. I fumbled for the seat belt and released it, then crawled through the window that wasn't there anymore. I slunk through the grass like a dying dog, around the tree and across the lawn toward Josh, who lay fifty feet away.

"Josh!" I screamed. I willed my body to move faster. Something was stinging hot and wet on my thigh, but nothing hurt. I didn't understand the smells; there were too many at once. Gas and rubber and burning smoke and too-hot skin and blood. I puked in the grass.

I wasn't sure that it was him at first. Of course it was, because that was his T-shirt, and who else would it be? But there was so much blood, and glass embedded in him like millions of diamonds in red velvet. It was hard to tell.

One minute he was, and the next he wasn't.

And I knew, not because his breathing was labored or he said his last words or reached for my hand or something dramatic like that. I knew because he was my brother. I loomed over him and stroked his face and his neck, blood-soaked and ribboned in places. His blood and my blood ran together, sticky down my skin. I watched him end.

I lay down next to him. Curled against his body until I couldn't feel the difference between us. We stayed like that until they pulled me away.

* * *

"I deserve to die," I tell Shrink now. Hearing it out loud, I know it's true. It sounds right. I expect her to leap up and freak out, to pin me to the ground while she calls for help.

Instead she says, "I know you believe that."

"It's the truth," I say.

"You've been carrying an incredibly heavy burden for a very long time now. I imagine that you're exhausted. That you just don't want to do it anymore."

She's right. I let myself lean into her. Just a little.

"The thing is, Stevie, you don't have to. If you would let me hold some of it for you while you get stronger—"

"You can't fix it." I stiffen.

"You're right. I can't fix it. I can't bring your brother back or magically transform your mother into the mother you deserve. I can't force you to feel like you deserve to get better. But I can sit here with you. And I can help you do the things you're not able to do for yourself right now. That's really the first step."

"I thought the first step was admitting you have a problem."

"Do you? Have a problem?"

I nod. My problem is being alive.

"I can't help you unless you let me take you back, Stevie. I can't help you unless you're willing to get some rest. Let me help you."

I nod again, because I know there's no other choice. I'm so exhausted I can barely keep my eyes open, and going back willingly is better than putting up a fight. I have no more fight in me. Whatever was left has leaked out, through the cracks in the floor tiles, leaving nothing but the faintest ghost of a stain.

day thirteen

Wednesday, July 16, 5:30 A.M.

WHEN I open my eyes, I don't know where I am. The bed feels the same—a hard single mattress covered in too-thin sheets—but the dark is different. Opaque. I blink and search for the familiar green glow of my digital clock. It isn't there.

I sit up. The pain behind my eyes comes in waves: a slow churning that builds, then dissolves in a milky froth. My throat burns when I swallow, and that's how I know last night was real. I am humiliated. I want to die.

"I'm going to turn on the light, Stevie. Might be bright." I inhale at the sound of Shrink's voice, and screw my eyes shut. Fluorescent light burns through my lids.

"What—" I blink, letting the light in slowly. I'm in a single bed in a bare, windowless room. Not three feet away, Shrink sits

193

in a wooden dining chair next to the door, one of the pillows from her office in her lap. And I remember: We came here, to this room in the villa last night. I passed out in my clothes. She must have stayed. How she could stand to exist next to me after everything she saw and heard last night, I don't know.

"How did you sleep?" She swallows a yawn.

"Best sleepover ever," I deadpan. "Want to play truth or dare?"

"No. But I would like us to have breakfast together."

I hate that she won't play. "Can you just tell me if I'm getting kicked out of here?" I snap. "Like, a 'one strike, you're out' kind of thing?"

"No. You're not getting kicked out."

"That's too bad." At the very least, maybe they could send me packing somewhere else, wherever they store the really broken dolls. I can't stand the idea of showing up to breakfast this morning. *Heyyy, girls. What'd I miss?* I couldn't bear the way Ashley would look at me. Especially if she's figured out what I did to her last night.

"You need to get weight and vitals done." Shrink consults her watch. "It's early, so if you go now . . . you can get them over with."

What she really means is: *If you go now, there will be fewer people out there, which will make this day slightly less awful for you. Not much. But slightly.* I sit up and press the soles of my feet into the floor. My soles are raw and crusted with blood.

Shrink reaches for the door. "I'm going to get cleaned up, and then I'll have one of the staff members bring us something to eat, okay? We can talk in my office."

I nod and shake my head at the same time, trying to clear my cottony brain. Being here is disorienting. I don't know where I expected to be by now. Thirty thousand feet over some other state, an empty mini bottle of vodka wedged between my knees. Eden's couch. My bed at home. Not here.

My welcome-back breakfast consists of scrambled eggs, a fruit cup with not one but three of those bloated hot pink cherries in it, and two freezer-burned turkey sausages.

"I hope you didn't go to too much trouble," I say politely. "I had a big dinner last night."

The line of Shrink's jaw deepens, then disappears. "I spoke with your mother just now. She's worried, and she asked to have a family session with you. Over the phone."

"I've been meaning to ask you: What's the deal with you and those paper birds? It's kind of weird." I stab one of the turkey sausages, and take my hand away. *Ta-da!* The fork stays frozen in place.

"I told her I didn't think you were ready."

"Listen," I inform her. "I'm obviously not ready for any of this."

"Stevie, I'd like for us to talk about what happened last night."

The last thing I want is to talk about last night.

"You said that you deserved to die."

"I don't—that doesn't sound like something I would say." The ink on my forearm burns with self-satisfaction. *Bitch.*

"Do you, Stevie? Believe that you deserve to die?" Shrink interlaces her fingers together, and her knuckles go white for a fraction of a second. Less, even. If I had blinked, I would have missed it. But I didn't, and understanding clicks into place in the base of my brain. I am walking on a razor-thin ledge here. One misstep and everything I've worked for will vanish in a cloud of smoke.

"Anna." I say it softly, fill it up with meaning. "You *know* me. I was upset, and when I'm upset, I get, like, dramatic. Right? I mean, hello?" My laugh comes out more like a cough. I reach for the remaining pillow on the love seat.

She shakes her head, slightly. "I don't think you were being dramatic. I think you meant what you said."

"Okay. I just—sometimes I do feel like that. Guilty or whatever. But I would never do anything about it. Nothing like that."

"Never actually hurt yourself, you mean? What would keep you from hurting yourself?"

Her question takes me by surprise, leaves me shuffling through index cards for an acceptable response. I didn't study for this one. I don't know what to say, so I respond, "Family." It seems like something a well person would say.

"Let's talk about that. How do you think it would be for your family if you killed yourself?"

If you killed yourself. It's weird how she says it that way, and not softer. Like, *if you weren't here anymore* or some bullshit. I almost want to thank her. At least we're speaking the same language.

"It would be hard for my dad." I let my face go soft. I imagine him slumped in the antique love seat in *Le Crâpeau*, smoking and alone. "He wouldn't have any family left." I hate the idea of doing to him what my mother did to him before me. But I love Josh and despise myself more. "And my mother would be upset, but mostly because it would make her look highly ineffective, parenting-wise."

196

"What about Josh? How would it be for Josh?" she asks. "What would he say if he knew you were considering suicide?"

I squint at her. "Josh is dead."

"I understand. But it seems as though Josh is still very much with you. Very much a part of your everyday thoughts. So I don't think it's fair to talk about the impact of your suicide on family without talking about Josh."

My mind goes totally blank. As if one-zillionth of a second ago, it was full of all these thoughts and memories and feelings and now there is nothing but quiet, white space. The truth is, I don't know what it would be like for Josh. I've been doing this for him—every self-denial has been in his name—but I've never actually thought about what he would have to say about it.

"I don't know," I mumble. "I don't know what he would say."

"I'm going to push you to think about this, Stevie. I think it's important."

"Why?" I drop the tray next to the love seat, untouched. "What's your deal? Are you just trying to make me feel like shit? Is that the goal here?"

"Of course not. But you don't need me to make you feel like shit, do you? Don't you already feel exhausted, and sick, and sad, and ready to give up?"

"Jesus." I close my eyes to block her out. It's a child's game, but it's all I have.

"I'm pushing you because I think you're strong enough to take it, Stevie. And I want you to hear this. Open your eyes, please."

I glare directly at her, into her bright green living eyes, and I'm so angry I could scream. And I hate her for making me cry

197

last night because now that I have, it feels like I am brimming. As if my body is nothing but water, constantly on the verge of dissolving in tears. She's made me weak.

"What? What do you want?"

She matches my gaze, but hers is soft and fierce at the same time. "If you kill yourself, it will not bring Josh back. It will not make his death any more acceptable. It will not lessen anyone's grief; it will only compound it. It will not make you feel any less guilty, because you will be dead. It will not make things any better for you, because you will be dead."

My breath comes in starts and stops, and I fix my gaze on the titles on her bookshelf. *Treatment Manual for Anorexia Nervosa, Second Edition: A Family Approach. Cognitive Behavior Therapy and Eating Disorders. Love's Executioner.*

"Stevie? I'd like to come sit next to you. Is that okay?"

I nod. *Interpersonal Process in Therapy: An Integrative Model.*

I feel her next to me on the couch. She rests her hand on my shoulder.

"You—look at me."

I do.

"You are too valuable to leave this earth before your time," she says. "And I know that if you want to kill yourself—truly want to kill yourself—I can't stop you. I can do my best to keep you safe while you're here, but ultimately your life is your own. But I hope, very much, that you will give treatment some time. That you will take your medication and continue to work in therapy and see—just see—if that changes anything for you."

When she stops speaking, I look at her. Her eyes are wet.

"You're crying," I say. I look down at my lap to see tiny dark spots on my thighs. I wipe my face with the heel of my hand. It's hot and salty. *Shit*, I think.

"Yes. I feel emotional. I care about you."

I bow my head in acknowledgment. "Did you know she didn't even cry?" I say after a while.

"Who didn't?"

"My mother. The day of the funeral. She didn't even cry. Not one tear."

The morning of the service, I stood in the bathroom of *Le Crâpeau*, dressed in an ugly long-sleeved black dress that was the only one I owned. I knew my mother would hate it, because it was faded enough and ill fitting enough to make me look like I didn't have a mother at all. My bare feet sealed themselves to the linoleum floor. I pulled my hair back, then let it down. How was a girl supposed to wear her hair when her brother was dead?

There was a knock at the hollow door. "Stevie?"

"One second." I turned on the hot faucet and stared at my hands under the scalding water, the skin growing a deep, repentant pink. The burn felt good, like crying underwater.

"Stevie." Another knock. "Your mother is here."

"I said I'm coming!" I turned off the water and wiped my hands on my dress. I rubbed my face with my hands, kneading the last bit of emotion from my face. When my face was pure and blank, I set it like granite. I would never let her see.

When I opened the door, she was standing in the front hallway next to my dad. She looked out of place: a fine porcelain doll shoved into a cheap plastic dollhouse. *One of these things is not like the others.* The first thing I noticed was her bare left hand.

Her suit was tailored: tight and black. Her hair was pulled back into a bun, her nails a lacquered red to match her lips. Next to her, a suitcase so small it made me cringe. Of course she wasn't staying. She was never going to stay.

"Oh, sweetness," she said, and she came to me and pulled me into her. Everything that touched me was cold: the heavy links of her gold bracelets pressed against the back of my neck, and her fingertips against my cheeks. My thigh ached beneath a thick white bandage. "Oh, baby."

"Hey, Mom," I said into her chest bones. She smelled expensive, like flowery French perfume. We stood there in the dim hallway for a long time, the only sounds her heartbeat and my dad's muffled, choking sounds. I let her hold me because I had killed her only son. I blinked and counted my breaths. *In, out. In, out.* The air in the apartment was stale and full; so much grief and anger there was barely room for us.

"Well." She exhaled and pulled away. "We should get dressed. Where can I—"

"My room," I said quickly. No one had been in Josh's room since he died. Not during the day, anyway. I'd slept in his bed once, inhaling him through the worn bed sheets. But when I woke up, the comforter was tucked around me differently than when I'd gone to sleep—tighter—and I never did it again. I couldn't stand the thought of Dad standing there in the dark.

I dragged her suitcase across the carpet and into my room. She sat on the edge of the bed—the tiniest sliver. She tried not to look at the heaps of clothes on the floor or wrinkle her nose at the sour sheets.

"So, how was your flight?" I chirped.

"It was—how are—how have you been holding up, my love?" She patted the bed next to her.

I pressed the Play button on my stock response, because she didn't deserve better.

"We're doing the best we can," I said.

"Ah."

"I have to brush my teeth, okay?" I ran my tongue over my teeth, smooth and minty. "I'll be in the bathroom." I stumbled out of my room and shoved through the bathroom door without knocking first. Sweat beads bulged angry at my temples, and I turned on the water and splashed my face again and again as she turned the knob and slid in behind me.

"Those transatlantic flights are just—" She sucked in a sharp, high breath.

"It's okay, Mom," I told her in the mirror. I said it the softest way I knew how. "Okay?"

Her face crumpled for the briefest of moments. Then she smoothed it out again.

"Yes. Yes." She set her makeup bag on the sink next to the soap dispenser. In her purse she found a pack of cigarettes. Only a few left. She tapped one out and lifted it to her perfect lips. I'd never seen her smoke. She took a long drag and blew a winding silver trail at herself in the mirror while I unjammed the frosted window. Sticky, wet summer air drowned the room.

"This apartment is not what I want for you," she told her reflection.

"Yeah, well . . ." I sat on the toilet lid, propped my bare feet on the edge of the tub, and watched her. "We had to. Because of you."

She pressed her lips together. "I needed to get away, and I didn't know how. Haven't you ever felt that way, like you just needed to escape?"

"What's his name?"

"Who?"

"It doesn't matter," I said. "I don't want to talk about it anymore." I felt like my insides were going to spill out of me at any second, and I would never ask her to hold me together.

"You're very thin," she said. Her lips twitched.

"Thanks." I looped my fingers around my wrist. "When are you going back?"

"Tonight, I think." She reached into her suit pocket for a tube of lipstick and applied a fresh coat. Before she put it away, she tilted it toward me and smiled a little. I tapped my ring finger against the rich color and dabbed it on my lips. We'd never done this kind of thing when I was nine. I felt greedy, having this kind of moment when my girl self never had.

"You're a beautiful girl, Stevie," she said.

Before she left, she bent over the toilet and pressed her cheek to mine. Then she kissed the top of my head. I imagined her lip print there, branding me.

"I'm sorry, Mom," I whispered. "I'm sorry."

"He made a mistake," she said. "There was nothing you could have done."

I didn't look at her. I just sat there, letting her blame him like that, because he wasn't here and it was easier. And I thought I deserved for something to be easy. Just this once.

day thirteen

Wednesday, July 16, 9:45 A.M.

"SHE didn't cry." When Shrink repeats the words out loud, I'm so ashamed I can't look at her.

"Not during the funeral, either. And neither did I." What was wrong with us? People cried at funerals. People cried at their dead brother's funerals; that was just how the world worked. But I couldn't. It was like my body refused to acknowledge his death that way. Maybe if the tears never came, he wasn't gone. Maybe this was all some horrible misunderstanding.

I stood at the mouth of the church until the last possible second. It was full—standing room only. I didn't recognize most people, and I wondered how many were here for the novelty of it. How many were just strolling by, and the marquis out front lured them in: Promising Teenager's Untimely Death! A hot ticket. If anyone knew that I costarred as the sister assassin, there would be a line down the block.

The organist played John Lennon's "Beautiful Boy," which made it hard for me to breathe. Hearing it on the organ was a terrible mismatch, just like the words *my brother's* and *funeral*. Like having the funeral in a church, instead of outside by the lake, where we could all read passages from his favorite books and then make sand angels on the bank. But my mother had insisted, and my father had obeyed. Josh's dying wasn't enough to change that.

A friend of Dad's stood by the door handing out programs. He had the good sense not to offer me one as I passed. I should have processed in with my family, but I couldn't stand the thought of walking behind my mother's reedy body, her fists clenched tight around a starched white handkerchief.

I could feel everyone's eyes on me as I walked, and I suddenly had the feeling that I wasn't supposed to be here, that I'd stumbled into the wrong classroom after the bell. It wasn't my brother who was dead. It couldn't be.

My parents sat in the front pew together. They'd never had anything in common except Josh and me. Now they had death, which was so much stronger. I sat on my father's other side. Without looking over, he patted my thigh, the unscarred one. He would never touch me if he knew this was my fault. I bit the inside of my cheek until I couldn't stand the pain. It felt good, knowing exactly where the hurt was, knowing that if I wanted to stop it I could.

When the song ended, Ben walked to the pulpit and adjusted the mic.

"I'd like to read from Philip Larkin's poem 'The Trees,'" he said. A sound came out of my father, but he sucked it back in again. My mother's jaw pulsed.

"*The trees are coming into leaf like something almost being said; their recent buds relax and spread; their greenness is a kind of grief.*"

Behind me, shuddery sobs. I recognized them almost before they started: Eden's. Fury burned under my skin. Josh wasn't her brother. He wasn't her anything. He was just the next guy at the bar. After the service, a bunch of people I didn't care about came to the apartment. They stood in clusters and talked in low voices and shook their heads over plastic plates of ham biscuits and potato salad. I went to my room and got into bed, shoes and all. I pulled the covers all the way to my chin. My mother's scent clung to the fabric, stubborn.

"Stevie?" A knock, and then Eden was next to the bed. She looked stoned—red eyed and there but not there. For once, she was wearing something appropriate: a sleeveless black dress that fell to her knees and was even a little too big. "Hey."

"Hey," I told the ceiling.

"I saw your mom out there, I think. She's pretty." When she sat on the bed, I turned on my side, toward the wall. "I've been trying to call, since—I've been trying to call." She sounded smaller than I'd ever heard her. Good.

"I have nothing to say to you." I scrunched my toes up tight and thought, *Oh, shit, what if I forget what he looks like?* and I shut my eyes and found his face in my memory: pixelated at first, then sharper. I would never have opened my eyes again, if it meant I could keep him like that.

Eden slid in next to me and matched her body with mine. Knees bent, head bowed. She raked the damp hair from the back of my neck and pressed her lips to my skin and left them there. I could feel my face collapsing, like my body just couldn't hold itself up anymore.

"It's okay," she whispered, rocking me slowly. Her breath was even, and it felt like she was breathing for me. "It's okay. I know."

But she didn't know, because her brother hadn't died. And I didn't know, either. Not really. Not yet. I only understood what his death meant later, in small life moments that piled up like rubble. I understood more every day.

When your brother dies, everything is different. You watch whatever you want on TV because he's not there to hog the remote, but you could give a shit about TV, so mostly you sleep. It's quiet all the time. No one wants to speak his name or laugh out loud—at least, not too soon. People take their Josh stories and their Josh memories and fold them gingerly, stack them high on shelf for "a more appropriate time." You play Scrabble alone. You stare at the tiles for so long the letters become meaningless.

And when your brother dies, everything is exactly the same. Your father asks you to go to the grocery store and he's too clueless to see the irony in it. You ask him for cash to buy your binge supplies and then you wander the aisles, wondering how people can buy frozen pizzas and read tabloids in the checkout line when your brother is dead.

We curled up in the hot sheets while the sounds of grief rose and fell outside my door. My mother's perfume and my dead brother slowly faded away. When I woke, Eden was gone and the space next to me was cold. My room was almost dark.

"Sweetness?" my mother's shadow said from the door. "Wake up, love. I have a flight to catch."

day thirteen

I am puddled on the love seat next to Shrink, empty. My face is hot and stiff; my scar is throbbing.

"Feeling feels like shit," I bleat. I press my cheek against the beaded pillow and stare at her office sideways.

"It does sometimes," she agrees. "But you're doing really important work. So what was the predominant feeling for you that night, after the funeral?"

"Anger." I don't even have to think. "Always anger."

"Anger is pretty easy for you to access, right?"

I sit up too fast, and the room spins. "You don't think I have a right to be pissed? My brother is dead and my mother left and Eden just wants to feel like she's part of the whole big dramatic show, and you don't think I have the right to be pissed?"

"Of course I do. I would never tell you not to be angry. Anger is important. Anger is part of grief. Have you ever heard the phrase, 'The truth will set you free, but first it will piss you off'?"

I shake my head.

"You have to speak your truth before you can heal." She gets up and settles back in her seat. Then she flicks the lighter on the side table—once, twice—and lights the candle. I focus on the flame.

"My truth," I say. "My truth is that I killed my brother?"

"That's not what I heard you say, Stevie. I heard you say that you and Josh were in a fight. I heard you say that there was a tragic accident. And then I heard you say that he died as a result of that accident."

If she wants to see it that way, she can. But I have carried the weight of his death for almost a year, for so long that it is part of me, fused in my bones. *I am the girl who killed her brother.* I don't know how to let it go, even if I wanted to.

"This is something that happened to you. A terrible event in your life. It is not who you are. And it does not have to define who you become. Do you hear me?"

"Yeah," I whisper. "I hear you."

"If you let this disease take you, you're giving up all the power you actually do have. Just giving it up, without a fight." She's quiet, but it sounds like she's yelling.

"I *have* been fighting."

"You're right. You've been fighting. You've been at war. Only you've been at war with yourself. All that anger, all that grief, you're funneling it right back into your body. Is it working?"

"It will," I snap.

"When? When you're dead?"

I say nothing.

"Will it be enough, dying?"

"I don't know yet. I don't know if it'll be enough. But it's all I have."

I think she's going to argue, but she says, "So ask him."

"What?"

"Ask him. Josh. Ask whether your death will be enough to pay for his." She drags her chair closer to mine, so that we're knee to knee. "What would he say?"

I close my eyes to escape her. And I search for him, because it's been so long and I just . . . miss him, in millions of the smallest ways. I miss how solid he was when we used to hug, and how he didn't let go right away. I miss how when he ate cereal, he scooped the flakes out first and then drank the milk. It kept the flakes crunchy and made the milk sweet, he said.

Most of all, I miss the biggest thing, the most important, enormous thing in the world: that he knew how to love me, and did. He wasn't selective like my mother, didn't hand out his affection in lean portions. He didn't thrive on drama like Eden. He just loved me, quietly when he could and angrily when he had to. And suddenly I'm so sad that I didn't understand this when he was alive. And I want to tell him how sorry I am, but my mouth can't even form the words.

"Stevie?" Shrink prompts me. "What do you think he'd say to you, if he could speak to you now?"

"Enough." Eyes still closed, I make strangled sound. The words flatten themselves inside my throat. "He'd say *enough*."

"Enough . . ."

"Enough . . . dying and leaving. Enough of this eating disorder bullshit. But he wouldn't say *bullshit*. He didn't curse."

"So he wouldn't accept your death as some sort of sacrifice. A penance for his."

"That's not the point."

"You're right. The point is not whether Josh would or wouldn't want you to die. He wouldn't, Stevie. He *wouldn't*. Do you know that?"

I swallow. "Yes."

"The point is whether you, yourself, want to die."

"I don't know what else to do." The truth comes rattling to the surface, and my eyes pop open. I don't know anymore. I've been working so hard to disappear that right now, at this moment, I can't imagine succeeding. And I can't image deciding not to. I only know this way of being, not quite alive, not quite dead. Not quite. "There's nothing else to do." I need to lie down. I need to sleep.

"Wrong."

"Don't you know you aren't supposed to say *wrong*?" I rake my hands through my cropped hair. *I must look like a boy*, I think. Suddenly, having Eden cut it seems like the stupidest thing.

"When something's wrong, I'm supposed to say *wrong*," she argues. "And I'm telling you that you have other choices. Like allowing yourself to grieve, and feel sadness. Like giving this whole treatment thing a real shot. Like living, Stevie."

"You make it sound easy," I say.

She shakes her head. "It's the hardest thing you'll ever do. But I am asking you to try, Stevie, knowing that you can always go back to your way if you want to. Would you be willing to try? If not for yourself, for Josh?"

"I—" I'm reaching for him, desperate to hear his voice. But he's gone, and without him, I am spinning and directionless. "I don't know if I can. I think it might be too late."

day fourteen

Thursday, July 17, 1:57 P.M.

I walk to group alone. Moving through the desert is like trying to run through water, the heat an invisible current. I'm tired. So tired I could curl up here, in the dust, and sleep while it blows over me like a thin, earthy blanket. I'm tired of Shrink telling me how to feel. I'm tired of hating my mother. I'm tired of being an only child. And I'm tired of being this pissed all the time. Only I don't know how not to be.

I've been thinking about what Shrink asked me yesterday, about trying treatment. And there's this miniscule part of me that thinks that nothing—not even treatment—could be harder than this: gunning full-speed toward total destruction.

I picture myself in the driver's seat: windows down, eyes closed, accelerator pressed to the floor. My lids frantic and twitching, my knuckles whitened as the Anniversary nears. And before I can stop it, my brain thinks, *I'm not sure I want to do this anymore.* I could blame it on Josh, say that he wouldn't want me to kill myself. But that would be a cop-out. I think maybe I'm scared to die.

Help, I plead silently. A prayer to my brother. *Help.*

I stop and wait, stupidly hoping I'll hear him. But all I hear is the wind.

When I get to the house, everyone is already there: Shrink, Jenna, the girls from Cottage Three, and a new girl from Cottage Two with bleached-blond hair, a nose ring, and full tattoo sleeves. Tempest, or Skye. Something weather related.

"We're going to have a group snack today." Shrink pushes herself onto the counter in the kitchen. Her bare feet swing like a careless girl's in summer. She's not wearing the toe ring today. "How does that sound to everybody?"

"What's the snack?" Teagan pinches the ends of her hair, then crosses her arms over her chest.

"Cinammon rolls," Shrink says.

My heart bats in my chest. So many questions—*the kind in the tube? I only know the numbers for the kind in the tube! Do we have to spread the icing on top? All the icing on top? I don't remember the numbers for the icing*—and I try to slow my breathing, like Shrink taught me. Practice the—what did she call them?—grounding exercises.

My name is Stevie Deslisle. It is Thursday, and I am in a treatment center in New Mexico because I have an eating disorder. I smell: the sharp, dry smell of desert dust settled in the cracks of the kitchen floor. Ashley's sugary-sweet body spray and Teagan's hairspray. I hear: the whirring of the ceiling fan above me, the other girls swapping cinnamon roll horror stories. I feel: the solid floor below me, holding me up. The sweaty canvas bottoms of my sneakers. I taste: the grainy icing coating my tongue. Wait. Not yet. I taste: my own sticky breath. I see: Shrink's small pink smile. Three tubes on the counter. Three.

Shrink says, "I'll preheat the oven, and, Ashley, if you'd grab the baking sheets? We can take some time to process before we eat. Stevie, why don't you pair up with Rain?"

Rain. Right. *Rain from Los Angeles. Thin but bulimic, like me.* "Uh, sure," I say, wishing I could be with Ashley or one of the other girls instead. None of them has mentioned my midnight dash the other night, but Ashley is dying to talk about it. Last night before sleep, she tossed and turned for almost an hour, clearly bursting with questions. Shrink probably told her not to bring it up to me until I was ready.

Ashley shoots me a *that sucks* look on her way to the oven. I cut my eyes at the new girl, who is squinting at my tattoo. I slap my palm over my mother's face.

"I'm not eating a bun," she says loudly.

The fizzy chatter in the kitchen goes flat.

"Whatever," I say. My face is getting hot. "You don't have to eat it all. We just have to make them and then you eat what you can."

She rolls her eyes at me. "Do you have any idea how much *fat* is in those things? How many *calories?*"

"Rain, no numbers talk, please," Shrink said sharply. She whips her hair into a too-tight bun and cages it with a rubber band. "I'd encourage you to talk about your feelings about the challenge, but not about the numbers."

Rain shoves back her chair and mumbles something that sounds like *give a fuck*. I catch Ashley's eye, and she grins and rolls her eyes. When Shrink isn't looking, I roll mine back.

"So what's up her ass?" Rain mutters under her breath. She stuffs her hands in her pockets before we get our tube of cinnamon rolls, which means I am the one to unwind the wrapper from the tube—slowly, slowly—and the one to press my thumbs just so against the perforated cardboard until *pop!* The dough oozes from its prison.

"Up whose ass?" *My name is Stevie Deslisle. It is Thursday.* I take in Rain's shoulders, her elbows. She has the perfect sharpness of the still sick. I can feel my belly hanging over the waistband of my jeans. I suck in, hard.

"Her. The therapist." Rain nods at Shrink, who is murmuring something to Cate in low tones on the other side of the kitchen.

"Nothing. She's fine." *I am in a treatment center in New Mexico.* I twist the canister open and slide out the doughy discs. They hit the slick, greased cookie sheet with a sickening thunk. *Help me, Josh. Help.* I wonder if Rain will even try to eat. Of course she won't. If I try, I may be the only one in my group to do so. *Because I have an eating disorder.*

"She seems like a bitch."

"She's not," I snap. "Put these in the oven?" I slide the cookie sheet in her direction.

The smell starts slowly at first, then overcomes the room in one big whoosh, like a fire spreading. Maybe it smells like Sunday mornings to some people, but to me it smells like the kitchen of *Le Crâpeau* in the dark. Josh and Dad are out somewhere, but I don't have much time so I yank the cookie sheet from the oven before the timer's gone off. Swallow them almost whole, sucking from a jug of milk in between. I almost want them to come home early and catch me, fat lips glazed with sugar and fear. It would make it easier. It would end this faster.

"Stevie?" Shrink ushers me to the table, where a frosted cinnamon roll sits on a plate. The other girls are already seated. Rain glares down at her plate with her eyes and mouth pinched. I know that look.

My name is Stevie Deslisle. I sit down at my place. I pick up my fork. I take a bite. And I swallow.

day fourteen

Thursday, July 17, 10:55 P.M.

IN bed in the dark, I ready myself for inspection.

First, the wrists. I wrap my middle finger and thumb around the opposite wrist, then slide the flesh handcuff as far as it will go without breaking. Not far enough. I can feel my body morphing cell by cell into what it used to be. As if I've pressed Rewind on my own body, sped up the process with each bite of the cinnamon roll.

I check the sinking collarbone, vanishing ribs, and lost hips. I've gotten soft, literally.

The door clicks open, and a light triangle appears on my bedspread. Then the flashlight on my pillow and Ashley's. *One, two*. The door closes. Footsteps, then the creak of another closing door. More footsteps. And our door opens again.

"We're here, okay? Both of us." I screw my eyes shut and bury myself beneath the covers.

Low giggles in the doorway. "You know I'm going to have to chart you for . . . insubordination, don't you, Stephanie?"

Across the room, Ashley snorts.

I sit up. "What the—"

"Shh." Cold, bony fingers clamp over my mouth.

"Cate?" I push her away, careful not to touch the tube. Teagan stands in the doorway.

"We've got an hour," Ashley says from the other side of the room. She slides out of bed.

Cate grins. "Let's go."

"Tell me!" I demand once we're outside, trudging down the hill. I should be used to the desert cold by now. I lift Josh's sweatshirt over my nose and breathe him in as deep as I can. There's less of him every time. "What are you doing?"

"Ohhh, no you don't." Cate giggles from the front of the line. Our fearless leader, in pink pj's with a permanent straw sticking out of her nose. "You're in this, too, now. You didn't actually have to come."

"It'll be fun. Promise," Ashley says without turning around.

I'm exhausted, but also a little excited. I've never snuck out with friends before, and it seems like this is some very important rite of passage, like the first time you lie to your parents. For a split second, I feel normal, and then I remember.

On the other side of the villa, Cate winds away from the main road. The desert floor is littered with large stones and low brush and the occasional piece of warped wood.

"There," Ashley says, and points.

Set back from the road is a chain-link fence painted black. Hanging on the other side of the chain link is a sheet of black mesh that makes it hard to see inside, like looking through a screen door. But I can smell what's on the other side, and it makes my stomach turn.

"A pool?" The chemicals sting the inside of my nose and remind me of a million things at once: me at six, standing hunched in a department store dressing room in a two-piece that didn't quite fit while my mother made a clicking sound with her tongue. Me at eleven, wearing a one-piece to the community pool, standing with my sausage toes wriggling over the edge of the deep end, watching the sunlight stream between the other girls' thighs. Me at twelve, me at fourteen, and now, me at seventeen: It doesn't matter. The feeling is always the same.

Ashley's smile is all teeth. "They won't let you go unless you're on green. But we wanted to, so . . ."

"Come on, guys." Cate tries the padlocked chain slung between the gate and the rest of the fence. "Locked. We'll have to climb." She hooks her tube around her ear and shoves up the sleeves of her ratty robe. Then she claws the fence, and Teagan boosts her up and over the side. Her flip-flops hit the concrete with a slap.

"You guys go next." I nod at Ashley and Teagan. "I'll be last."

Teagan is breathing too hard as Ashley shoves her over, then starts to climb herself.

"Oof." She wobbles at the top, but makes it. Then it's my turn, and it's harder than it looks. Especially with the other girls watching. My body is weak from all the sugar. The metal presses into my skin as I climb. When I get to the top I swing one leg over the side, then the other, my ass spilling over the cold, hard bar.

"Just let go and jump," Cate says. "It's not that bad."

"I'm doing it." My head knows that the jump isn't far, but my body feels like it is.

"Oh, come on." Ashley grabs my ankle and yanks it. I scream and let go, hitting the ground.

"Shhh," she hisses. "Quiet."

Cate fishes something small out of her pocket and secures the end of her tube with it. Then we stand in a huddle in our pajamas, next to the quiet black rectangle, staring at one another and then at the ground like nobody knows what to do next. I shiver, even though I'm not really cold.

"This is stupid," Ashley announces, kicking off her Keds. "I'm going in." She pulls off her pajama pants but leaves on her T-shirt. "Cannonball!" she whispers, then takes a running leap— *slapslapslap*—and jumps in. Water explodes over the side, soaking my pajama pants. When she surfaces, her curls are plastered to her pink cheeks.

"Me, too." Cate turns her back to us and strips down to her bra, tank top, and underwear. Shoulders hunched, she hurries around the side and down the front steps. She doesn't go under.

"Cold!" she announces with a blue-lipped smile.

Teagan dives in with all her clothes on, and again I'm the last one.

I don't want to mess up Josh's sweatshirt, so I pull it over my head and drape it carefully over the fence. The pajama pants are my only pair, so I hang them next to the sweatshirt. The long scar from my hip to my knee glows white-hot. I hurry to the edge of the pool, knowing the darkness is not enough to cover me, and slide into the deep end as fast as I can.

The cold water takes my breath away. My legs are covered in goose bumps and prickly hair.

Ashley's dark round outline bobs toward me. "On the website, they say it's heated, but I feel like they lied."

"Guys!" Cate's silhouette shudders in the shallow end. "Come down here."

Teagan and Ashley suck in heavy breaths and dive under, their shadows gliding across the bottom of the pool. I cut through the water slowly, lowering my lips to the surface. I'm almost weightless. I let myself relax into the feeling of being not quite here. I wonder how much I weigh in water.

"Thanks," Cate says gratefully when I reach the steps. I don't know if she can't swim, or if she's just scared about the tube.

Ashley and Teagan surface together.

"Let's play a game," Teagan says.

"Oooh! Chicken fight!" Ashley's eyes get wide.

I picture Cate and me perched like birds on Ashley's and Teagan's shoulders, but I'd be too scared to rip out Cate's tube. So then I picture it the other way, with Ashley and Teagan wrestling each other while Cate and I sputter for breath. It makes me laugh so hard I suck in a mouthful of water.

"Yeah. I guess that won't work," Ashley admits.

"Handstand contest!" Half of Cate's face shines in the little bit of light from the moon. "You guys go. See how long you can hold your breath. I'll be the judge."

"One! Two! Three!" Ashley dives under, and Teagan follows. Cate's practically shaking with excitement, so I follow. I plant my palms on the rough pool bottom and press my thighs together, trying hard not to think about them ballooning huge and white above the water. Instead I try to remember if I know how to do this, if I've ever done it before. I dig for a memory—a pool party, maybe, or a day my mother took me swimming—but there is nothing.

When my lungs start to burn, I flip to the surface. Ashley and Teagan are already standing.

"I win," I announce. It's stupid, but I feel kind of excited. I glance across the pool, pretending for a second that Josh or even my mother is there, crouched on the edge and smiling and proud of me for something real.

"Cheater!" Ashley shoves me before I can find my balance.

"How can I cheat under water?" I shove her back.

"You didn't go down till, like, two seconds after we did."

"But I stayed down longer than that, right?"

We turn to Cate.

"Stevie wins," she decrees.

"Yes." I grin and shape my short wet ends into a Mohawk.

"Hey. So what's that, um, scar on your leg?" Teagan asks, trying to sound casual. The other girls' eyes are on me, too.

My fingers fly underwater, to the raised white line. "It's—" I should have left my pajama pants on. "Nothing."

Everyone is quiet and still.

Then Ashley closes her eyes, leans back in the water, and starts to float. "I like it out here."

The four of us, even Cate, let our feet find the surface and spread our arms and legs out like points on a star. I spin slowly around and around, a human pinwheel. With my ears underwater, the sound of my breath is the only sound. There aren't many stars out. Twisting in the cold, weightless dark, I wonder if this is what being dead would feel like. I flop upright again, fast.

The air is starting to smell like something, but I can't tell what. Burnt summer. It reminds me of the night before Josh died. Eden and I got wasted and made out in the lot behind the Stacks. It was desperate, chaotic. She pressed me into the ground and ran her hands everywhere and the sky twisted above us and I felt a little sick. But I didn't stop. I let her touch me and my body rose up in response. One of the many unthinkable ways it betrayed me.

The memory isn't right. I should be remembering running through the sprinklers with Josh when we were kids. I should be remembering standing over the spray, blinking with wet lashes at the millions of rainbows. That's what Eden took from me; that's what I gave away: the sacred importance of the real things. The things that mattered.

Suddenly I realize these girls are the closest things to friends I've ever had. They're closer than Eden, anyway. They don't want anything from me. They don't suck the energy out of me like air from a balloon.

After a few minutes, Ashley splashes next to me.

"What?" I jerk myself upright, shaking the water from my ears. Cate and Teagan follow.

"Shhh." Ashley's face goes pale.

"Girls?" A nurse voice, one I don't recognize. "Who's out there?"

"Oh, *shit!*" I whisper. We scramble out of the pool, and I cram my feet into my flip-flops and grab Josh's clothes. I'm first over the fence but a sharp pain lights up my calf. I break into a sprint in the dark, the soles of my muddy feet slipping and sliding against my shoes. The brush stings my shins as I duck away from the flashlight beam.

"We're so dead," Ashley wheezes behind me.

"Shhh!" Cate hisses behind her. "Just run!"

I run as fast as I can up the hill, sending a gravel shower behind me, then tear open the front door of the cottage and dive inside. When the others tumble in behind me, we slam the door and lock it.

"Wait. No." Cate giggles, bending over and gasping for breath. A puddle of pool water expands around each of us, and a tiny river of blood snakes its way down my calf. "Do they leave it unlocked at night? We have to leave it like it usually is."

"Girls? I can hear you in there." Footsteps on the porch.

"Go!" Teagan shouts, even though we know it's useless. We're busted. But we scurry to our rooms and I slam the door behind Ashley and me. Ditch my clothes on the floor by the bed and take a running leap onto my mattress soaking wet, whip the covers over my head and bury my face beneath my pillow.

"She's coming!" Ashley's squeal is muffled.

"Shhh!" My body is shaking, laughter I didn't even know was in there leaking out through my nose and mouth.

On the other side of the room, Ashley starts laughing, too, and then she snorts, which makes me laugh harder. It's ridiculous, being soaking wet and almost naked under the covers, but I can't stop laughing and my body aches. And I think, if Josh were here, he'd be laughing, too.

day fifteen

"I know, okay?" I sit cross-legged on the love seat in Shrink's office, my journal in my lap. I reek of chlorine, even though I washed my hair three times this morning. She can smell it, I'm sure. "I know."

"You know . . . what, exactly?" Shrink's tone is teasing.

I give her a look. "I know we weren't supposed to sneak out like that."

Shrink settles into her armchair. She looks amused. "I did hear a little something about an impromptu field trip last night, come to think of it."

"Okay," I say. "And?"

"And . . . did you have fun?"

"What do you mean?"

"Like . . . did you enjoy the other girls' company? Did you find yourself smiling, or even laughing? Did you have a good swim? That kind of thing."

"Are you making fun of me? I feel like you're making fun of me."

Her eyes find my eyes. "I'm not, Stevie. If you had a good time last night, if you were able to get outside of yourself and away from your eating disorder for a little bit, then I think last night was a success. Truly."

"Oh."

"Of course if you do it again, we will have a problem. Understood?"

I nod.

"Good." She leans back in her chair and waits. I've learned this: Therapy is more about waiting than anything else. I am surprised to realize that a tiny part of me wants to tell her about swimming last night. If only to prove that I'm not a total freak. Somewhere inside me there's a fragment of a normal girl who sneaks out and laughs too loud and gets caught doing things that aren't so bad.

"I don't think I like the new girl," I say, because I don't know what else to say.

"Who? Rain?"

I nod. "She's kind of a bitch."

Shrink's expression stays neutral. What did I expect, for her to lean in and whisper, *Seriously, I know. Did you see the way she*—?

"To you? Kind of a bitch to you?"

"I don't know. Sort of. Mostly, I think she's just pissed about being here, which I guess I get."

"And how are you feeling about being here?"

I position myself in the corner of the love seat and survey her bookshelves. I've never really looked at the pictures she's arranged in various junky frames. There's a full-body shot that reeks of self-discovery and weed: Shrink on some mountaintop, squinty-eyed and proud. Then there's a faraway shot of Shrink and some other lady with their arms slung around each other on a beach. The sister, maybe.

"Stevie?"

"I don't know."

"Don't know . . ."

"How I feel about being here." I want to ask her which *here* she's talking about: here, as in treatment? Or *here*, as in alive? "Actually, I've been thinking about what you said. About trying treatment or whatever."

"And what do you think?" Shrink leans forward and rests her chin in her hands. Everything about her is soft: her eyes, the wispy red-blonde resting against her cheekbones. Her mouth. Even her words are soft: doughy and floured.

She would make a really good mother, I think.

"Maybe I could try," I say. "For Josh. Just to see."

"I'm glad to hear that. You've been thinking about him a lot? Josh?"

When she asks, my body gets tight, as if she's tugging the end of a string that binds up my throat and heart.

"Just . . . how I miss him," I whisper.

"I know, Stevie."

Then she's quiet, which is the best thing and the worst thing. She doesn't try to fill the space up with words or prayer and she doesn't try to pretend. She's the first one to do that, really. We sit together in silence, just Shrink and me and Josh's death so heavy it's crushing. And it hurts so bad I can't imagine it ever not hurting.

"I don't know what to do," I say.

"You're doing it. You're grieving his loss, and that will look different every minute of every day. But I think a really important part of your process will be learning to honor him."

"I'm trying, though."

"I mean learning to honor him in a way that's healthy for you. I just believe, really strongly, that he would want that for you."

I let myself nod. "Yeah. Okay."

"I wonder what that could look like. For you to honor him in a healthy way."

"I don't *know*, okay? I don't know." Just thinking about living past the Anniversary fills me up with fear. I wouldn't know how to do it: how to wake up and sit across from Dad, sipping shitty coffee and knowing that Josh was still gone and he would be tomorrow, too. How to go to school another year, wandering the halls alone and pretending I don't notice the pity whispers. Going home to face Eden.

"He was just a really good friend to me." My voice is too loud.

"How?" she asks.

"Like, he was just there to talk if I needed to, or whatever. And he supported me. Whatever was best for me."

"Do you think he'd be supportive of your being here?"

It's a leading question, but I allow it. "I guess so. Yeah."

"You've made some friends during your time here, it seems. Ashley, in particular."

"Yeah. She's . . . it's weird. I wasn't all that nice to her when I first got here, but she was nice anyway."

"So her friendship isn't conditional. On your being in a good mood, or even your being kind."

I shake my head.

She sits back a little, and her eyes flit to the ceiling. "How do you think your relationship with Ashley is different from your relationship with Eden?"

"I can't even—they're nothing alike." I slide down the love seat. I remember my first hours here at the center, the way Ashley seemed to breathe me in, desperate for a smile, a story. Approval. Or maybe it wasn't approval. Maybe it was connection. Maybe she was just a little girl trying on her mother's lipstick after her brother died. Maybe she was just like me that way.

When Eden breathed me in, it was different. Eden never wanted to connect with me. She wanted to eclipse me. And I let her.

Most nights after Josh died I spent at her place, lounging drunk on her couch and wanting to kiss her but knowing we could never do that again, and listening to records on the brand-new old record player her parents had bought her. We'd stay that way until she got a text from some guy she wanted to hook up with, and then she'd head for the Stacks and I'd drive home. I'd grit my teeth, angry and silent. Even then, I knew what she was doing: owning me. Taking me out when she was lonely and putting me back when she didn't need me anymore.

The thing was, I needed to be owned. I needed someone to say, *This girl is mine.* That's what family is for, but mine was almost gone. There was no one to claim me but Eden and my sickness. So I gave myself to both.

"Well?" I say, when Shrink is too quiet.

"Well, what?" she asks.

"Well, aren't you going to say something like *sounds like you were engaging in some pretty self-destructive behaviors, Stevie?*" I squirm on the love seat, irritated. Her office feels too small. The air stinks of chlorine, and that stupid candle.

Shrink presses her hands together like she's going to pray.

"I mean, I know I was. Obviously. The thing was, Eden was the most destructive part of the whole thing. She was, like, this . . . virus."

"A virus."

I nod, because it fits. She is a virus, and I have been fevered with her since the first day of seminar. I thought she was the cure. I thought she could fix me. But instead she's kept me sick, and needing her, because that's what she needed.

"How's your letter going? You were writing her, correct?"

"Yeah." I open my journal and flip to the letter. I read it to her, out loud.

Eden,

I got your letter. Obviously. Maybe sometime we could talk on the phone or something. I don't really use the phone here, but I could, if I wanted to. After dinner, which is going-out time at home, I guess.

I've been thinking about you. A lot, actually. About what happened to Josh, and why it happened. I think it started that night at the Pit. I keep replaying the night again and again in my head and every time I want to know: Why did you do it? Just for fun? To prove you could?

Here's the really shitty thing about it all, Eden: I was going to apologize to him. Can you believe it? For being a bitch to him that night and storming off. I'd thought about it, thought maybe he was just trying to be a good big brother, and I was going to skip time with you to apologize to him. God, I was so stupid.

"Huh. It seems like you're holding back a little," Shrink says. "What do you really want to say to her? After all the processing you've done around your relationship, what do you want to say?"

I try to organize the words, but they won't stay in line. There's this sudden, weird surge of energy in me and I ask, "Could I write it?"

"Write out what you want to say to Eden?"

"Sometimes writing is . . . I don't know. Easier." It's the first time I've wanted to write—really, truly wanted to write—in more than a year. I can feel the words welling up in the tips of my fingers, pooling there like ink.

"Of course. Take your time." She gets up and meanders over to her bookshelf. I know she doesn't have anything to do there, really, but I'm grateful that she's giving me some space. I slide down to the tile floor, the love seat at my back. Rip the letter I've started from my journal and crush it, leaving it at my hip. I turn to a fresh page.

The words run out on the page, instantly.

Eden,

You didn't ask, but I am learning some things, here at the treatment center where I am being treated for the eating disorder you have never asked about, not in over a year. I am learning some things about me, and some things about us. I am learning

*that I needed someone to cling to when my mother left and you
needed to be clung to. So we fit, and it felt good.*

*You needed to be the eye of the hurricane, the center around
which chairs and roofs and whole families spin. And I let you, and
that's my fault.*

You never loved me; you loved the sickness in me.

You never loved Josh; you loved how it felt to be wanted by Josh.

You stuck around after he died because I was wounded.

I kept you around after he died because I was wounded.

I'm tired of hurting and being hurt by you.

I'm tired of being angry and letting you stroke my hair.

*I don't know what comes after this, but whatever comes I do
it alone.*

Without you.

Never call me, never text me, never write me.

*You and I—whatever we were—are through. Even though
you didn't ask.*

Stevie

I read it through, once. And I fold it and ask Shrink for an
envelope, which I address. I press a stamp Shrink gives me in the
corner—it says *love*. And on my way out of session, I drop it in the
mail bin by the front door.

day fifteen

Friday, July 18, 7:47 P.M.

AT evening snack, I make my selections at the window: pretzels, an apple. Supplement. Somehow the tray doesn't seem quite as heavy in my hands. Somehow it's easier to move. I am heavier and lighter, both.

"Hey, guys." I drop my tray at my usual table and sit between Ashley and Jenna. Ashley's trail mix is arranged in a swirly mosaic design on her tray. It's only a matter of time before Hannah charts her, and she doesn't seem to care. Her eyes are glazed and pink.

"What's going on?" I glance from Cate to Teagan to Jenna and back to Ashley. The space between them is taut. "Did Kyle get pissed at you for sneaking out or something?"

"No." Ashley sniffs. "I mean, yeah. But it's not that. I thought my parents weren't coming for my Ninety-Six. But this morning, Kyle said they're thinking about coming."

"What? As in, you have to do sessions and have meals and stuff with them?" I grip her wrist. I can feel her pulse, panicked and thready.

"Yeah." Silent tears roll down her cheek.

"Could you tell them not to come or something?" Maybe I could talk to Shrink. Ask her to talk to Kyle. I'm almost positive that one or both of Ashley's parents put those marks on her.

"I don't think so. They pretty much . . . do . . . what they want." She breathes in little gasps, like she doesn't have a right to the air.

"But you don't *have* to leave with them, right? I mean, if you want to stay in the cottage and stuff at night, you can?"

"Maybe. I haven't asked Kyle yet."

"I'll ask Anna, okay? I'll ask."

"Yeah. Okay. Thanks."

I search her face, which is puffy from crying and deflated at the same time. It's strange, seeing yet another version of her. It hasn't been that long since she woke me up, journaling and organizing her clothes and puttering around the room like there was some sort of turbo engine inside her. And now this. It reminds me of these painted Russian nesting dolls my mother used to have on the mantel in the house on Broad. You opened one and found another. You opened that one and found other still.

"Hey. You want to go for a walk or something? Go see the horses?"

"We can't. It's still snack time." She looks at me funny.

"Yeah. Right." I pick at my pretzels and the table goes silent.

Teagan finishes first, and Cate's really trying. I can tell from the way she pinches her lips tight and forces the peanuts onto her tongue.

I lock my gaze on Ashley again. I feel the tiniest spark of anger—she's supposed to be the cheerleader here, she's not supposed to get upset—but then it goes away and I reach over and flick a dried cranberry at her.

"Got plans the rest of the summer?"

"Huh?" she sniffs up a giant wad of snot, which makes me laugh, and then she does, too.

"You could come visit after this if you wanted. Stay with my dad and me for the rest of the summer." I can kind of picture it: us stretched out on ratty towels around the soaked concrete edge of the neighborhood pool. I can see my reflection in her cat-eye sunglasses, and I'm laughing so hard my stomach hurts. The concrete burns through my towel, so hot it feels real. My hair is a little longer, in that awkward stage, wispy and stubborn around the temples.

"Oh," she says, and starts crying again. For real this time. "Yeah. That would be nice, Stevie. Thanks." But she says it almost wistfully, the way I used to think about having a houseful of girlfriends over for a sleepover when I was a lonely kid: It was a nice idea, but I knew it would never happen.

In group the next day we sit in a "Kumbaya" circle on the floor: Shrink, me, Ashley, Cate, Teagan, Jenna, and Rain. Underneath her sweatshirt, Rain is doing ab work. Her forehead is wrinkled in concentration. She thinks no one notices. She thinks she is not us and we are not her.

"We're going to try a body image activity today," Shrink says. She's sitting cross-legged, her maxi skirt stretched tight over her knees. She dumps the contents of her straw bag onto the floor in front of her, and everybody cranes their necks. There are a few balls of colored yarn. Real scissors, which I haven't seen since I got here. A measuring tape, the soft kind.

"I'd like you all to take the string." She lifts a pinky-red ball. "And with it, I want you to estimate the circumference of your hips, at the widest part. How much string do you think you would need to wrap all the way around your hips? Remember, this is just a guess. Don't measure it against the actual circumference of your hips. When you've finished, let me know and I'll cut the string for you."

We move syrupy slow, all of us, reaching listlessly for balls of yarn. I take the green, because that's what's closest. I tear the paper sleeve and start to unwind the yarn. It's cheap and acrylic, scratchy between my fingers.

"Wait. Our hips now, or they were like before?" I pat mine. They are thick, meaty. I try not to think about it, for Josh, but my mind keeps coming back.

"Your hips as they are right now."

"Oh." I cut my eyes to the left, at Ashley. She's just staring at the yellow ball of yarn in her lap. My yarn will be shorter than hers, longer than Cate's. Shorter than Teagan's, too, but Teagan's will be just a little shorter than Ashley's. Rain's will be the shortest. I don't want to care about that, but suddenly it feels like the most important thing in the universe.

That's the strange thing about life in this odd plastic bubble. One of the strange things, anyway. Here we're supposed to be focusing on big-picture issues, like learning how not to despise our lives, learning how to love our bodies, how to make peace with who we are. If Shrink has told me once, she's told me at least ten times: I'm supposed to use this time to retrain my brain, my thinking, the way I perceive myself and the world around me. If I have to, if all of us have to, we're supposed to go back in time to examine our childhoods. To discover how we learned to hate ourselves with such intensity. *We're not born hating*, Shrink insisted once.

But we are a group of girls so overwhelmed by our mere existence that it's almost paralyzing, the idea of dealing with the "big-picture" issues. It's the reason we got this way to begin with. The reason a single caloric unit takes on such importance, the reason the pound becomes our currency of worth. These are things we can manage.

Here in this artificial world, it is the same. Self-worth, relationships, abuse, parents, families, expectations, dead siblings: they're the dark, low clouds that loom so close not even we know how big they really are. We can't step back to see them in their entirety. And so we focus the little things. Stashing bobby pins to pin our hair back while we wash our faces, because it makes us feel like any other teenage girl for just a second. Rolling the cuffs of our too-loose shorts high on our ghost thighs to get a little sunburn. The little things make us feel human. I get it now, why all the other girls spend so much time curling their limp, brittle hair and applying lip gloss to their flaking, starved mouths. It's what we have.

"This is hard," I announce. The space inside my head feels electrified.

"What's the most difficult piece for you?" Shrink looks up. She is crouched next to Cate, holding a tiny notebook and a pen.

"I just . . . I have no idea how to do this."

"It's difficult, isn't it, trying to estimate what your body actually looks like?" Shrink stands up. "Ready for me to cut your string, Stevie?"

I shake my head. "Hold on." I stretch a length of yarn into an oval, widening it until it looks right. "Okay."

"Here we go." Shrink bends over and snips the yarn. Then she measures the length of it and makes a note on her notepad. "Stand up for me?"

I obey, and she wraps the measuring tape around my hips. I try to suck in, which is impossible. I'm aware, suddenly, of how tight my jeans are.

"Come here, Stevie." Shrink pulls me outside of the circle, and tilts the notebook in my direction. The numbers should be comforting, but they mean nothing because I never really measured in inches. Pounds, yes. "So if we look at the difference between the measurements—what you think your hips measure versus what they actually measure—we can see that you view yourself to be about forty pounds heavier than you actually are."

My head is throbbing and I can't focus. Ashley is finally undoing her yarn, draping it in different shapes: a circle first, then a triangle, and a lopsided little-kid star.

"So what's that like for you, to see the difference there?" Shrink asks.

"Sad?"

"Sad."

"No. I mean—" I shake my head a little; try to focus. I have to give her an answer, or she'll never move on. "Weird. Or unsettling or something. I feel like I have a good idea of what my body looks like. So the difference is just . . . weird."

It's enough. She moves on to Ashley. Bends over her, talks in hushed murmured tones. I try, but I can never see Ashley's face.

When we come back to the circle, Cate draws her knees to her chest and crosses her bird ankles and says quietly, "I hate this."

"Which part?" I ask.

"I know we're not supposed to say this . . ." Her eyes flit to Shrink, and then to me. "But I miss my old body."

"Before you were sick?" Jenna asks. Rain has moved on to legwork, the thready muscles in her thighs jerking beneath her yoga pants.

Cate pinches her tube. "No. Before I got here. When I was skinny."

Some of us nod. It's been sixteen days for me, and I don't need a mirror to know that the negative space between my thighs, between my belly and my waistband, along the hollows of my cheeks, is melting like precious ice.

"It's a grieving process," Shrink agrees. "When you make the decision for health, for recovery, you make the choice to let go of your eating disorder. Have any of you ever felt that that the eating disorder was almost a companion?"

I think back to the sitting at the dining room table, when we were still at the house on Broad. In bed, beneath the sheets, or standing in the kitchen in the dark, wincing at the sucking noise the refrigerator made when I opened it. The thoughts were always there with me. Warm and pulsing. Suffocating. There. My name. My companion.

"If you choose to let it go, then it could feel almost like a death. And it is absolutely okay to grieve that loss," Shrink says, mostly to Cate. "For each of you, letting go of your eating disorder would mean letting go of many things. Who you thought you could be with it, what you thought you could change, or fix."

Next to me, Ashley ejects a puff of air.

"I wonder what some of those things are for you. Maybe we could talk about that. What will you have to let go of as you make the choice for recovery? Teagan?"

"Approval or something?" Teagan's fingers skitter across her scalp. Then she sits on her hands.

"Could you say a little bit more about that?" Shrink asks.

"It's really messed up, though."

The room gets still, except for Rain, who is clenching and unclenching every muscle in her body. She looks too familiar. I look away.

"My stepdad. Or ex-stepdad. They aren't together anymore, Frank and my mom, so it's fine. But he liked my sister Liz better, from the start. Even when we were little and stuff, he would read us bedtime stories and she would curl up in his lap and I just sat next to them, which made sense because she was littler than me, and skinnier. And blond."

It's the most I've ever heard her say. I imagine her as a little girl, shoulders sloped beneath a dingy, too-tight T-shirt.

"It felt like . . . rejection?" Shrink says gently. Around the circle, we are all doing everything we can not to look at Teagan. We are picking at toenails and adjusting bra straps and blinking at the world outside the window, because to do anything else is just too much.

"And when we got older, it just got worse," Teagan says. "Like he would hug her, and he never hugged me. And he would laugh at her jokes and take her to the mall whenever she wanted. It was like I wasn't even there."

"You felt invisible." Shrink again. The air sours. I curl my toes tight in my sneakers. Next to me, Ashley's shoulders are shaking.

"It wasn't just him. Everybody paid more attention to her. She was pretty and skinny and bubbly. Everybody was always telling her she should be on TV and stuff. And even when I was purging a lot, nobody said that about me."

Shrink nodded. "But his attention bothered you most. Frank's."

"It's so stupid." Her voice is like smoke. "Even after Liz told my mom about him and we moved out, I kept thinking *why didn't he pick me? What's wrong with me?*

"Your stepdad's a piece of shit, by the way." The words slither out of me.

Shrink rises up a little. "Stevie—"

"It's okay." Teagan looks up at me with her face like a blank sheet. "He was. That's what makes it . . . confusing."

"Yes," Shrink says. Even she doesn't seem to know what to say.

"Can somebody else say something?" Teagan asks.

"The confusion is the thing that pisses me off the most." Jenna jumps in. "This thing screws with your head and you wind up going literally insane. Which sucks, but sometimes it's not any worse than your actual life, so—"

"My life was fine," Cate interrupts, and all the heads turn her way. "My parents are very nice people, and I don't know what to tell them, about why I'm like this. They think it's their fault." Her perfect face is pinched and red. "I'm almost *jealous*. Because at least if something really bad happened to you, you get to have a reason."

"My brother died," I snap. "Would you rather have a dead brother for a reason?"

Her face goes white, like I've slapped her.

"That's not what I meant," she whimpers.

Rain looks up from her exercises. Suddenly, there is something here that interests her.

"Stevie." Shrink jumps to Cate's rescue. "I need you to use your voice respectfully, please. I understand that you're angry."

"I just meant that I feel messed up, like, inside," Cate tries again. "Nothing happened to make me this way, so maybe I was born this way. And if that's true, then I don't really know if I'll ever get better." She draws her knees to her chest and balances her forehead there, too afraid to look at me.

"Whether or not you had a traumatic event before the onset of your eating disorder , you have all experienced real loss as a result of your illness." Shrink keeps her eyes on me.

"Fine," I say tightly. "Okay."

"Sometimes I think about all the time I've lost." Ashley clears her throat. "And I get mad at myself for wasting so much energy on food and purging and everything. Like, so much time."

"Me, too," says Jenna.

I nod, and think what we are all thinking and not saying. Yes, the illness took away. It clawed at family and time and the very beating of our hearts. But it gave, too. For me, it was the only way I could move through life blurry, without having to see things as they really were. It would have been too much that way, having to stare at my life head-on. It just would have been too much.

day seventeen

THERE'S a knock at my bedroom door.

"It's me." Cate pushes the door open and stands in the hall. "Can I come in?"

"Yeah."

She talks too fast. "I just wanted to say sorry. About group yesterday. I didn't mean to say anything about your brother. I just meant that sometimes it's hard to be sick when there's no reason." The words are prepackaged. She's been mouthing them to herself in different combinations.

"It's okay." I've been mouthing my own words. "I know that's not what you meant. I'm sorry, too."

"And I wanted to give you this." She takes another step and lifts up the corner of her T-shirt. Tucked between her jeans and her pale belly is a pink plastic razor. Disposable, the kind that comes in a zillion-pack.

"For real?" I lunge forward on the bed and swipe it as soon as she holds it out. I roll my jeans up. My leg is disgusting: the hair is dark and prickly, not long enough to be soft. "Where'd you get it?" I ask.

"There are a couple floating around," she says. "Just don't give it to anybody else, and don't get caught with it. And if you do get caught with it, don't rat me out."

"I won't." I roll my jeans down again. "Thanks, Cate. Really."

The outside door slams open, and her eyes go wide. I shove the razor under my pillow just as Ashley comes in.

"Hey," I say, too loudly. Cate rolls her eyes and flops onto my bed.

"Hey."

"How was your meeting?"

"They switched my meds because I can't, like, sleep with these." Ashley kicks off her Keds. "We'll see."

Cate and I exchange glances.

"I'm gonna take a quick shower, okay?" I say.

"Sure. Can I go ahead and turn off the light?"

"Yeah. No problem." I fumble around for my towel and pajamas, and at the last second, I slip the pink contraband in the nubby folds of my towel. I grin and speed walk all the way down the hall. I shut the bathroom door and strip quickly, without standing on tiptoe to get a glance of my belly in the mirror.

The water is hot, and my skin feels dry. I lather my legs with conditioner and drag the razor in careful, even lines. When I've finished a strip, I run my fingers over the smooth skin. The razor reminds me of the single summer I went to camp, in the mountains of North Carolina. I was ten. Josh was at computer camp somewhere and my mother had to work in London and so she sent me away. She had my dad pack my outfits, complete with underwear, in gallon ziplock bags. One for each day, labeled with permanent marker.

The popular girls (there were popular girls even in the mountains, which should not have surprised me) were always trading things in the dark after lights-out: gum, scented lip gloss, folded paper sculptures that predicted who you would marry and how many children you'd have. I waited, stared at the upper bunk above me. Nobody ever passed me anything. Until now.

The water runs cold too soon. I reach for my towel, dry off, and change quickly into my pajamas. The thin cotton of my yoga pants clings to my legs. They're smooth, and for the first time all day, I feel good. I wrap the razor in my jeans and head back to my room.

It's dark, and I hear muffled sobs.

"Are you okay?" I slap the wall, feeling for the light switch.

"Don't turn the light on." Her voice is broken, thick with tears. "Close the door?"

"Okay." It's pitch-black once the door clicks behind me, and wavy gray lines rise up in front of my eyes. "But I just—do you need anything? Do you want me to call one of the nurses or something? Are you sick?"

"No," she says quickly. "I just . . . my dad called tonight and he said they're definitely coming for my Ninety-Six. They'll be here tomorrow." She sniffs. "I don't want them to come, Stevie. I'm not ready—" The sobs drag her words under.

"Did you tell Kyle?"

"He can't do anything. They're—my—*parents.*" The bed shakes beneath her.

"Hold on." I drop to my knees and find the drawer. Cram my folded jeans and T-shirt and bra into it, and feel around until I find the pointy metal underwire. Then the pills. The sleeping pills are slick, with shiny plastic coatings. I take two, and slam the door shut.

"Here." I feel my way across the room, moving slowly, awkwardly. My big toe slams into the side of her bed. I swallow the pain. "Move over."

The bed creaks beneath her, and I sit on the edge. "Swallow these." I find her hot wet hand in the dark and press the pills into her palm. I hear her gulp them down. She says something—I'm not sure what—in shuddery gasps.

"I'm getting in," I say, and slide in next to her. "And you better not hog the covers." I pat the mattress until I find the bunny. I wedge it between us.

She laughs a little at the ceiling. Her body is still shaking. The pillow is wet, but I don't know if it's from my hair or her tears.

"Sorry," she says.

I roll onto my stomach and rest my hand on her, in the crook of her elbow. I wait for her to fall asleep. I can feel the throbbing of her pulse, steady beneath her skin. Her breathing evens out after a while.

"Yeah. Me, too," I say.

day eighteen

Monday, July 21, 5:45 A.M.

ASHLEY is still sleeping when I wake the next morning. I'm careful not to disturb her. I sit up so slowly that a minute, maybe two, goes by before I can see the red digits on the face of her clock. Time for weight and vitals, exactly. My body has slipped into the routine here without asking my permission.

"Ashley? Time for vitals and stuff, okay?" I slide out of bed and slip the toes of my right foot under my left pajama pant leg, just to check. The skin is still smooth. I smile in the dark.

"We can walk over together if you want."

She makes another mushy sound and buries her head beneath the pillow.

"Okay." I find my way to my side of the room and find my jeans bunched up in the drawer. I tuck the razor in the very back, between layers of sports bras. I dress in the dark, run my fingers through my hair, and rub the crusty sleep from my eyes. I think about waking Ashley again before I leave, but then I remember that her parents are coming today. They are moving this way like low yellow clouds before a storm: Her mother applying lipstick in the airplane bathroom. Her father checking his cell one last time before a mauve-lipped flight attendant with plastic hair asks him for the third time to *put it away, please. Sir.*

I let her sleep.

"Stevie? Can we check in briefly, please?" Shrink waves me down after breakfast. She's signing charts at the nurses' station.

"Oh. Yeah." I draw my belly button toward my spine, or try to. It's does nothing; my stomach is disobedient. Somewhere in me, the acidic, stringy pineapple is growing. The quarter of a cold, hard waffle sits unmoving. I try to focus on something else, anything else. *Distracting*, as Shrink would call it. I assess her clothing: loose jeans, white T-shirt. A fitted blush-colored blazer. She looks comfortable.

"Are we supposed to have a session?" I ask.

"Well, it's been an intense couple of days for you. Just want to see how you're doing. Want to take a walk?"

"On *red*?" I jangle my wrist in front of her nose.

She gives her head a little shake, but I think she's smiling.

Outside it's hotter than usual, the clay hard beneath my feet. I run two fingers over my mother's face. It's hot enough that I should be sweating. At home, I'd be sweating. We walk along the edge of the yard and I toe the line between the grass and decorative stone like it's a tightrope.

"So how are things going this morning?"

"I'm kind of worried about Ashley. Her Ninety-Six starts today."

"Worried that it's going to be a difficult time for her?"

"Yeah. But not just that. She's been all over the place lately. Up and down." I don't tell her about the crying last night. Too personal. "She won't sleep all night and she has a ton of energy, and then it looks like somebody sucked the air out of her."

"Ninety-Six can sometimes be tough. But it also has the potential to be incredibly rewarding. To make space for healing." A glossy non-answer, straight from the brochure. She should be riding a horse when she says that.

"But I don't think Kyle gets how upset she is."

"I hear that you're concerned about her, Stevie." When we get to the edge of the riding ring, she stops at the fence and rests her forearms in the space between the bars. The rusty paint is chipping, and I run my fingers over the irregular border. "I can assure you that Ashley's treatment team will continue to give her excellent care."

"Don't do that."

"Do what?"

"That. *Assure you*, and *excellent care*, and stuff. I'm just telling you she's upset. I'm telling you like a normal person."

"Okay." She looks at me in a real way. "I hear you, and I'm glad you let me know. But I want you to be able to focus on yourself, so I'm telling you that we will take care of her. But I do hear you."

Ashley's parents are scheduled to get to the villa after afternoon snack, during the second reflection time of the day. Ashley and I sit together on the patio, her back to the lawn so she can see them when they come through the doors. We're bouncing together like birds on a wire, our eyes furtively clicking from each other to the door each time it opens.

"Is this dress okay?" Ashley wipes her palms on a melon-colored T-shirt dress. She curled the hair around her face with a skinny silver wand this morning. She's wearing too much mascara, but I don't tell her that.

"Yeah. You look great." Around the lawn, it seems like everyone is on alert: sitting a little more upright, a little more tense. Some of the girls roll their jean shorts down to an acceptable length. Some roll their shorts even higher. It's quieter than usual out here.

"It's always like this when a new set of parents come." Ashley wriggles her painted toes. "Isn't that weird? It's like, it's my parents, but everybody gets nervous or something."

"Yeah. Weird." Somehow I'm nervous too: my stomach keeps flopping around in my gut like a dying fish on land. *It's not my mother walking through those doors. It's not her.*

Ashley's parents are only partly what I expected. When they come through the doors, the mother is wringing her hands, which I didn't think anybody did anymore. She's older than I pictured, wearing mom jeans and a perfect white shirt and a black blazer. Gold drips from her wrists and knuckles and ears. She could be pretty beneath all the makeup. The father is what I imagined: tall, good-looking, wearing a golf shirt that's meant to look casual and unbearably expensive at the same time. He smells like woody cologne and tobacco.

They're not so bad, I think first. And then I remember what they've done.

"Hey, Mama. Hey, Daddy." Ashley stands up and her face freezes in this kind of panicked grin. I reach for her hand and squeeze it. It is sweaty and limp.

"Hey there, Ash." The mother's voice breaks a little. She doesn't move, except for the hand-wringing.

The father clears his throat and looks at me.

"Oh. I'm Stevie," I say. "Ashley's friend."

"Pleased to meet you, honey," says the mother.

The father nods.

"Stevie and I are roommates, too," Ashley chirps. "She's from Atlanta."

"Outside of," I say.

"That's lovely," says the mother. She stretches her neck and looks around the grounds. The other girls are trying to pretend they're not watching. But everyone is staring at the strange animals roaming the grounds—and we all know what parents are capable of.

"Well, this is just . . . lovely," the mother says again. "The grounds are beautiful, Ash. You didn't say how beautiful it was here."

"Should be, given what we're paying," grunts the father.

Ashley tenses.

"How was Spain?" she asks. I've never seen her so careful.

"Well, we left early, you know," says the mother. "To come here."

"Right," says Ashley. "Sorry."

The four of us stand there. The father checks his cell phone and doesn't try to hide it.

"I should probably go journal or something," I say.

"No, that's okay!" Ashley says. So I stay and watch them watch each other. They look like confused strangers standing in a lopsided triangle, like the one Ashley made out of yarn. It makes me wonder what makes anybody family. I think that maybe for some people, family is just the people you're standing next to when awful things happen.

day nineteen

Tuesday, July 22, 9:45 P.M.

WHEN I get back to Cottage Three after evening snack, there is a thin ray of light fanned out beneath my door. I frown at it. Ashley should be out, with her parents.

"Hello?" Carefully, I nudge the door open. Inside, Ashley is pacing. Lapping the room with the bunny bunched awkwardly in her fist.

"Hey! What are you doing here?" I stay close to the door.

She doesn't stop. Just marches to the closet and back. She's wearing jeans and a T-shirt and a tailored blazer. I don't recognize any of it. "I couldn't, you know? It was just, like, too much. I didn't want to stay with them again tonight."

"Your parents?" *Duh.*

She sniffs and looks up, and my breath stalls at the back of my

256

throat. Her face is so made up, it's almost grotesque. Caked on foundation and circular pink cheeks. Slashes of bronzer across her cheeks, as if she'd been slapped. Twice, and precisely. Her curls are exact. Crisp. The part that makes me want to cry and scream all at once are her eyes. Lined with black waxy liner, the lids filled with a bruised purple. Lashes so thick, her eyes are at half-mast. The color creeps down her cheeks, like she's melting.

"Oh my god." It's a whisper.

"My mom, like, wanted to take me for a makeover or whatever. She thought it would be a fun girls' thing or something, and my Dad wanted to watch the game back at the hotel, so . . ." She starts pacing again, silent tears burrowing through the layers of color.

My hand shoots out, but I retract it, knowing I can't stop her.

"Come home with me," I blurt out. "After this. You don't have to go back there, Ashley. You don't."

She lets out a sound like she's laughing or dying. I can't tell which. "Right. You really want me coming home with you."

"I *do*," I say forcefully. "My dad's a nice guy, okay?"

That makes her cry harder.

"Don't," I say, and hate myself instantly. "I mean . . ."

There's a soft knock at the door.

"Get out!" Ashley's scream is strangled.

"Do you want me . . . Should I call someone?" Cate's voice is small on the other side of the door.

Ashley's eyes go wide, so I say, "It's okay! She'll be okay."

"Uh . . . okay?" I hear nothing, then the quiet click of the door down the hall.

"Ashley. Come here. Let's get you cleaned up, okay?"

"I'm okay. I'm okay," she says. "Sorry. I'm okay." She wipes her nose with the back of her hand, smearing snot across one cheek.

"No. I know," I say gently. "Can I . . ." I reach out to touch her, but she stiffens. "Just . . . hold on a second, okay?" Kneeling next to my bed, I take my last fresh towel from the drawer. "Come on."

She nods furiously and follows me down the hall to the bathroom. I guide her to the toilet and nudge her to the seat then rummage through my shower caddy on the sink and find everything I need.

"You'll feel better," I promise her, which sounds like a lie even to me. I twist the sink faucet all the way to hot and dip the bunched up corner of the towel beneath the spray. Then I squirt some of my face wash on the edge, and rub the fabric together. "Here." I lean over her, pushing her hair back, and wipe her face in slow, small circles. The colors swirl like watercolor.

"Thanks," she says. She keeps crying.

I rinse the towel and start again, with a fresh corner.

"It wasn't . . . my parents." Her breath is shallow. "If that's what you think."

"Huh?"

"It wasn't my parents who did . . . that to me. The stuff on my back? It was my brother."

"What?" I crouch in front of her. Try to meet her gaze with mine, but her eyes are everywhere, and they won't settle. "What are you—you don't have a brother."

"Yeah, I do. I just never talk about him because it gets me too upset. He's four years older and he's always been kind of . . . messed up. My parents sent him to psychiatrists and stuff, but he wouldn't take his meds."

I have to force myself to breathe.

"When we were little, he would hit me, and at first I thought that was a normal brother-sister kind of thing because my friends said their brothers hit them, too. But I don't think it was the same. And then when he got older and my parents would leave us alone to go out, he would wait until he thought I was asleep." Her face crinkles up, but there are no more tears.

I don't know what to say. I have no idea what to say because when you have a brother like the brother I have—fuck, *had*—the words she's saying just don't make sense. You can't imagine, you can't possibly understand, and you know it. So you keep your mouth shut.

"And it's like, I would hear the match and smell the smoke and I wanted to scream."

I press the cloth to her cheek, catching tears.

"But I couldn't, you know, because I think he wanted that? I think he wanted me to scream."

I think I might be sick. "Did your parents know?"

She shakes her head, then nods. "Not for a while, I don't think. My mom walked in on me in the bathroom once, when I was like ten. And she just stared like I was some sort of freak and then she said, *you should put on lotion. I'll get you some lotion*, and then she walked out. And after that my brother was out of the house, but we never talked about it."

"Have you seen him since?" I want to kill him. For real.

"No," she squeaks. "But on this trip my parents keep, like, bringing him up. They're like, *so Rick's doing really well with his medication* and I'm like, *fuck Rick and his fucking medication, and fuck you for ever talking to him again*."

"Yeah. Yes. Fuck them."

She makes a swallowing sound and then jumps up quick, pushing me back. Then she bends over the sink. The tiny bathroom fills with the sour smell.

"It's okay," I say quickly. "It's okay. You go back to bed, and I'll clean up."

"Noooo," she wails into the sink.

I find her shower caddy—purple with sparkles—and rummage through it. "Where's your toothbrush?"

"At the hotel."

"Okay. Just put some toothpaste on your finger, then." They don't allow mouthwash here, either. The alcoholics get desperate.

She obeys begrudgingly, like a small child at bedtime. I rinse out the sink, wipe it clean with my bath towel, and stuff the towel in the trash can. I guide her down the hall and into bed.

"Want a pill? I'll get you a pill."

She doesn't argue, so I bring her a sleeping pill, and one for myself. She sticks out her tongue and I place the capsule on its bumpy red tip. She tilts back her head and swallows. I do the same.

I start to go back to my own bed, but she makes a whimpering sound, so I crawl in next to her with the lights still on.

"My brother hurt me," she says.

"I know. I think you're really brave," I say. "For telling the truth."

"Tell me about your brother," she says.

My eyes well up. I clench my fists around the covers.

"Please? I think it would help," she whispers.

"His name was Joshua. He was really, just . . . good. It's hard to explain. He died almost a year ago. In a car accident. I was in the car, too. I've always felt responsible."

I can't say any more than that, and she doesn't ask. We lie there, one next to the other, pinned to the sheets by grief.

day twenty

ASHLEY bucks in her sleep, restless and sleep talking into her pillow. After a while I leave her bed and find mine. My brain buzzes, heavy and veiled as the pill starts to creep in.

I dream about the accident, only Josh isn't there. I'm in the passenger seat, staring through the glass.

"You're just like Mom, you know that?" When I look over, it's Ashley sitting in the driver's seat. Her face is puffy, painted purple and bronze and pink. War paint.

"What are you *talking* about? Fuck you."

"Please. Like you don't know." She makes a wide right turn, swerving onto a deserted one-way street. "You think she just left, moved to Paris for no reason? Are you seriously that naïve?" Another turn, barreling onto the two-lane road that stretched

262

through the dark like a thread, stringing nameless towns together. The Buick's headlights like two white pearls, rolling fast.

"I don't know why she left!" I screamed at the windshield, clawing at the ugly cloth seats like an animal. "Nobody tells me anything!"

And then we're in the pool together, at night, our faces bobbing close. Under the water, my scar burns.

"My brother hurt me," she whispers. Her words skip across the water like weightless pebbles.

"I know." I glance up at the edge of the pool and Eden's there, crouched over the surface like a bird hunting prey. She laughs and dips one toe into the water.

"Haven't you ever wanted to be something . . . extraordinary?" she asks.

The Buick weaves in a seamless dance with the yellow line.

"You're the same, Stevie. You're just like Mom. A heartless slut." Ashley sobs.

"Shut up, Josh. Shut the fuck up."

The Buick weaves.

I scream. The whoosh of the car, airborne, a cheap aluminum toy.

Weird, I think.

And then the screaming begins.

I bolt upright in bed, shivering and sweat-soaked. My throat is dry. I lick my lips and press them together until I taste blood and it takes a few seconds to realize that the screams haven't stopped, that they aren't mine. My hand hits something soft. The one-eared bunny. I don't remember stealing it. Not tonight.

"Ashley?" I croak. The clock says five something.

I trip out of bed and paw at the wall until the light comes on. Ashley's bed is empty. My head is stuffed and thick and it's hard to *think* so I stumble into the hall calling "whaaa" and following the screams. I pass Teagan on the hall phone, bellowing *please* again and again. She looks straight at me without seeing.

At the end of the hall, the bathroom door is open. Steam leaks out, smelling like puke and metal. Cate is crouched in the shower, the water still running, plastered slick to her skull. Cate is soaking wet, holding Ashley's head in her lap. Rocking her. Cate is screaming something, but I can't make it out. Her tube and nightshirt and ratty pink pajama pants are soaked in blood.

Jesus, there is so much blood. It runs like water.

The floor sways, and I bend at the waist, resting my hands on my knees. I taste bile.

"What did you *do?*" Cate screams. "What did you *do?*"

"What? What happened?" I should move. But I just stand there, holding the bunny while the smell of blood balloons up, pink steam rising.

Cate looks up at me, her face frozen, accusing. "Did you give her the razor? Did you—" The rest of the scream bleeds out of her, unrelenting.

And then I know: She's talking to me, not Ashley. She's talking to me.

The bathroom door slams against the wall. A team of nurses barges in, shoving me out of the way.

"Back to your rooms, girls." A male nurse drags Cate from the shower. "Come on, honey. Let's go."

"No! Don't you touch me!" Cate's is the horror screech of a

dying beast. It takes two nurses to hold her, one at her wrists and one at her ankles, and another to drag Ashley onto the pink tile floor that used to be white.

"Back to your room." A nurse I've never seen before ushers me down the hall.

The hall phone is dead, hanging by its cord, nearly grazing the floor. The nurse guides me into my room. Outside the window, red lights are circling and the grounds are crawling.

"I'll send someone to sit with you, but you absolutely must stay in your room until you hear otherwise. Do you understand?" the nurse asks.

I think I nod yes, because she closes the door behind me. Somehow I drop to my knees. The drawer beneath my bed is ajar, and I know without looking, but I look anyway, once, twice, again and again, raking through everything, but I know I won't find it. The razor is gone.

The shrinks—all of them—arrive quickly, sweeping patients into deflated huddles in various places on the grounds: the villa, the houses, any of the cottages but Cottage Three. Shrink herds Cate and Teagan and me to the treatment team house. In the kitchen, breakfast is waiting on taupe-colored trays, along with two cups of supplement. No one looks at the food. Not even Shrink.

We sit on the very edge of the metal folding chairs, curled into ourselves in jeans and dirty T-shirts. I stuffed the pills from my drawer in my jeans pockets, and pulled on Josh's sweater over my tank top. After this, I know they'll scour the room for contraband. I'm thinking only of myself while Ashley's lying on some chrome table, water still dripping from her lifeless corkscrew curls. That's the kind of evil I am.

"I know that there is nothing I can say to make this any less traumatic for you all—for us all—right now." Shrink's voice is so low, I can hardly hear her. Her voice sounds bubbly, like she's been crying.

I told you I was worried! I want to yell, but she didn't do this. I was the one with the razor.

"In times like this, it's incredibly important to stay grounded in the present moment." No one's listening, not even Shrink herself.

"Is she dead?" Teagan's watery voice rises.

"As soon as I have more information, I'll let you all know."

I slip my hands under Josh's sweatshirt, feel the reassuring ridges of the pills in my pockets. I don't look at her. I don't look at anyone. I couldn't stand it, seeing Cate's wet, red-eyed hatred or Teagan's vacant stare. The three of us know: I killed her.

"Would you all take a deep, slow breath for me? In through your nose, and out through your mouth?" Shrink breathes a cartoon breath, but no one follows. It seems cruel, breathing that deep and big when Ashley can't.

I should feel something, I think. I rattle through Shrink's list of emotions: anger, sadness, shame. But they are nothing more than words.

Shrink's phone rings, and everyone jumps.

"I should . . ." she says, as if any of us would stop her. She pulls her cell phone from her pocket and checks the screen. "I'll be right back, girls."

We sit in silence, Teagan sucking gobs of snot down her throat every few seconds. I say nothing, not a thing, because I deserve this quiet hell for as long as it lasts. I wait for the blame.

"I'm sorry," Cate whispers.

My head snaps up. "What are you talking about?"

"I should never have given you the razor. I should have thrown it out. I'm sorry. I'm sorry. Oh my god." Her face shrivels.

"Who gave it to you?" Teagan asks her.

Cate shakes her head. "Doesn't matter."

"I didn't know . . . I never showed it to her," I say desperately. "I swear, okay?"

The other girls' heads dip.

"I hid it in my underwear drawer, wrapped up tight. I don't know how she—"

"Okay, Stevie. We get it. It's not your fault." Cate's voice is glinting.

"It's not anybody's fault." Teagan strokes the bald spot above her ear, rubs it almost forcefully, as if she's trying to rub the memory from consciousness.

"I know," Cate squeaks, shrill like metal on metal.

I shake my head. It's making me feel worse, what they're doing. I hate that they're carving up the blame, each girl taking a bloody, pulsing piece for herself. It belongs to me, all of it.

Shrink returns, and clears her throat behind me. She rests her hand on my shoulder, and I whimper. "I just spoke with one of Ashley's doctors. She's alive. They're . . . optimistic."

My shoulders sag. "What does that mean, *optimistic*?"

"It means that she will live, most likely."

Cate starts to sob, burying her face in Teagan's shoulder. I stay stoic, unmoving. I should have known better. I thought I had changed, but I am still the girl who brings destruction wherever she goes. I am the girl who disappeared my mother and my brother and very nearly the only real friend I have ever had.

"Stevie?" Shrink's voice, too kind. "Can I see you in the other room?"

"No. No. Just . . . I want to see her." I slide my hands beneath Josh's sweatshirt again, for reassurance. The pills are still there. My heart slows every time I touch them. "Can we go to the hospital?"

"Not today. I'm sorry." She squeezes my shoulder.

"Then could I have my supplement, please?" I say without looking at her.

"Of course." She disappears, then returns with the plastic cup of chalky chocolate milk.

"Thank you."

"Stevie." Shrink crouches down next to me. "Tell me what's going on for you."

I could sit here, say nothing, but that won't do the trick. I have to play the game. Have to hold up the shiny black-and-white die for all to see before I cast it.

"I'm just really . . . shocked. Like, fidgety or something. I think I need to take a walk."

"We can't leave the house right now, Stevie. Later, perhaps."

"Anna. *Please.*" I turn in my chair and find her eyes. My desperation isn't contrived. I *am* desperate. I have to go, now. If I don't go now, if I don't do it now, I never will.

She searches my face.

"Just for a few minutes, and I'll come back. I'll go crazy in here if I have to stay. *Please*."

Her pink mouth opens, and she closes it quickly.

"We can go with her, if you want," Cate mumbles.

"No. I want to be alone." I take an agonizing sip of supplement.

Shrink glances at the doorway, then back to me.

"You may walk to the riding ring and back. No detours. Got it?"

I nod. "Thanks. Thank you, Anna." I feel like I should hug her or squeeze her hand or something, because the truth is she has done a good job and she deserves the recognition. She might even have saved me, if I weren't so far gone by the time I got here.

"If you're not back in ten minutes, I send Hannah on a golf cart." It's supposed to be a joke, but even she doesn't smile.

"Deal," I say.

Outside it feels the same as any other day. But it's not any other day. I hold the supplement cup in one hand, and count the pills through my jeans pocket with the other. I don't know if they will be enough, but they are my only chance.

I walk quickly toward the horses. This is all wrong, every bit of it. It's supposed to be the Anniversary, not eight days before, and I'm supposed to have more time and I'm supposed to be sure that what I have is enough. For the past three hundred and fifty-seven days, I've pictured what it could be like: me, lying still between white sheets, a collection of bleached, hollow bones arranged in perfect formation. I would stare, wide-eyed at the ceiling and everything around me would stop: the noisy chatter in my brain, the merciless pounding of my heart. My last breath would be slow. My body would shut down dutifully, one organ after another after another until it all went dark, like fluorescent lights in a vacant room. I wouldn't need pills. I could do it myself.

When I get to the ring, I scoop a handful of pills from one pocket and examine them. *I deserve* this, I tell myself. *Do it*. I picture Ashley in the shower, water running, blood flowing from the stripes on her arm.

Do it.

Mechanically, I toss my head back and pop the first handful into my mouth, chalk and plastic melting fast on my tongue. But they taste wrong in my mouth, and I realize: I don't want this. I don't.

After a few seconds I spit them out, all of them, a syrupy pink-red wad. I kick dirt over them. For the first time all morning, I feel something real: humiliation. One simple task, one crucial, simple task. And I can't do it.

"Stevie. Stevie." The squeak of sneakers on dirt, and then Shrink's hand is on my back. "What are you doing?"

"Nothing. What are you doing here?" I kick more dirt.

"I shouldn't have let you go," she admits. "I wasn't thinking. And then I got worried, so . . ." She looks me up and down, searching. "Everything okay?"

"No." I shake my head. "I'm tired. I don't think I can do this anymore," I say, not entirely sure what *this* is.

She cups my face in her hands. I can feel her fingers, strangely cold, pressed against the side of my neck. My pulse throbs. She hugs me and I just stand there, pressed into her, stiff and embarrassed.

"I know you're tired," she says. "I know."

day twenty-three

"LET me go," I beg Shrink, without knocking on her office door. "Please." I stand in the threshold of her office, hands clasped, begging. I'm wearing a pair of god-awful ugly jeans that Shrink made me take from a closet in her office since I can't fit in mine anymore. A kind of skinny-jean cemetery, where girls are supposed to leave their thin clothes to wither and die, until another girl can use them. I wonder about the girl who wore these before, and the girl before her. I wonder if they are alive. If they're happy. If they think about food and numbers or remember the name of their horse.

Three days have passed since Ashley tried to die. For three days, I've been asking Shrink to take me to her. I'm close: I can feel it in the heavy pauses, in the pursing of her lips. She wants to give in.

Today, she stops writing and looks up from the chart in her lap and says: "I'm working on it, Stevie. It isn't as simple as all that, okay?"

I slump in the doorway. "Come on. You could do it if you wanted to."

She motions me inside, and I take a few steps and collapse onto the love seat. I hold one of the pillows in my lap. Pick at the metallic beads until we both hear one ping against the tile.

"Oops," I say. "Sorry."

She flips the chart over so I can't see the name and slides it onto the chessboard side table. "I've put in a request for us to see Ashley during visiting hours this morning. I'm waiting to hear back from our clinical director."

I bob my head. "That's good, right?"

"Ultimately, she'll be the one to make the final decision. I've pled your case because I'd like for you to be able to see your roommate, but I have to tell you, Stevie, the fact that you tried to run away less than a week ago . . ."

"I know." I cut her off, irritated. God, I hate these ugly jeans.

"If she says no, it's no."

I nod my understanding.

She reaches for the closest paper crane, then decides against it and clasps her hands in her lap. "How is everything in Cottage Six?"

"Well, nobody's tried to kill themselves yet, so . . ." Instantly I wish I could slurp the words from the air, swallow them like they never happened, but it doesn't work that way. "Sorry," I mumble.

She nods, a quick, gracious *let's move on*. "I've been . . . concerned about you, Stevie, I have to say."

"What do you mean?"

"I just mean that I was starting to feel like you were on the verge of a major shift, thinking about committing to your treatment plan." She looks at me, questioningly.

"What do you want me to say?" I pinch the flimsy red bracelet.

"Am I correct on that, or did I misread you?"

I shrug. "I don't know. I guess I was starting to feel . . . different or something."

"I saw you moving," she says. "Contributing in group, accessing your emotion, processing in our sessions together. And all of these things are incredibly significant."

"Okay." I'm uncomfortable, and not just in these ridiculous jeans. How am I *supposed* to feel when she says these things? Ashamed that it's taken so little time for me to abandon the goals I've had for nearly a year?

She wants me to feel proud, I can tell, but that's not right. If anything, I'm more confused. I could still kill myself on the Anniversary, only five days away. But what I said to Shrink was real: I'm tired. I'm too tired. I don't want to do this anymore, the planning, the readying myself for death. It's exhausting, fighting my body this way. I want to lie down. Pull the covers up.

"I wonder about the impact of Ashley's attempt. I wonder where that's left you. How you're feeling about treatment."

I think about it for a while, but then my head starts to throb, so I say, "Mixed."

"Mixed."

"The Anniversary's coming up, you know. Of Josh's . . . the accident. It's Thursday."

"Yes. I do know."

274

I slide down the love seat a little and prop the pillow on the arm of the love seat. Try to rest my head there, but it's an awkward angle and it doesn't feel right. But it was my choice to sit there, so I stay there for a while before I sit up again. "I keep thinking, like, it's going to be this big event. Like it should be, you know?"

"What do you mean, event?"

"Like something big should happen on that day."

"Something . . . like what?"

"I don't know."

She shifts in her chair. "Well, it's an incredibly significant day. And you can make it what you need it to be. But what if that day feels, in some ways, like—"

"Any other day?" I finish. I don't want to hear her say the words. "That's what I'm scared of."

"What would that mean, if Thursday felt like . . . a Thursday?"

"It would be fucked up." I rest my hand on my throat. I can feel my pulse. "It would feel like I didn't care or something. Like I wasn't sorry. But I do care and I am sorry. I just don't know—"

"It won't feel like any other day, Stevie. I can promise you that." She takes a long, slow breath. "I don't know what it will feel like. You'll know when you get there. But it won't feel like any other day."

It's bizarre, thinking about the day as anything other than the day of my death.

On the desk behind her, the phone rings. She lifts her eyebrows at me and I think she says *fingers crossed* on her way to answer.

"Anna Fredricks," she says into the phone.

Oh, I think. *Fredricks.*

"Thanks, Linda. Appreciate it. I'll check in when we get back."

I'm grinning by the time she turns around.

We sit side by side in the middle seat of a white minivan, behind a male driver who barely grunts when Shrink tells him our destination. I tuck the one-eared bunny under my seat belt. I think maybe this van is the same one Cotton Candy drove, but I can't be sure from the backseat. I wonder about the lady who drove me here on the first day. I would ask about her, but I don't know her name.

Shrink talks for a while as the van pulls onto the road. She tells me Ashley will be weak, that it will be difficult to see her, that our time together will be short. She asks what I think it will be like.

"I don't know." It's still and hot in the van, and the vents in the ceiling are blowing lukewarm air.

"How are you feeling about seeing her?"

I consider that. "Mixed," I say again, staring out the window. "Like relieved but also . . . upset."

"Upset angry? Upset . . ."

"Upset fucking pissed," I tell the window. My cheeks look puffy in the glass. I look past my reflection. Outside, the desert looks the same as it did on the first day. Like somebody pressed Pause and the whole world's been waiting for me to get my shit together. "I mean, I know it's not about me, but still." *It is about me. It's about me and what I did and if I had just told Cate no, thank you, no razor for me, none of this would have happened.*

"Pissed," she says. "That's . . . yes. I can understand that. Betrayed?"

"It's not her fault," I say. "Did you know she has a brother?"

"I didn't."

"Yeah. But not a brother like Josh."

"Hm," she says.

"It would have been better for her to have a woman therapist, I think. Like you, maybe."

She smiles. "I've been really proud of you, Stevie," she says in a way that tells me she means it. "I think you're starting to work, and the relationship you've developed with Ashley is . . . admirable."

Don't say nice things, I beg her silently. *I'm not ready for that yet.*

"I want to let you know something, Stevie. Moving back into the outside world after spending any amount of time in a treatment center can be difficult. Overwhelming in some ways. I want to make sure that you know I'm right here. And if the hospital starts to feel like too much—"

"It was mine." I widen my eyes at my reflection.

"What was yours?"

"The razor." I swallow the excuses: *It wasn't mine to begin with; I was only using it to shave my legs; I never told her about it, I don't know how she . . .* Noise. Irrelevant. I hold my breath, half expecting her to morph into an angry mom—*I will turn this van around, young lady, so help me*—but she doesn't.

"I appreciate your telling me, Stevie."

Shit. She's disappointed. Angry would have been so much easier.

"I'm sorry. I'm really sorry, obviously."

"You realize that we will have to address this when we get back to the center."

"Yeah. Okay."

"It will mean suspension of several privileges, and you'll likely have to meet with our clinical team."

"I'll do whatever." My voice is small. I don't tell her about the pills I buried next to the riding ring. Maybe she already knows. I flushed the rest down Cottage Six's toilet. I watched them circle around and around. I watched them disappear. I didn't feel some sweeping, magnificent sense of relief. But I could breathe just a little easier, and that was enough.

The first thing I notice about the hospital is that it's the loudest place I have ever been in my life. Shrink and I walk quickly down the hall, toward room 346. I repeat the number again and again—*346, 346, 346*—to have something to focus on. It's too much, all of it: the whiter-than-white halls and the lights overhead and all the noise—my *god*, doesn't anybody else hear that? The blare of the loudspeaker coming from nowhere: *Paging Doctor Kildair, Doctor Kildair to the* . . . The screech of the broken wheel on a gurney, someone's laugh, untethered and bouncing through the halls. I ball my fists at my side.

"Doing okay?" Shrink slides a glance at me.

"Yeah." I stare straight ahead. My body is vibrating with all the noise. Seriously, doesn't anybody hear that?

"It will take a while to get used to," she says. "Just breathe. It's a lot, I know."

When we get to the end of the hall, she holds up one finger and leans over the counter at the nurses' station. She shows a woman her ID and says something in a voice so low, I can't hear.

Then she's next to me again. She squeezes my shoulder and nods at the door.

"Can I go in by myself?" I ask, knowing the answer is no. Grateful for it, even.

She shakes her head.

"Okay." I grip the handle and pump it slowly. The door is heavier than I imagined. Inside, Ashley is propped up in bed. Her blond curls are matted to the side of her head, clear tubes snake around her, and her hospital gown looks almost exactly like the one we put on every morning for weight and vitals. The side of her face is bruised. Finally, I look at her arm. It's bandaged with pure white. The other is fine, unsuspecting. As if nothing bad ever happened to its mirror image.

"Hey," she murmurs. "You came. Hi, Anna."

"Hi, Ashley."

I stay by the door. The room is tiny, with a window into the hall but no real windows that let in light. In the corner next to a beeping machine are three balloons. One of them says Get Well Soon, which seems like the most awful thing, but I guess they don't make suicide balloons. There are also a couple greeting cards with sweeping cursive and pastel backgrounds propped open on the table next to her.

"Where are your parents?" I demand.

"They went out, to get something to eat. They've been here, though. Like, most of the time." I think she tries to smile. Her lips are chapped. She's pale. I wonder if her skin feels clammy. I wonder if this is what I would look like, if I actually tried to go through with it. The thought makes my stomach turn. Maybe this wasn't such a good idea.

"Can you, like, come a little closer? It feels weird, you all the way over there," Ashley says.

"Okay." I take a few small steps until I'm standing at her feet. Shrink sits in the chair by the door. I hear her bag hit the floor.

"I'm sorry," I say. I force myself to look at her.

"Yeah. Me too," she says. She moves her legs a little and pats the edge of the bed. I sit.

"Did you mean it?" I ask.

She glances over my shoulder at Shrink, then back at me. She nods. "Yeah, and then no. I did at first, like I really thought maybe it would be better than going home because I hate the idea of going home. I *hate* it. And then things started to get fuzzy and I got really panicky, but I couldn't move. And then I just felt really warm and that's the last thing I remember."

"Oh." I lower my voice. "How did you find the, um—"

"Girls," Shrink says gently.

"Sorry." I give a forced, twisted smile, and she smiles back. "Cate found you," I tell her.

"*Stevie.*"

"I know," I say, without turning around. "Sorry." I wasn't going to tell her the rest. She doesn't need to know the rest.

"You're lucky, you know," she says quietly.

I frown at her.

"Having a dad who made you come to treatment. It means he wants you to get better. It means you're worth getting better." Her eyes get red and glassy. "You have somebody to go home to. Some *worth* going home to."

I look at my lap. "Well, I'm glad you're okay."

"Me, too, I think."

"I brought you this." I wiggle the bunny around, make it dance in the air.

"Cool." She smiles with cracked lips. "Thanks."

I tuck it in next to her.

"I'm going to be here for a while," she says. "Probably."

"Probably."

"Do you think I could still come visit, after?" she asks.

"For sure. After." Then I hold my breath and pat her arm, above the bandage. It's warm and pulsing. Alive. Nothing like what I expected.

day twenty-eight: the anniversary

Thursday, July 31 , 7:45 A.M.

"ARE you ready?" Shrink asks.

Just like that. We're sitting on the lawn, on her ratty picnic blanket at the very edge of the green and the sky is so blue it could be the ocean, vast, with just a few white caps. Breakfast and supplement sit on a tray in front of me. Quesadillas, which means past-their-prime bananas mixed with generic-brand peanut butter and brown sugar, slathered on wheat tortillas and grilled. I'm full, up to the very back of my throat, even though I haven't taken a bite.

I press my lips together. I shrug.

"I want to empower you to use your voice to express whatever you need to express to him today." She sits cross-legged, in loose black pants. "First off, where do you feel it in your body?"

"Feel what?"

"Your words. Your story."

My hand flies to my throat. She nods.

"Your throat chakra. The home of honest expression. Speaking your truth."

"Jesus, Anna. Today?"

"Today is the perfect day to speak your truth, Stevie."

I don't want to speak my truth. It will hurt too much. I thought about calling Dad this morning but didn't, for that very reason.

"I'm going to challenge you to speak without judgment," she tells me.

I take a breath, a free breath, but it feels like I'm breathing through a straw.

"Okay. I hate that this is a day," I begin.

"Tell him."

"Josh." I stare at the empty space next to her. I'm supposed to imagine that Josh is there, to see him in his faded jeans and T-shirt, his messy towel-dried hair and his freakishly long middle toe. I want to see him, I do. *Please, Josh*, I plead silently. *Just today. I'll never ask again.*

"Josh," I say again. "I hate that this is a day. I hate that there is any reason to remember this day, and the truth is that almost all of the time I feel like it's my fault, that this will be a day every year, forever."

"Good, Stevie."

"You probably know I was going to kill myself today." I can feel Shrink's eyes on me. "Of course you know." I touch the blanket.

"And I've thought a lot about it and I'm just wondering, if it would be okay if I didn't. If I didn't do that. Today."

I wait for an answer. The air is hot and thick, sagging with anticipation.

"I mean, I know you wouldn't actually want me to die. That's not what I'm saying. I guess I'm just telling you that I don't have anything for you today. To, like, honor you. Or whatever. I don't know what that would be."

"I wonder if it would be possible," Shrink says carefully, "to honor him with your life. Instead of your death."

"The truly shitty part of all this is that if I don't die today, then I have to deal with this . . ." I rub the back of my neck. "This."

"What's this?" she asks. "Tell it to Josh."

"I'm sick, Josh. And it really sucks to be sick without you here." I laugh, more of a choking sound. "Oh, fuck. I'm really sick."

"Okay." Shrink stops me. "What does it feel like to say that out loud?"

I shake my head. Jump when the tears hit my collarbone. "I don't know how to get unsick, you know? It's been a really long time."

"I know. And it will take time to get healthy." Legs still crisscrossed, she scoots closer to me. She stops once our knees are touching. Rests her forearms on her thighs. "I believe, Stevie, that human beings . . . we're oriented toward health."

"Meaning . . ."

"Meaning, your body wants to heal. Your mind wants to heal. If you can get to a place where you let your mind and body do what they want to do, you will start to move toward health."

"Yeah." I sniff and stare over her shoulder. "Can I ask you a question?"

"Of course."

"What's the deal with the paper cranes?"

"There's not a deal, really. I like the process. I like making something with my hands. And the cranes themselves are meant to symbolize peace. Some believe that they symbolize recovery. I like that idea."

"Oh."

"If you'd like, I can teach you."

I nod. "That would be . . . Thanks." If I let my eyelids drop just a little, the desert gets hazy. I try to conjure up an image of Josh. Not even Josh as a teenager. I'll take Josh as a little kid, at the lake. With the Mickey Mouse towel and the paperback. I'll take any version. I'm desperate that way.

"I also want to tell him I'm sorry. Not just for the accident and for not saving him. But for Eden, too."

"Tell him." She reaches out, and squeezes my arm.

"She sucked me in, Josh. It's not an excuse, I know. But I think you get it."

"She manipulated you both."

"Yes."

I steady my breath to tell him the most important thing. "I love you, Josh. I never loved her. Not . . . I love you in a real way." My head is thick with tears and all the waiting for the Anniversary. This day that can't be erased or unremembered.

"So what has the day been like for you so far?" Shrink asks.

"Different." I pluck two blades and twist them together.

"Different how?"

"Different like I thought I'd be dead, for one." I keep talking fast so she won't have room. The last thing I need today is to end up in that tiny room in the villa. "And different like I just pictured myself crying a lot and getting really mad and stuff."

"Maybe those things will come. Grief is like that. Cold and fast and insanely unpredictable. But right now, it sounds like you're in a place of acceptance."

"Acceptance . . ."

"Acceptance of the fact that your brother is dead. Acceptance of your eating disorder, of needing to be in this place for a little while. Acceptance doesn't mean you like something, doesn't mean you're comfortable with it. But it does mean that you acknowledge it for what it is."

"I guess."

"And today marks the one-year anniversary of the night your brother died."

"It does." I'm exhausted suddenly, like I could flop back into the grass and let it swallow me up. Sleep for days.

Shrink checks her watch. Noticeably, which has to be some sort of rookie mistake. "Listen, Stevie. I have a little something for you. Something to acknowledge the day. I'd like to give it to you, if you don't mind."

"Huh? Okay." I push myself to standing and brush the dried bits of grass from another girl's jeans. Then I pick up my tray and follow her into the villa and down the red-tiled hall. She unlocks her door.

Inside, there's a paper crane sitting in my seat. It's gold, and heavy when I pick it up and turn it over in my palm.

"Hey. It's beautiful. Thank you." I swallow the lump in my throat, but it bobs right back again. It takes effort to keep my palm flat, open. Not to crush this beautiful thing in an effort to keep it close.

"My pleasure. And one more thing."

I look up. Look away and look back again, even though I was right the first time. "Wait." I'm not dreaming.

He's standing in the doorway. "Hey, Stevie. Hey, little girl."

I forgot how much he looks like Josh, or Josh looked like him, with his wavy, almost curly hair and broad shoulders. He's wearing a dress shirt. He never wears a dress shirt.

"I'm not supposed to say you look good," he tells me. "But I'm . . . you . . . it's good to see you."

I walk slowly, afraid that if I move too fast, he'll be gone. I wind my arms around his neck and press my face into his chest.

"Okay. Me, too." I press my palms against his cheeks, his neck, his shoulders, and every time he's still there. "What are you doing here?" I pull back and glance behind him, half expecting to see her lips: perfect and red like desert dust. "Where's—"

The corners of his mouth fall just slightly, and I feel stupid. *Of course.*

"She's still in Paris," he says. "She wanted to come."

"It's okay." When I whip my head around, I see Shrink standing in her office, and suddenly I'm embarrassed.

"What are you doing here?" I ask again. "When did you—"

"Well, Anna here called. And she said that she knew it was gonna be a tough day today, with—" His voice wobbles. "So she asked if I wanted to come out and start the family part early."

Shrink raises her eyebrows. "What do you think? You'd have

to stay here for meals and sleeping and such. But we could start early with your family sessions."

I can't take my eyes off him. "So, like, when?"

"Now?" Shrink says.

"Fine by me." Dad's laugh is shaky. Nervous. I can't blame him, and I don't.

"Me, too," I say.

"Let's get started, then." Shrink sits in her red chair.

Dad closes the door behind us and I carry myself across the threshold, suddenly, hopelessly aware of my weight. The weight of all the parts of me: beating heart and bone and flesh and things that have happened and things that are happening now. And Josh, resting still between the folds. I carry it all, and it's heavy enough that I'm tired and need to rest. Just heavy enough that I know: I am here. I am alive.

note from the author

I have done my very best to make Stevie's story authentic, in terms of her experiences of enduring an eating disorder and in terms of the realities of life in a treatment center. That said, her story is just that: a story. The characters that make up her world and her treatment journey are fictional, even if this fiction is based in large part on what I believe to be true as a writer, a therapist, and perhaps most importantly, a survivor.

If you or someone you know is struggling with an eating disorder, I hope that you will educate yourself about available resources. The National Eating Disorders Association is a wonderful place to start. You can visit NEDA's website at www.nationaleatingdisorders.org, or call their help line at 1-800-931-2237.

acknowledgments

THIS book has almost existed for what seems like a very long time, and without the faith, expertise, and tough love of an incredible team, it might never have come to be. Sara Shandler, Josh Bank, and Les Morgenstein at Alloy Entertainment have had enthusiasm for this project from the start, and have showed continued faith in the story through the many lives of the book. Lanie Davis is the sharpest editor and loveliest LP on the block, and I feel so blessed that she chose to see this book through to the end. It would not be the same story without her intelligence, deep heart, and empathy. Jen Klonsky at Harper was passionate enough about this story to threaten violence with a tire iron to get it, which makes me want to cry (mostly tears of gratitude, and only *some* tears of fear). Rebecca Friedman has been not only a brilliant agent, but also a tireless reader and an advocate for Stevie's story in its truest form. Thank you for helping me to give Stevie a voice. Natalie Sousa created a beautiful, nuanced cover that fits the story perfectly. Christina Colangelo, Elizabeth Ward, and Kara Brammer showed faith and confidence in this book as they introduced it to the world, and I'm grateful for their hard work.

Laura, Erin, and Melody formed an unbreakable circle of support for me at a crucial time, and I am indebted to them for their wisdom and care. Megan, Jess, Becky, Alison, J9, Jamie, Lindsay, and Emily occupy a special place in my heart.

Writing is always an emotional and personal endeavor. Writing this book has been a particularly emotional and personal process for me, and the support of my loved ones has sustained me through it. My parents, Mimi and Hugh, have walked with me through the ups and downs of life and of writing, and they never miss a step, even when I trip and face-plant. My sister, Molly, and my brother, John, are dear and constant cheerleaders. And last but certainly not least, David has been an incredible partner. He has cared for and about me through my writerly madness, delivering dinner and pep talks at all the right times. He has endured long hours, early writing mornings, and my questionable work-life boundaries with grace. I'm not sure how to thank him exactly, except to say this: More love, more better.

M.H.